# *Love's* LOST STAR

# Love's
# LOST
# STAR

CAITLIN M. SMITH

Ambassador International
GREENVILLE, SOUTH CAROLINA & BELFAST, NORTHERN IRELAND

www.ambassador-international.com

# Love's Lost Star

ISBN: 978-1-64960-110-0
eISBN: 978-1-64960-160-5

Cover Design and Interior Typesetting by Christy Perry of Mercy's Hue
Edited by Katie Cruice Smith

Scripture quoted from the Holy Bible, New International Version®, NIV®
Copyright ©1973, 1978, 1984, 2011 by Biblica, Inc.® Used by permission. All
rights reserved worldwide.

This is a work of fiction. Names, characters, and incidents are all
products of the author's imagination or are used for fictional purposes.
Any resemblance to actual events or persons, living or dead, is entirely
coincidental. Any mentioned brand names, places, and trademarks remain
the property of their respective owners, bear no association with the
author or the publisher, and are used for fictional purposes only.

AMBASSADOR INTERNATIONAL
Emerald House
411 University Ridge, Suite B14
Greenville, SC 29601
United States
www.ambassador-international.com

AMBASSADOR BOOKS
The Mount
2 Woodstock Link
Belfast, BT6 8DD
Northern Ireland, United Kingdom
www.ambassadormedia.co.uk

*The colophon is a trademark of Ambassador, a Christian publishing company.*

*To my wonderful husband, John.*
*I appreciate your heart for Jesus and*
*am so blessed by your love.*
*Thank you for believing in me.*

# Prologue

July 18, 1983

She sat in the darkness of her room, holding her knees to her chest. The only light was that of a soft glow issuing forth from an outlet on her wall. She looked out the window from atop her bed. It was a black night. Intense rain had wreaked havoc on her life the past two days, and the storm clouds still hovered tonight, blocking any light that the moon or stars tried to offer. When it rained outside, it poured inside. Rain meant Papa and Mama were bored, and bored parents spent more time with her.

Slowly, she released the hold of her knees and let them drop to the side. She stared down at her forearms. In the dim light, she could see large, black and purple marks from all the time she and her parents spent together. The biggest ones were from Papa. From what she understood, it sounded like he had lost money this week—from a race, or poker, or something. Anyway, if she hadn't been such a distraction, he would have been able to focus and win. She had to learn her lesson somehow, and Papa deemed this way best.

She shifted her eyes toward the meek light coming from the wall to her right. It was a star, the nightlight. She had always liked stars. They were sparkly; and somewhere along the way, she heard that if she saw the first star of the night, she could make a wish. She sighed. She couldn't see any stars out tonight. Instead, she gazed at the plastic imitation on her wall, closed her eyes tight, and made a wish. She knew it wouldn't come true, but it was worth a shot.

Her eyes steadily moved to the left of the light and settled on a little, pink backpack. Its contents made the bag puffy, and the light purple zipper was slightly opened. She pulled her knees back in and tucked her head forward to rest upon them. Tonight. She should just do it tonight. What was she waiting for? As she continued to think, she heard a door open and close.

"Where's my briefcase?" The thunderous voice rolled through the house. Papa was home. He had gone out for a few hours and didn't say why.

Suddenly, there was silence. She slid off her bed and crept toward the door. Putting her ear to the wood, she could hear the muffled sound of talking downstairs. Needing to know what was happening, she slowly turned her doorknob and tiptoed toward the banister railing.

"Where is she?" Papa's voice boomed.

"In bed," Mama answered softly. She was probably looking down as she spoke, a customary behavior nowadays.

"What? She doesn't want to greet her father when he comes home?"

"You wanted her to?" Mama questioned sarcastically.

The sound of several quick steps was followed by a thud. Mama groaned. Papa laughed.

She could hear Papa moving toward the stairs. She scurried backward and rushed toward her room. Quietly closing the door, she thrust herself under the covers. Maybe Papa would see her sleeping and leave her alone.

Suddenly, the door flew open, and the heavy steps of judgment came closer. On his way to her bed, she heard Papa stumble.

"You little piece of nothing!" he roared. He reached for her blanket and yanked it off her body. She sat up and turned toward him in a panic. He smirked. "You want to hurt Papa?"

Shaking her head, she slid from her bed and backed up.

Stopping, he glared at her. "Come here!" He pointed to the floor beside him.

She looked at Papa's finger, up at his face, and over at her tiny backpack sitting on the floor. Without another thought, she raced around the bed and toward her bag. Papa reached over and grabbed her arm as she struggled to pass.

"Ow!" she shrieked. Papa's hand was wrapped around two big bruises on her right arm. He squeezed.

"Oh, does that hurt?" He squeezed harder as she wailed.

"Well, perhaps you know how Papa's ankle feels now, huh?" He reached for the doll over which he'd stumbled and threw it against her bed.

Tears streamed down her face as she jumped, driving both heels into Papa's foot as she landed. He gasped; but before he could stop her, she'd ducked between his legs and lunged toward her bag. After grabbing it by a strap, she raced out the bedroom door.

"Hey!" he hollered as he chased after her.

She hopped on the banister rail and slid down the stairs. Landing swiftly on her feet, she glanced right and made eye contact with Mama—curled in a ball against the floor. Mama's eyes were surrounded by puffy, red skin, her thick tears concealing the once-golden flecks within her auburn eyes. The gold had faded years ago, and it seemed her light would be gone forever. Although she looked at

Mama for only a split second, it felt like an hour. The frozen moment shattered when Mama shook her head and looked away. She was right to leave. Nobody cared anymore—not even her own mother.

Spinning her head around, she saw Papa wobbling down the stairs. There were no more seconds to waste. She quickly turned and ran out the front door. Papa's yelling followed her down the sidewalk, although he wasn't close enough to catch her.

"You come back here this instant! Do you hear me? I mean now!"

Still shocked by what was happening, she kept running. She'd been planning her escape for months, and although she had desperately wanted to leave, she questioned if she actually could. In her final strides down the front yard, she could faintly hear Papa's last words.

"Young lady, there will be nothing for you if you don't return this instant! Your mama and I won't love you anymore!"

Her heart sank, and she slowed to a walk. She had heard Papa use that word only a few times in his life. Whenever he said it to her, it was in conjunction with punishment. If Mama and Papa's way of loving meant pain, then perhaps she didn't want their love after all.

She glanced back at the house. Wiping the tears from her cheeks, she frowned. She was done caring about people. She didn't need "love." As far as she was concerned, all she needed was herself. She was done with that house and would never go back. Rubbing a wet hand against the soft fabric of her leggings, she huffed and started running again. This was the last time she'd ever let someone make her cry. From now on, nothing would break her heart.

# Chapter 1
## Darkness Speaks

March 12, 1994
Saturday, 4:00 a.m.

Darkness lingered on the riverbank. It sank deep into the long, moist grass and hovered around the willow trees that followed the river for miles. Though the moon was full, a thick blanket of clouds forbade it from shining. An occasional star broke through the cloudy fortress, offering a glimpse of hope to whomever saw its light.

Along the river, a baritone frog, with the time-keeping skills of a pendulum, croaked every three seconds. The harsh screams of crickets responded to the frog's cry, and it was while the crickets screeched that Cece's eyes shot open.

Cautiously, she lifted her head. Complete darkness. In fact, she didn't quite remember when she last saw daylight. Somewhat dazed, she blinked a couple times before realizing that her vision was hampered by something covering her eyes. Slowly, she lowered her head back to the ground. She thought for a moment before moving her hands. Her wrists were stuck together. Suddenly, the previous night came back in flashes of memory: the blindfold, hands tied behind her back. She didn't recall her feet being bound. She wiggled her toes. *When did that happen?* Never mind. First, she had to find a way to relieve her eyes of their burden.

As she lay on the ground, a solution came to mind. About to execute her plan, she froze. Where had the people gone? Was it possible they were still here, right beside her? Perhaps they were sleeping and hadn't noticed her return to consciousness. Or were they watching, laughing to themselves as they calmly awaited her feeble attempt to escape? Regardless, she couldn't risk *not* trying to escape.

Slowly, she pushed the side of her head deeper into the mud until the ground felt firm against her cheek. She put pressure where she thought the blindfold rested on her temple and moved her body down. After repeating this process two or three times, she painfully rolled over and continued on the other side of her head. A few more times and her eyes were free. Forcefully shaking the blindfold off, she breathed.

Cece gently lifted her head and shifted her eyes from right to left. She was alone. She looked down. The side of her body still lay in the grass, sinking deeper into the muddy ground. Her scraped knees were bent, her delicate, pale feet pressed together. Her stomach, legs, and shoulders hurt with a throbbing pain, but it was nothing she couldn't handle. Carefully, she rolled to her back. She groaned as the weight of her body pierced her thin arms. Grinding her teeth, she lifted her knees to her chest and brought her restrained wrists to the front of her body. Immediately after, she released her jaw of its anxious clenching and breathed. The exhaustion she felt surprised her, but after all that had happened, she figured she had ample reason to feel this way.

Now her hands and feet. She determined she must stay focused if she had any chance of escaping before the people returned. To her right, she noticed a large rock. Instead of attempting to stand, she rolled toward it like a used mattress flipping across the ground. When she was close enough to the rock, she saw a sharp point at the top. Lying on her back, she lifted her legs into the air and positioned the middle of the rope against the rocky point. Back and forth, she moved her legs, bending and straightening her knees until the rope finally broke.

She maneuvered onto her rough knees, which sank slowly into the grass and mud as she raised her torso to begin the same process with her hands. Finally, she was free. Untying the remaining bits of rope that dangled from her ankles and wrists, she threw them in the river, letting the current sweep them out of sight. Placing one hand in the mud, she rose to her feet. Her knees wobbled, but balancing quickly, she lifted her shoulders upright.

It was dark all around, but her eyes had already adjusted to the night. She looked up and saw a star. It, too, had squirmed free from a cloudy bondage. The star's reflection shimmered on the black river, and for a moment, Cece smiled.

The reality of her situation abruptly returned. What mattered most was finding a way home and out of this place, but where was she? Where did her captors go? Thoughts raced through her mind, and she determined that the safest thing to do was move far away from here. She couldn't take the chance that the people might come back.

Stealthily, she crept along the riverbank, her muscles aching with each step. Tattered, silk strands of her dress shivered in the night's cool breeze, caressing the flesh of her bruised legs. The gown shimmered when struck by the moon's occasional light. As she traveled onward, the soreness within her bones pulsed through her body, causing her to pause against the intermittent willow trees.

Dawn was quickly approaching. The night felt like it lasted but a moment. Adrenaline seared through her veins as she fled. *I have to get home. I have to.* She stumbled toward another tree and fell limply against its bark. She panted, digging her fingers into the creases along the tree trunk. As she lowered her head, she squeezed her eyes shut. Each eyelid was a dam, preventing tears from flooding forth onto her dirt-stained cheeks. How could they do this to her? How could anyone treat another human being this way?

Blood rushed to her face. With each additional question, she felt heat rising until she couldn't contain herself. She opened her mouth to unleash her frustration toward the rising sun. She intended to scream; but when her lips parted, her voice was just a faint whisper: "Why?" She grabbed her throat. *My voice. What happened to my voice?* Struggling to recollect the events from earlier, she recalled the dinner, family, people dressed-up. She remembered leaving the restaurant. It was a ten-minute walk home from Bartinelli's, and she had decided to go alone. It was a cool evening with a gorgeous sunset, and she had wanted to enjoy every minute before the big day. But she didn't make it home. What happened? She remembered being in a room, tied to a chair. *There were two men . . . no, three. There must have been three.* The memory was fuzzy.

She looked down at her legs and fell to the ground. She stroked the scratches on her kneecaps and thought. The dusty street back home in an alley near her house—she had fallen trying to escape. They still hurt. Closing her eyes, she fought to contain the tears that begged her for freedom. She rolled her head in a circle, hoping the emotion would go away, but it triggered a headache and dizziness instead. Taking a deep breath, she opened her eyes and waited for the ground to steady.

*I don't remember,* she thought, trying to piece together fragments of memory. *There was a vehicle. One of them carried me along the river.* She squinted and tried to concentrate. It felt like the intense effort was overloading her brain. *I heard them talking . . . What did they say?* She lifted her hand to feel the back of her head. "Ouch!" she whispered. Her head was tender, and the smallest touch sent a pounding pain to her temples.

That was it. That was all she could remember. She looked up and laid the side of her head against the willow tree. She sighed. Wait. There was something else. A person. She had seen a fourth figure at the end of the alley as she was being forced into the back of a vehicle. She couldn't make out a face, but she had wondered why the person didn't help her. It certainly wasn't the good Samaritan she needed. Perhaps it was one of them.

Cece clenched her teeth. She hated the idea of what had happened to her. She wasn't even sure she wanted to remember the rest. What she desired more than anything was for everything to go back to normal. She froze . . . Her mouth suddenly became dry. Today was supposed to be special. It was supposed to be the happiest day of her life. She lifted her eyes to heaven, pressure building against her chest. Somehow, she would make it out of this; but in the deepest chambers of her heart she wondered if she really deserved to go back home.

## Chapter 2
# One, Two, and Three

9:01 a.m.

"I can't *believe* you." Marley curled his fingers, shook his hands in Jackson's face, and walked away. He could feel a glare against his back, but he didn't care. Jackson had failed him, and there were consequences.

"Now, looka here, Marley," Tommy inserted himself. He was nothing but a big goon. "You's always doubtin' us, but we can do our job!"

"Yeah, what happened to trust in a partnership, huh? I thought we were a team." Jackson's thick, Italian accent made Marley cringe. People who messed up should not be allowed to speak.

"A team?" he whipped back around. "No, Jackson, *this* is not a team!" Heat rushed to his face. "I expect this stuff from him." He nodded at Tommy. "But from you . . . oh no, not from you. I want to rip your head off!"

"Wait a—"

"Not another word. You hear me? Nothing!" Marley threw a finger in Jackson's face. It was enough that he had to tolerate their incompetence. He didn't have to hear their excuses, too. As he walked away, he was forced to an abrupt stop. Pain shot through Marley's head as someone yanked his hair backwards, cracking his neck.

"You know, Marley, I'm sick. You hear me? Sick of your mouth!" Jackson pulled harder. "You think Tommy always blows it, huh? You expect *this* from him, do you? And now, you're blaming me, too? Well, guess what? You aren't the boss of us!" He released his grip and wiped his hand on Marley's shirt. "And relax with the gel. You're short— porcupine hair won't change that."

Marley looked down at the spot and cringed.

"And what about her, huh?" Jackson motioned to a slender woman who was leaning against a wall, her hands stuffed in the pockets of her green cargo pants.

Marley paused. He watched as a large, pink bubble popped in front of her face, covering her nose. She sucked it back in and kept chewing, seemingly unaffected by Jackson's malicious attack, though she kept her eyes averted.

"What about her?"

"She's more of a screw-up than any of us!" Jackson fumed. "Yet you keep her around to replace your precious, little—"

"Don't!" He knew where this was going. Those jerks always called her a replacement, but nobody would replace a selfish slimeball like . . . His fists clenched. Stepping forward, he swung at his unruly subordinate. Jackson caught it and glared at him.

"Wendy had nothing to do with your mistake," Marley roared. "She wasn't even at the river—had other plans, remember?"

"What other plans?" Jackson chuckled. "She's weak!"

Before he could respond, Jackson grabbed him by the collar and lifted him up. "I'll tell you something else! Tommy and I don't need you! You can wave goodbye as we leave, begging—*begging*—us to come back!" Spit flew into Marley's face as Jackson spoke. "We thought you wanted the girl dead. Turns out, we were wrong." He dropped him and started walking away.

"Wait." Marley stood. He could feel a restoration coming to their partnership. Staring at the back of Jackson's leather jacket, he thought for a moment. It was nearly silent as the wall clock ticked, reminding him of the time he'd lost. Straightening his shoulders, he continued, "You didn't tell me you still have a way to kill her." He was skeptical but hoped for a favorable answer.

Jackson turned around. "Have a way?" He stepped toward him. "The girl's dead."

Marley glanced at Tommy, whose eyes shot around the room. He looked back at Jackson. "But you left her there . . . "

"You bet we did. Dead."

"No, no." He kept his attention fixed on Jackson's black eyes. This guy was the best liar he knew, which was one of the reasons Marley found him useful. "I left her with you. You and Tommy were watching her. Tommy got hungry. You made sure she was out. You left with Tommy to eat. You went back by the river, and she was gone." He recalled the precise story from when the two had reported what happened. He grinned, knowing he had Jackson trapped. "If you knew I wanted her dead, why didn't you tell me you killed her in the first place?"

Jackson returned his stare with an arrogant smile. "Well, *Boss*," he began, "we knew how badly you wanted to do the deed yourself; we thought you'd be mad. After all, it was our idea to keep her alive."

Marley realized his checkmate wasn't what he made it out to be. "Ah, yes. What changed your mind?"

"She deserved it," Jackson replied. "After what she did, she deserved to suffer."

Pacing the room, Marley scratched his chin. He didn't feel the exuberant joy he anticipated upon the death of that treacherous brat—probably because he didn't believe it happened.

"You're right. I *am* mad," he said. "I suppose my relief that she hasn't escaped outweighs my disappointment that you did the deed without me." He paused. "So, she's in the river?"

"Yes."

"Did you drown her, like I wanted? You secured the body, right? The last thing we need are cops involved."

Jackson hesitated. "Yes."

"You mean if I went to the river, I'd find her sunk in the spot where you dropped her?"

"Of course."

"Good," sneered Marley. "I guess if I can see for myself, I'll let it go." He hurried out the door. "Let's go, boys!" He could hear Jackson and Tommy whispering as he waited outside the door. "Something wrong?"

"Not at all." Jackson strolled past him, hands in pockets, with Tommy close behind.

The latter kept his eyes forward. "She'll be there all right," he added, wiping sweat from his forehead. "Dead. Not alive. Dead."

Rolling his eyes, Marley sent them ahead to start the van. He moved back to the door and peeked inside. "Wendy, you busy?"

"Nah. Not for you," she said with a wink.

He felt his cheeks flush. "I've got something for you to do back in Ichacar. You up for a drive?"

"Always."

He watched as she pushed herself from the wall and sauntered over. Her hips swayed with each step. She pulled a set of keys from her pocket and shook them in his face. "Wanna come?"

Grinning, he pulled the door open and extended a palm toward the hallway. "I'll catch up with you later, but this first part is all on you. Can I trust you?" he asked jokingly, though for some reason, she froze. "Wendy?" he barked.

She jumped, as though abruptly awoken from a quick snooze. "What?" Her voice: so deep and beckoning, even with that one word.

Marley instantly regretted his tone. Proceeding softly, he repeated, "Can I trust you?"

"Of course. Why would you even ask?"

"Then I need you to go back to Ichacar and handle that punk."

"That punk?" Her left eyebrow rose. "I'm gonna need you to be more specific."

He let a smirk escape before following it with his business face. She'd know what the look meant. Narrowing his eyes, he stared at her.

"Uh, Mar? Are you okay? Your face is doing that weird thing again—"

"What? Yes, I'm fine!" He shook his head. "The punk—you know, the one that wretched, little traitor was going to . . . you know . . . be with. I need you to . . . distract him. Give him something . . . *someone* . . . else to think about."

She glanced down at the glistening rock on her left ring finger. He'd found it in a Cracker Jack box, but his girl was so good, she didn't care. She wasn't the diva that Cece had been. Wendy actually listened. She was reasonable. She was—

"Did you hear me?"

Apparently, he had zoned out. Whatever. It probably wasn't important, anyway. Grabbing her hand, he gently pulled her down the hall.

"Marley, wait." Wendy yanked her hand away, forcing him to stop. "You're really okay with this? I mean, I know it's part of the reason you brought me on, but it doesn't bother you now?"

Turning his face away, he rolled his eyes, then returned his attention to the brown-eyed woman before him. Man, could those big beauties melt a man's heart. She was perfect.

"Yeah, sure it does. But on the job, you're just acting, like a movie star."

Bingo. He watched as her straight lips bent into a smile. It was too easy. Wendy loved the movies, which made it an effortless way to her heart. He turned to catch up with Jackson and Tommy, this time leaving her hand behind. "I'll meet you there later, sweetheart."

"How much time do I have?" Her voice echoed against the bare walls behind him.

"None," he answered, pushing open the steel door that led outside. He heard the van's engine rumble as Tommy beckoned him with gestures from the passenger seat window. He paused, still addressing Wendy. "It needs to happen now. We need the insurance."

"But—"

"Remember what this woman did. She doesn't deserve to be alive, let alone loved; and after we're both done, she'll be neither."

Wendy nodded. "You got it, babe."

He let the door slam shut as he strolled to the van. "You're in my seat."

"But I called shotgun," Tommy whined. "I thought you liked drivin' anyways." Candy wrappers spilled on the pavement as he opened the door to obey.

"I don't drive the bus to Disaster Town."

Jackson and Tommy looked at him as he climbed in the van.

"Just go!" He folded his arms and the van pulled away, his teeth clenched. Soon, he would find out if Cece really was dead; and if she wasn't, he would fix that.

# Chapter 3
## Going Back

10:32 a.m.

The three men trudged through thick grass as they traveled along the riverbank. Marley led the way, followed closely by Tommy and Jackson.

Marley refused to wear boots, but instead insisted on tackling the rough terrain in his Italian loafers. Although he claimed to be a skilled outdoorsman, it was far from the truth. Instead, he stumbled over tree roots and fallen branches. At one point, he tripped over a hole, complained about the upkeep of the riverbank, then kept going as if nothing happened. Jackson would have been annoyed, but he was used to Marley's stupidity. The man always tried to be bigger than he really was. He was clearly overcompensating for something.

Shouting expletives, Marley tripped again. Jackson watched as the man in front of him fell forward. At this rate, it would take a year before they reached the spot.

"We better be getting close! You punks are driving me crazy," Marley yelled as he sprang to his feet.

"You want me to take the lead?" Although he already knew the answer, he couldn't resist antagonizing the hot-tempered man. Unlike Marley, he could walk without falling over.

"We're almost there, Boss." Tommy's voice was muffled as he chewed a stick of jerky. "That there tree coming up—that's the one."

Marley stomped toward the tree, lifting his knees up high over the grass. "You sure this is it?" he growled.

Jackson sauntered over and glanced around.

"Yep, that's the one. Right there's your boulder."

Marley stared at the rock. "*My* boulder?" he snarled.

"Yeah, Boss." Tommy stepped forward. "It's the one you wanted to sink and crush her with."

Jackson drove a hard elbow into his comrade's side, sending him hunching over.

"I take it you found another rock to sink her with then, huh?" Marley's voiced oozed skepticism; and although he was right to doubt them, there was no way he'd get the satisfaction of being right.

Jackson gestured toward the river. "Yeah, you should find your girlfriend in the water there—that is, unless the current dragged her elsewhere."

"Stop smiling! I'd rip that smug look of yours right off your face if I could!" Marley wove his fist in the air. "And she's *not* my girlfriend!" His voice softened for a moment. "And I'd appreciate it," he began quietly, "if you would stop calling her that!" Slipping his precious shoes off, he jumped into the water and began flopping around.

The sun's reflection shone in the river as Marley searched. Droplets of teal water splashed about, causing ripples in every direction. Jackson watched, somewhat amused by the crazed man's obsession. He wished he had hidden a mannequin in the lake. The self-proclaimed boss wouldn't know the difference.

After he'd had enough, he leaned toward Tommy and whispered something in his ear.

"She's not here, is she?" Marley questioned, still kicking his legs underwater.

"Well, Mar, I guess the current must have taken her. But you just started . . . keep looking." Jackson turned back and began his trek to the van.

"Where you going? Get back here!" Marley slammed his fist into the water and looked up at Tommy, who was now leaning against a willow tree, watching. "Where's he going?"

"To pick up a package from town," he reported. "He'll be back later."

Before he was out of earshot, Jackson hollered back at Tommy, "If we don't cross paths sooner, remember: Monday."

# Chapter 4
## *Ichacar*

1:00 p.m.

Although the afternoon had the appearance of a regular day, there was far more gossip on the streets of Ichacar than usual. Practically every tongue dripped with the names "Cece" and "Jason."

"How could she do somethin' like that?"

"That gal oughta be hunted down and punished for what she done!"

"Poor Jason—what a nice young man he is."

"If ya ask me, Jason Porter's better off without her!"

Whispers and outbursts flew from person to person as the day progressed. Even those who barely knew the two wanted to have their say. The only person who didn't want to talk about what had happened was Jason.

The Porters lived in a small home on the east end of Ichacar's Main Street. Mrs. Porter had been gone for twelve years now. She'd moved away when he was only thirteen. Mr. Porter, on the other hand, had departed more recently. Six years ago, after he'd determined that Jason was man enough to take care of himself, he left, hoping to leave the memories behind. Now, Jason, Uncle Ed, and Auntie May lived in the cozy home.

Jason stood beside the kitchen window. Focusing on the large pane bordered by limp, pastel-blue curtains, he raised his eyes and gazed toward the street. As he stood, he heard Auntie May hustling about the kitchen behind him. Dishes crashed into the sink as she cleared the table.

"Come now; you've been standin' there for hours. You didn't even touch your lunch."

Jason turned to see her scrubbing a ceramic plate. She lifted her eyes and looked at him. He could have sworn she was about to cry, but instead, she shook her head and kept cleaning. "I know you're upset, honey. But we can't let what happened ruin our lives. We gotta put our grown-up pants on and keep going." Frowning at the plate that she just cleaned twice, Auntie May jammed it in the drying rack and proceeded to sponge the table.

Jason sighed. He hadn't said much since earlier that morning after he realized Cece was gone . . .

*The moment he received the news—relayed to him by an usher—he shook his head. There was no way his bride would desert him; she was probably just running late. He determined that he would wait; but after every guest had left, each of them awkwardly rising to their feet, looking at him, and walking out, he acknowledged that she wasn't coming. Withholding eye contact, he asked his remaining family and closest friends to leave. Struggling to remain composed, he walked up the aisle of the church and into his dressing room.*

*Why, God? He slumped onto a tiny plastic chair that was created for a five-year-old. Holding his head within sweaty palms, he pulled his hair. Why? He hated this feeling. Pressure beat against his insides; his stomach twisted; and his veins felt pinched, limiting the blood flow to his brain. But I love her. . .*

*He shot to his feet and hollered as he sent a table to its knees. He picked up the chair and threw it across the room, grunting at the stuffed animals it knocked over. Those ridiculous creatures with permanent smiles knew nothing about life. Jason collapsed on the floor. He had to get out of there. Taking a deep breath, he walked over to the disheveled animals, put them back on their shelves, and left the church.*

"Honey!" Auntie May snapped. It wasn't like her. Her patience must have been wearing thin. It was amazing what pain could do to a person. "Look, I know this is new—and we're all feeling a little raw—but you gotta talk to me."

"That's not true," he mumbled, wishing he could escape to one of those distant clouds in the sky. If Cece wanted to get away, he was sure that's where she would go. The thought made him smile, though he was instantly dragged back to reality.

"Come again?"

"We're all a little raw?" he began. "Please! Nobody's upset that she's gone." He could feel her stare against the back of his neck, but he knew what to do about that. Auntie May was one of the nicest people on earth, and despite his own feelings, he hated seeing her this way. "Besides, I think some folks down the street wanted to throw me a party. Look," he said as he leaned forward and pressed his forehead against the glass. "Are those balloons I see?"

Auntie May appeared behind him and swatted his back with a dish towel.

"Oh, come on," he smirked as she huffed at him. "You fell for that?"

"Well, I'm glad to see you haven't lost your sense of humor," she answered, sarcasm oozing.

"How come I don't believe you?" He turned and wrapped his arms around her. Normally, she would put up a fake fight—a playful back and forth that had them both bursting with laughter, but not today. Today, he felt her muscles soften as he embraced her.

"Jason?" She started slowly, resting her head against his shoulder. "I'm so sorry. As sure as the sun rises, I thought she was the one."

"So do I—I mean, I did. I mean . . . " Exhaling, he gave up on finishing the thought. Of course, she was the one. But if that were true, she would have met him at the altar.

Before he knew it, Auntie May was crying. He hugged her tighter as her back shook.

"It'll be okay." How he wished he believed those words. Turning his head, he looked back out the window.

The sun was bright and mocked his pain. It was truly the perfect day for a wedding—a wedding that he wouldn't have. How could the woman he loved—who he was so sure loved him back—do something like this? Had he so drastically misjudged her? He never imagined she would change her mind—not after all they had shared. As he began thinking of what might have been, the struggle intensified. *Why would she leave, God? All I ever did was love her.*

# Chapter 5
## *Stranger*

3:23 p.m.

Cece's feet dragged as she slunk along the riverbank. Each weary step felt like her last, but somehow, she kept moving. Despite an occasional stop to catch her breath, she hadn't rested much. The sunlight made it easier for her to navigate the uneven terrain. More than that, it offered hope. It was bright, exposing a vast stage of blue sky upon which birds danced. Dance. She would've had her first dance as a married woman today.

She shook her head as if to erase the thought. She had been walking for what felt like days. Originally, she hoped to reach a town or road by now, but that didn't happen. The people must have dropped her off from the other direction. Retracing her steps and escaping the opposite way was not an option—it was much too possible that she'd encounter her captors on the way back. Her best choice now was to cross the river, though she had hoped to avoid it. She studied the trees on the other side. They were thinner in that area, revealing a field behind.

She crept to the edge of the bank. There, the land dropped off into the river. She sat down on the muddy grass and let her bottom sink. Any other day, she would have cringed at the thought of her lovely dress being soaked with mud, but today was different.

Cece forced a leg down and stuck her toes into the river. The cool water tickled her skin and massaged her sore foot. Although the chill startled her, it's what she'd expected for a spring day. *Help me, God.* She lowered her body into the river, gasping at the frigid shock that gripped her. Relieved that her feet touched the ground, she started walking.

Step by step, she reached a foot forward and cautiously tapped the wet ground before transferring her body weight. The last thing she wanted was to step on a sharp stone—or worse: a fish or slimy snake. As she broke through the current, something brushed her skin. Its slippery surface scuttled past her leg. She shrieked, though no sound came out. Without hesitation, she picked up her legs and began swimming frantically. "Don't touch me; don't touch me!" she pleaded through a noiseless whisper. Another fish slapped her squirming foot as it hurried passed. Cece jerked her head in the other direction and sank under the water. Her heart beat like a jackhammer as she flailed her arms and forced her head above the surface. She stood and quickly searched the water. It was dirty, and she couldn't see much. Throwing precaution aside, she ran. It felt like she was moving in slow motion as she dug her feet into the ground and attempted to propel herself forward. *You can do this.*

She pushed and pushed, finally reaching the river's edge. Once there, she folded her arms and laid them against the stony wall of dirt that stood between her and the riverbank. She let her head drop against her arms and stood panting, trying to muster the energy to hoist herself up.

"Ya in need of some help there, Missy?" The friendly, Southern voice startled her, demanding her attention. She looked up to see a man squatting down, smiling. He looked steadfastly in her eyes, which made her uncomfortable enough to look away.

"No, thanks," she forced through her strained vocal cords. She turned her eyes back toward the stranger.

"A bit shy, are ya? Never mind that. I see you're in a bit of a fix." He continued to smile. "Sure ya don't want some help?"

Her uncertainty was outweighed by her desire to be on dry ground. After a deep sigh, she raised an arm to the stranger, and he pulled her from the water.

"You're a light gal, you are. I reckon you can't weigh more than a hundred pounds," the man declared as he released her onto the ground.

He wasn't right about her weight, but Cece was used to that by now. She presumed his guess was affected by his large, athletic body. Lifting her was like nothing to him. As she sat ringing water from her dress, she assessed the man. He wore what appeared to be thick, brown pants that had black streaks throughout. His t-shirt was adorned with sweat stains and dirt—probably from some kind of physical labor. In a way, he reminded her of Jason—the tan skin and muscular build. Only, Jason's face was much more handsome with deep brown eyes that made her heart warm and gooey.

"Am I close?" the stranger asked in a surprisingly kind tone.

"No," she retorted.

"Well, I do apologize there, ma'am. So, where you headin'?" He walked about, casually glancing at the scraped-up woman in her disheveled gown.

Cece finished ringing out her dress and stood. She had no desire to sit below this man. In fact, she wanted to stand taller, but that wasn't physically possible.

In an effort not to be rude, she thought she'd thank the man and move on, but the stress on her vocal cords was too much. Finally, she heard herself almost silently declare, "I'll continue alone."

"Continue?" The stranger lowered an eyebrow and stopped. "You runnin' away or somethin'?"

She was not amused. The nerve of this man! Running away? Really? She could feel her face growing red.

"Oh, I see. You're upset because you think I'ma try to take you back. Well, don't worry your pretty, little head about that. I ain't takin' you nowhere you don't wanna go." The stranger shoved his hands in his pockets and began moseying around.

"Take me back? I'd give anything to . . . " She stopped. Each word felt like a knife slicing the back of her throat. She wanted to yell—to give this guy a piece of her mind. How he could possibly think that she didn't want to go home was mind-boggling. Look at her! Did she look like she didn't want to go home? She glanced down at her soggy dress and dripping, scraped legs. They were scabbed-up enough by now, so the water didn't sting like it could have. She raised her eyes. This guy had it all wrong. Home was the one place on earth she desired to be.

"What's your name?" she gently asked, mindful of her throbbing larynx.

"Name's Bart." The man smiled at her.

She looked away. She didn't want to see another man smile at her. She didn't even want to look at him. She wanted Jason.

"Don't worry, Miss. I know a cozy place where you can clean up and get yourself together before continuing on whatever journey it is you got yourself on."

"Is it close?"

Bart pointed. "Through them trees, past the field, and into town a little ways. It's not the nicest of places, but it'll do. 'Bout an hour's walk."

Her heart leapt. An hour? She was moments from finding a way home.

"What's the town called?" she whispered.

The man paused. His eyes traced her face, probably analyzing her expression. "Brandoon," he said at last. "You may have heard of it, but most haven't. We Brandoon folks like to keep to ourselves. It's a small, little place."

She nodded. She'd anticipated recognizing the name. She thought she knew every town within one hundred miles of Ichacar, but apparently, she was wrong—that is, unless Bart was lying. Narrowing her eyes, she glared at him. Her former relief had dissipated. There was a time she had known that people like this couldn't be trusted, but then she met Jason.

"Yikes! What's that for?"

Realizing her prolonged silence, she blinked, as though attempting to wipe scales from her eyes. The old her had always been so quick to judge. In fact, her survival depended on it. That wasn't who she was anymore. "I'm sorry." She refocused. "They must like privacy."

"Uh, yeah." He smiled. "They sure do."

That part was not a surprise. From her experience, it was true that small towns looked questionably upon strangers, and rightfully so. Strangers were dangerous. She, of all people, should know.

"Is there a phone at your place?"

"Of course, Miss . . . ?"

"Smi . . . " She paused, startled by the involuntary response she had thought was long gone. "Burbin," she corrected.

"Ah, yes. Miss Burbin."

# Chapter 6
## *The Call*

4:40 p.m.

As Bart and Cece approached the town, Cece struggled with her conflicting emotions. She was excited to finally be around people. Her plan was to find the nearest convenience store, ask to borrow the phone, call Jason, and await his gallant rescue. She wouldn't have to clean up or step one foot in the place Bart mentioned. Although he had helped her, she still wasn't sure she could trust him. Plus, if Bart tried to force her to do anything that wasn't in her plan, she could make a scene, and someone would come to her defense. It wasn't perfect, but it would work.

She forced a smile, although she couldn't shake the queasy feeling in her stomach. She kept telling herself that this was it: she would be rescued. Despite it being late in the afternoon, she and Jason could still be married, spend a wonderful night together, and go on their honeymoon tomorrow. Everything would be as it should.

"Excuse me, Princess, but did you hear what I said?" the newly familiar voice interrupted her thoughts.

"Huh?"

"I said, try not to talk to anyone, okay? People here are real particular 'bout who they associate with." Bart kept his eyes forward. There were people moving in the distance, probably hustling to get home for dinner.

It was a Saturday, which meant many offices would be closed. It was likely that nothing but the grocery store and town pharmacy were open.

"What do you mean?" Cece questioned. "I want to call someone."

She frowned at her rescuer as he continued to look ahead. His wide-set jaw appeared to be clenched beneath the dark stubble growing across it. He was so peculiar, and she didn't trust his help. In her former life, she would have followed her suspicions and continued alone—that is, until Jason had taught her to give others the benefit of the doubt. He'd said that undeserved kindness isn't always used to conceal ulterior motives. Sometimes, it's a gift. She wanted to believe him, but acting on that belief was proving to be difficult.

"What does that have to do with not talkin' to people? You can use the phone when we get there," Bart responded after an awkwardly long pause.

Cece thought for a moment. "I need a store phone. It would save you the trouble of stopping at the place you mentioned," she explained, frustrated by the meekness in her voice.

"You mean, my house?" He shot her a sideways glance.

"Yeah."

"Fine. McGreggor's is open. It's a convenience-type store with food and whatnot. He's a decent fellow. You can use his phone."

The response surprised her. Perhaps Bart wasn't so bad after all. She glanced down at her dress. Could his concern and instructions really be for her benefit?

After a few more minutes of walking, they reached the town. Bart strolled confidently through the streets, smiling and nodding to people as he passed. Cece noticed the pleasant looks he received, as well as the judgmental glances that darted her way. Men, youth, and mothers holding baby bundles seemed disgusted by her appearance. Trying not to notice, she continued forward.

"Here's McGreggor's," Bart announced, and the two went inside.

A gray-haired man stood behind the counter folding newspapers and chewing bubblegum. Cece could smell the sugary scent as it emanated from the owner's mouth.

"Hey, Big G!" Bart approached the counter and opened his arms.

"Bart! Good to see ya, my friend." The men exchanged a loose hug, patting each other on the back.

"How's Betty doing'?" Bart inquired.

"She's doing well, yessir! I'm blessed to have a wife that puts up with me the way she does."

The men laughed as they continued in conversation. Cece gently tapped Bart on the shoulder.

"Oh yeah, Big G, this is Miss . . . Banks, Mary Banks, and she'd like to use the phone."

Cece gave him a puzzled look. "My name's not Banks," she began. The man—whom she presumed was the storekeeper—looked at her as he handed over the white desk phone.

"What's that, honey?" he questioned.

"I said my name's not—"

"Hey, listen here, Big G," Bart's voice boomed, capturing the owner's attention. "We're fixin' to have a horseshoe tournament next weekend out by Martha's lawn. You in?"

The two began adamantly discussing horseshoes and the talent required to play. Although it disappointed Cece that she couldn't be louder to regain the man's attention, her call was more important. After dialing carefully, the phone rang.

"Hello?" a scruffy voice answered on the other end. She recognized the voice as Mr. White's.

"Hello, may I please speak to Jason?" she whispered.

"What's that?" the man questioned. "You're gonna have to speak up."

She mustered all the sound she had for one more plea, "Jason! I need Jason!" She could hear people talking in the background.

"Jason . . . Jason! I can't hear a word this person's saying. Can you take this?" There was shuffling, and finally, a new voice took over.

"Hello?" It was deep and wonderful.

Her heart smiled. "Jason! It's me, Cece!" As she tried to yell, a throbbing pain shot up her throat. She had to endure it. Jason needed to know she was okay.

"What about her?" He sounded irritated. "Just let it go!"

"No. It's me." Alarm gripped her; she must find a way to communicate her identity. "I'm her, Jason! Cece!" The words left her lips like gusts of wind dotted with tiny chirps.

"Huh?" He paused. "Who is this?"

"It's me!" She wanted to lash out—to reveal her identity loud enough for the world to hear. She wanted to scream about her intense feelings for him. Here she was, on the phone with the love of her life, and he couldn't hear her voice. She stood still, clasping the phone as she awaited a response. The sound of Jason's breath came through the line.

Finally, he responded, "Cece? Is that . . . you?"

"Yes, yes, it's me!" She beamed. Noticing Bart's eyes dart toward her, she turned away from him and squeezed the phone.

"Cece? Where are you?" He sounded puzzled, as though he questioned his own words.

"I'm in Brandoon!" She glanced over her shoulder, surprised to see the storekeeper's raised eyebrow looking her way.

"Braintoon? What?" Jason asked.

"No, Brandoon!" There was a short pause, but she couldn't take the suspense. "Can you hear me?"

Suddenly, Bart's arm emerged and yanked the phone from her clenched hands, throwing her into a panic.

"No! I'm not finished yet!" She tried not to cry, choking back the shaky sensation in her throat.

Bart stood, holding the base of the phone in one hand and the receiver in his other. He looked at her.

"Tell him I love him. Tell him to come get me!" she pleaded.

Boldly, he lifted the receiver to his mouth. "Haha, pranked ya!" He hung up the phone and handed it back to Mr. McGreggor.

"No!" She collapsed against the hard floor, its cold tiles mimicking the winter inside her. Her heartbeat raced as though trying to pump life into her frozen limbs. Her tongue was stuck to the roof of her mouth. Why couldn't she say something—anything? Sure, they wouldn't hear her, but she'd make certain they *knew* what she said. If only.

Both men stood silently until Bart attempted to salvage the situation.

"We can't stay here too long. We gotta get you home!"

She squinted and looked up into the man's repulsive eyes. How dare he mess with her emotions that way! Just like that, a heatwave swept through her.

"What?" she asked through clenched teeth.

"I mean, you can't expect coming to visit and then leave right away 'cause you're homesick, now can you?" He winked at her and turned to McGreggor. "Young lady's been looking forward to this trip for months; it'd be a shame for her to leave her Uncle Bart now 'cause she's missing home."

McGreggor gave an understanding nod.

"It's okay. Your brother will still be there when you get home, honey," Bart stated, justifying his actions to the storekeeper.

"Don't worry, Miss," McGreggor chimed in. "I'm sure Bart's right. I bet that Jason fella will be right there to meet you when you get back!"

Cece's stare hadn't left Bart. She pursed her lips. "He'd better be."

Her anger fumed. Had she foolishly chosen to trust someone who was part of this whole thing? In her desperation to get home, had she overlooked the obvious: Bart was one of *them*? She rose to her feet, still glaring at him. She'd never seen him before today. What could he possibly want?

"Well, shall we get going?" Bart motioned toward the door.

She lifted her chin. Bart—if that was his real name—had no idea who he was dealing with, and he'd be sorry. Going with him was a risk; but without money, shoes, or connections, her options were limited. Although she was resourceful, her voice used to play a big role in getting what she wanted from people, but that wasn't an option. Even if it was, she wasn't that person anymore.

Her stomach grumbled. She would go with Bart. If he wanted a favor from her, he would need to win her over. Perhaps he'd continue hiding his real self if he thought this new approach was working. She'd bide her time. Her face softened.

"Shall we go, Bart?" she whispered, placing a special emphasis on his name that spurred a frown from McGreggor.

Bart forced a laugh. "Ah, yes, come on, Mary; you've had a long day." He extended an arm to Cece; and with renewed confidence, she took it.

\*\*\*

At the other end of the line, Jason hung up the phone. Still unsure of the identity of the caller, he squatted into a brown, suede sofa chair and rocked back and forth. She didn't have Cece's sweet voice that he loved so much: that voice like the song of a blue jay. He stared at the phone. *"Pranked ya!"* The second voice echoed in his mind. It was a man—clear as day. He shook his head. Someone was probably getting a good laugh at his expense. People had too much time on their hands. Still, there was something peculiar about that call. He just couldn't put his finger on it. Relaxing his head against the sofa, he sought to rock his cares away, although he knew they weren't leaving anytime soon.

# Chapter 7
## *Memories*

6:30 p.m.

Cece sat, carefully taking in her surroundings. After the incident at McGreggor's, Bart brought her straight to his place—a tiny log home at the back corner of town. The house was a ten-minute walk from McGreggor's, a fact for which her feet were thankful. Upon arriving, Bart showed her the shower and gave her a fresh set of clothes. The plaid shirt and sweatpants swallowed her petite frame, but she was nevertheless grateful to be in something clean.

After showering, she exited the bathroom to discover that Bart had prepared a small dinner for her. She folded her legs and sat upright on the couch. Slowly bringing the bowl of soup to her lips, she smelled it and proceeded to eat with caution. She wanted to give Bart the idea that everything was fine—that she didn't constantly fight an urge to go running for home. Thus far, her efforts appeared to be working.

It was almost bedtime. For the past half-hour, she had been assessing the situation. If this were a normal visit, what questions would she ask at a time like this? Inquire about future plans, perhaps? Ask about Bart's family? No, she didn't want to get too close, even if she was pretending.

"So, is the weather usually like this in Brandoon?" she whispered, kicking herself inside. Really? The weather? A go-to topic when two people have absolutely nothing else to talk about. *Smooth, Cece.* She tried to save her comment. "I mean . . . has Brandoon always had weather?" *Ugh.*

Bart lowered his newspaper and gave a half smile. His peculiar green eyes met hers, then drifted away. Cece watched as he stared straight ahead. He was clearly somewhere else, and she envied his absence.

Relieved that he hadn't paid attention, she decided to keep her mouth shut. If she couldn't articulate an intelligent thought, it was best to just observe.

"What was that, Miss Burbin?" Bart blinked and looked over.

She folded her hands together and sighed. "What do you usually do this time of night?" she asked, pleased with her choice of question. She sat upright and looked kindly toward Bart, or so she thought.

"Well, Miss Burbin," he began, "I usually head to bed about now. That is, if there isn't some kind of game or entertainment fixing to be done. How about yourself?"

"Oh." She nodded. "I do the same," she whispered, "except for the late-night entertainment." She shifted her eyes across the room and gazed out the window. She couldn't see much at this time of night, except the reflection of the room against the glass: the bookcase, couches, fireplace, and Bart with his newspaper.

"You kidding me?" Bart laid his paper on the coffee table and picked up a drinking glass. "A young lady like you not going out at night?"

"Well . . . " She prepared to clarify herself. "I mean I don't go *watch* things for entertainment. I entertain myself." She smiled, remembering times when she and Jason would walk through the streets at night, marveling at God's creation and naming the stars they saw. Jason would look at one and say, "What's *his* name?" Cece would follow the line of Jason's finger and analyze the star carefully.

"*His* name? How do you know it's not a girl?"

"A girl?" he would question as though astonished by the thought. He'd pull her in close, holding her tenderly in his arms.

"What should we name her?" she'd ask playfully, catching his gaze and then turning her head away. She really wasn't shy, but Jason made her feel like a school girl. She got butterflies when he smiled.

"I don't know. I'm still not convinced it's a girl. How do you determine these things?" he would continue, holding her as he swayed from right to left—

"Well, that's certainly nice." Bart's voice brought her attention back into the room. "Have friends that you do stuff with?"

She shrugged.

Without notice, Bart stood and walked to the doorway. "Feel free to use that there blanket. I'm going to bed."

Surprised at his abrupt departure, she summoned what little sound she could and forced it up her throat. "What are the plans for tomorrow?" She lifted her hand and feigned interest in her fingernails.

"I don't quite know, Miss Burbin. I'm expecting a phone call between now and then. Someone wants to meet me in the morning."

Cece watched as Bart disappeared down the hall. The wooden floor creaked with each heavy step he took, a fact she noticed mere seconds after she first arrived. The loud nature of the floorboards would inhibit her ability to sneak around the house.

She wanted to find a phone. She would have asked Bart but refrained, considering what happened the last time she made a call in his presence. *It has to be here somewhere.* As she stood, raising her chin to get a better look over the kitchen counter, she heard a door open. Quickly, she sat back down, yanked the blanket off the back of the couch, and closed her eyes.

Bart's thunderous footsteps grew louder as he approached. "Sorry to disturb you, Miss Burbin, but I forgot to show you where the light switch is located. There's one for the first floor right back here."

She watched as he reached behind the bookshelf to indicate where the switch was.

"I'll just get that for you, since you're already sleeping."

***

The lights were off, and the house was dark. Everything was quiet, except for a gentle breeze outside. The wind brushed against the side of the house as if giving each log a soft handshake. Cece rose from the couch, wrapped the wool blanket around her shoulders, and approached the window. Although the night wasn't cool enough to warrant the use of a warm covering, she was comforted by the illusion of protection it created. The blanket felt like a big hug, holding and shielding her from the outside.

She relaxed against the wood on the right side of the window and gazed through the panes of glass. There were only a few stars out tonight, but the ones that were out shone more brightly. *Jason.* The memory of that night on the street flooded back—she in his arms as he looked into her eyes.

*"Well," she began. Her wheels spun rapidly in an attempt to develop a creative yet solid explanation as to how one could tell male and female stars apart. After a brief pause, she continued: "The really bright ones are women, naturally!"*

Jason chuckled. "'Cause women are blinding, right?"

"Blindingly beautiful," she responded with a tinge of attitude. She smiled at her love as he stepped back and took a hold of her hands. His palms were rough and calloused, and they made her feel safe. He gazed at her through intense, sparkling eyes. She looked away and took it upon herself to fill the silence. "Of course, I'm joking, but you knew that."

"Eh, maybe you were, but you didn't need to be."

She cocked her head to the side and wrinkled her eyebrows.

"You are beautiful, Cecelia."

Having heard this before, she knew the polite response. "Thank you."

Jason drew her into his arms again. "I mean it," he said. "You were fearfully and wonderfully made by God. You're one of a kind, created with a special purpose in mind, and there's no one like you."

She beamed as warmth rushed to her cheeks. She laid her head against Jason's chest, her affection thanking him for the kind reminder. After what she'd been through, it was easy to forget who she was in God's sight. Jason would never let her forget. Somehow, he constantly made her feel like the most special woman in Ichacar. As she rested in his arms, tears glossed over her eyes.

She blinked as she noticed movement on the street. She was no longer captivated by a memory, but now, by another stranger. On the roads of Brandoon were several lanterns suspended from rooftops. Underneath one of these lights stood a man in a dark jacket. He appeared impatient as he paced in front of the building, his black hair flapping in the wind. She squinted and leaned her head against the glass. She wanted to see the man's face, but he never turned in her direction. Soon, an elderly woman opened the door. The man's composure shifted. After exchanging words with the woman, he extended his arm as if offering an explanation of some sort. The woman nodded as the man entered her home.

Something about that man seemed strange, and yet, familiar. The jacket, the hair, the way he carried himself: they reminded her of someone from her past—a man whose memory she'd locked away. A man whom she would never see again.

# Chapter 8
## *Reasoning*

8:05 p.m.

Jason didn't sleep the night of his wedding day. Ever since the mysterious person with her indistinct voice had called claiming to be Cece, he'd been thinking. That night, he made a trip to the local convenience store, enduring the public barrage of pity and opinions, to get one basic thing: maps. When he had arrived back home, he proceeded up the stairs and into his bedroom without a word to Uncle Ed or Auntie May, who were preoccupied in the family room below.

Upon entering his room, he closed the door and laid out a map of the state upon his desk. He dragged his finger down the map, methodically reading the name of each city, both large and small. When he came to a city that had no possibility of holding Cecelia, he eliminated the option by crossing it off with pen. Possible locations, on the other hand, he circled. "Something like Braintoon . . . Brundan . . . Brodan . . . Banfoon . . . " He repeated these words as he searched, trying to make sense of what the woman had said. Realizing that he didn't know the location's name for sure, he circled any city that began with a B. Eventually, he had seven names circled within a one-hundred-mile radius of Ichacar, after which he opened a map of the country and continued searching.

After several interruptions for hydrating, bladder relief, and accidental catnaps, he had compiled a list of locations by 6:30 a.m. the next morning. Despite its 186 names, Jason was not satisfied. Although he identified a town that sounded like the one given by the mysterious caller, it was in Vermont, which was much too far away to be Cece's location. Being that she had disappeared yesterday morning, he reasoned that she wouldn't have gone that far. She didn't have money to travel like that, which eliminated most of the other towns that he found, except for maybe Bakersville, Burnsville, Brevard, Benton, Byrdstown, and Bomilton.

He sat back in his wooden chair and sighed. There weren't any towns close by that sounded remotely similar to Braintoon; and even if he did want to check them out, where would he possibly begin? Either Cece really wanted to get away, or someone knew how to play a cruel trick.

He leaned forward, resting his forearms on the map. He shook his head and issued a frustrated smile at the little information he knew for certain. In fact, he wasn't sure of *anything* except that Cece was gone. What if the faint noise on the phone wasn't her at all? He shoved the map off the desk; his pencils, pens, and a magnifying glass crashed to the floor with it.

"Ugh," he grunted, looking up at the ceiling. "Why can't I just know? I just wanna know!" He lowered his eyes, clenched his fists, then raised his head again. "Why did she leave me?" His head collapsed against his arms as he fell upon the desk. Tears ran down his cheeks for the first time since his fiancée had vanished.

*** 

Downstairs, Ed and May White sat comfortably in their normal places. Ed lay in his suede recliner, bare feet propped up as usual. He held Ichacar's daily paper in one hand, a mug of coffee in the other, and was still dressed in his shabby robe. May also sat, quietly rocking in the chair her brother-in-law had made for her years ago. Occasionally, she'd wander off into the kitchen, peek in the oven to ensure her cinnamon buns were rising, then return promptly to her knitting. If she started now, she could have three new scarves and one full blanket ready for the family come fall.

May had just returned from a trip to the kitchen. She approached her rocker with a sense of discomfort, placed her hands on the armrests, and slowly lowered herself down. She was so preoccupied in her thoughts that she didn't think to move the pink yarn from her seat. Immediately recognizing her error, she reached beneath her to remove the uncomfortable bulge. Although she knew Ed preferred not to be interrupted during his morning reading, she couldn't stand the silence any longer. The cinnamon buns had approximately three minutes left to cook, and she couldn't wait that long to reveal her thoughts.

"Well, Ed," she began naturally. "I just can't wrap my head around it, can you?"

Her husband kept his eyes on the paper. Raising his coffee mug to his mouth, he sipped and calmly returned it to its place on the rickety end table. "We've been over this, May," he responded.

"Yeah, I know." She looked down at her fingers as they twisted the hem of her sundress. "You think it's for the best, but I don't understand why that sweet, young lady would leave. I mean, she was like family. I thought she never wanted to leave Ichacar. She said she could live here forever." She let out a long sigh. "I don't know. I just really thought she was the apple to his pie."

Ed glanced up from his reading. "What are ya trying to say, May? That our boy's life is ruined 'cause that girl made a mistake? That she's the only one who could make him happy? Jason had no control over what she did," he declared, returning to his paper.

"Of course, his life isn't ruined, Ed. But I mean, the situation is rather odd." She rose and walked toward her husband. "She was all smiles at the rehearsal dinner. I wonder what changed her mind."

"Probably some other guy. Who knows really." He asked the question with a period, and May recognized this attempt to end the conversation.

Walking about the room, she frowned. "You'd think she'd at least have left a letter or note or something, if she didn't have the decency to say goodbye. You know, Jason isn't the *only* one she left behind." Her voice skipped as pressure built against the back of her eyes. She swallowed hard, hoping the tears would escape down her throat instead of her face, though she knew that wasn't how it worked.

"You'd think that of decent folks, but Cecelia Burbin ain't a decent person." Ed raised the paper to read a section on the bottom half of the page.

"Fiddlesticks! You've been saying that for years, but until yesterday, she's proven to be nothing but kind. How do you know that all that nonsense about her associations and all is true, anyway?" May's voice became firm. She realized that her questions were completely justified. Why should she *not* challenge such notions? The kitchen timer buzzed. As she hurried to the kitchen, she continued, "People and their vicious rumors! Why would Jason, a smart man, get mixed up with a person like who you *claim* Cece to be?"

There was a long pause as she bustled about the stove. She could hear the wrinkling of paper in the living room and presumed Ed had finally finished reading. The scent of freshly made cinnamon buns had that effect on him. Warm sugar never failed to beckon the men in her life, who had noses like bloodhounds when it came to food. Jason should be joining them any minute.

"I'm not making it up, May."

She turned and faced her husband, who was standing within an inch of her body. She looked at his stern expression. "What do you mean?"

"Cecelia's been seen with some shady folks."

"You saw her?"

He shook his head. "No, but when she first came around, Marty said he recognized her as some girl he'd seen pretty regularly when he did deliveries to that large town south of here. He'd see her shopping every Thursday morning when he arrived."

May didn't see how shopping could be such a crime. "So?"

"He said he wouldn't have thought much of it either, except that she'd leave with a mean-looking fella each time. Some guy waiting outside the window."

"Oh, Ed! It was probably her boyfriend."

He put his hands on his wife's shoulders and looked her in the eyes. "Turns out, after a month or two, Marty saw this guy's picture in the paper—arrested for armed robbery." His serious tone made May think. He released her shoulders and stepped toward the table.

"But, Ed, that doesn't mean she was involved," she tried to reason.

"No, it doesn't."

She turned back to the buns and dished them onto three plates, moving effortlessly as she carried them to the table.

"Three? Is Jason joining us this morning?" Ed asked.

"I hope so, though I reckoned he'd be here by now."

# Chapter 9
## A Visit

8:33 p.m.

After Jackson had left his comrades, he had proceeded with his plan to retrieve Marley's package from town. It was a reasonable drive once he hiked back to the main road. No doubt the fellas would be mad he took the van, which was a bonus for his trouble. In no hurry to appease his boss, he drove the speed limit, careful to follow traffic laws and not draw attention.

It had still been early in the day when he arrived in Bomilton, so he spent most of his time perched on a rocking chair outside the town's only bar—the one place a guy like him might avoid arousing suspicion. He had watched the people, making mental note of their interactions and tendencies. Overall, they seemed like an unimpressive bunch, which was good. It would make his job much easier.

When darkness fell, the little town was nestled in a foggy haze with small spouts of light issuing forth from street lanterns. It was time for him to turn in for the night. Uninterested in paying rent, he had arranged over his lunch break to stay with an elderly couple, whose home sat at the edge of town. Standing, he stretched his arms and let a series of cracks cascade down his spine. As he was about to descend the porch staircase, he overheard two men talking as they passed.

"I'm telling ya, she looked like she'd just fought a bear and lost!"

The second man chuckled. "Is she at least a looker?"

"Not bad. Small and blonde—not like the women we got around here!"

"Give 'em time. They'll fatten her up like the rest of us."

The first man slapped his oversized gut. "You got that right. Before I got married, I used to be smaller than she is!"

They belly-laughed as they pulled open the bar doors, music spilling into the street.

Jackson grinned. That was her. He had taken two breaks all day—once to eat and arrange lodging and once to use the facilities—and somehow, she had arrived when he wasn't watching. It was almost poetic—just like old times.

Shoving his hands in his pockets, he leaned against a wooden post, the chipped paint fraying against his jacket. Bart had found her, and soon, it would be time to make good on their deal. Realizing he was now late, Jackson glanced at his watch. He couldn't disappoint his hosts.

Moving down the street, he approached the house and tapped the door with his knuckles. Figuring it would take them a while to answer the door, he used the time to concoct a reason for his late arrival.

After a few minutes, he heard the door creak open. A thin beam of light pierced through the sliver and disbursed in the dark air. The door opened a little more as a large eye made room to peer out.

"Who's there, Elma?" An elderly man's raspy, muffled voice questioned the woman standing behind the door.

After scanning him up and down, the woman greeted Jackson with a warm smile. The corners of her mouth thrust her excess skin upward, revealing a wealth of deep wrinkles. Her cheeks were grandma-pink, and her large eyes had an innocent sparkle. Jackson smirked. He could walk out of this place with anything he wanted. Naïve people were the easiest targets.

"It's the kind man from earlier today—Mr. . . . . " Elma frowned, hesitating for a moment as she thought. "Connor, is it?"

"Yes, ma'am," he said, still smiling at his future donor. Her benevolence would look as good as a new pair of leather boots.

"Ah, yes, Mr. Connor," she repeated, beaming. "My, oh my, I love that accent of yours! We thought you'd decided not to come! What time is it, anyway?" She cocked her head sideways and hollered back into the house, "What's the time, Earl?"

"I beg your pardon," Jackson politely interjected. Elma returned her attention to the guest. "I would have arrived sooner, but I had car troubles and had to walk a good ways." He looked down at his dirty shoes and then lifted his head. "Now, don't you worry about me. I'll take care of it tomorrow. For now, I'm just grateful for your hospitality."

She nodded, opening the door wide. "Of course! Please, come on in."

He entered, wiped his feet, and removed his shoes before proceeding to the living area.

"Can I get ya anything to eat, Mr. Connor?"

"No, thank you, ma'am. I had quite a walk and should probably be getting some sleep." He removed his coat and laid it over the back of a tiny, cream-colored sofa. The couch would have been large enough for him to sleep comfortably had he still been twelve. Now, his legs would certainly dangle over the edge, but it was no trouble. He didn't plan to sleep much.

"Ah, yes, of course you should," replied Elma as she disappeared, then reappeared with a crocheted blanket. She carried it over to the couch where he stood. "Made it myself!"

He politely received the blanket and spread it gently across the sofa as Elma watched. He turned his head and gave her a wide grin. "Why, thank you, ma'am. It's lovely!"

By now, Earl had shuffled down the hall and was standing in the doorway to the living room. Elma looked over at her husband and bade Jackson goodnight.

"We'll see you in the morning!" she said as she followed her husband.

"You will indeed."

***

Faint light poured through the window from the lantern outside. It was just enough light for Jackson to cast shadow puppets against the wall—a level to which he stooped only in complete boredom. He wanted to leave the house now, take care of business, and return before anyone knew he was gone. But he knew better than to rush things. That's how mistakes got made—that and Tommy's relentless stomach. He smirked. No, he would wait a few hours to be sure his hosts were sound asleep. That was the smart move.

He sat twiddling his fingers. He knew better than to sleep, which was fine, because he wasn't tired anyway. Years of sleeping during the day did that to a man. Regardless of being tired or not, sleeping in someone else's home wasn't ideal—they lacked his perfectly flattened pillow.

Staring forward in a daze, he thought back to the moment when he first met Cece: a young, scrawny girl with an eagerness to rebel against everything.

He and Tommy had been playing a round of Go Fish in the alley behind Cameron's Bakery in Vicktown, a large city far south of here. The noise of traffic accompanied their games, cars driving endlessly back and forth across the alley's entrances. He and Tommy sat against opposing brick walls, tossing cards toward each other. They were eighteen at the time, out of school, and unemployed—except for their night job.

Marley had been gone for longer than usual that afternoon, which could be a very bad sign in that neighborhood.

*"Yo, man, what time did the Marley brotha leave again?"* Tommy was still in his *"cool guy"* phase.

*"Must you, Tommy?"* He shook his head. *"If you were any closer, I'd smack you one."*

*"You gonna smack me?"* Tommy questioned, as if the whole idea were completely ridiculous.

*"Yeah, I'd smack you!"*

*"And how you gonna do that, huh? I'm bigger and stronger than you."* Making a muscle with his arm, Tommy kissed it and winked at Jackson.

*Furious at the outrageous claims, he rose to his feet. "You want some o' this?"* he challenged.

*Tommy stood and moved forward.*

*"Huh?" Jackson gave his friend a light shove across the shoulders.*

*"Yeah, I do!"*

He grinned as he sat on the couch, replaying the incident in his head. He liked this memory of Tommy: tough, confident, funny. He was a real neat guy until Marley started digging his teeth into him for every little thing. Now, Tommy seemed more like a three-hundred-pound mechanical teddy bear. He was a softy who did what he was told, but you wouldn't want him to jump on you. Jackson shook his head. *Man, Tommy. You could have really been something.*

*While the two wrestled in the alley, Marley approached with a small girl. "Hey, idiots!" he yelled.*

*They stopped. Stumbling about, Jackson felt a hard hit to his face and put a hand up to his nose and felt blood. He turned to Tommy, who was bent over catching his breath, and punched him across the face.*

*"Ahh! Dude!" Tommy wailed as he grabbed the side of his head. Jackson shook his throbbing hand and placed it in between his knees, trying desperately to contain tears.*

*"You got a hard head, man," he forced out.*

*"Perhaps you shoulda thought about that before you punched me!"*

*"Guys!" Marley yelled. He, too, was eighteen and obviously considered himself the epitome of cool, though the closest he got to cool was the way his breath made everyone's face freeze in disgust. "We have a guest." He smiled as he pushed Cece forward.*

*They stared at the child.*

*"She's like, what? Seven?" Jackson walked over to the girl and, putting his bloody hand on her head, yanked her blonde hair back. Her eyes shot upward.*

*"Ouch!" she hollered with a frown. She frantically threw her fists at him but to no avail.*

*"Don't hurt her!" Marley scolded. "And no, she's fifteen."*

*"Fifteen?" Tommy scratched his head. "I think that's still kidnapping."*

*"I didn't force her, you idiot! She wanted to come with me."*

*"She wanted to come with you? Why would she wanna do a thing like that?"*

*"I dunno," Marley began. "I guess I'm that incredible!"*

*"Yeah, incredibly stupid!"*

*Tommy busted up laughing as the two continued to argue; however, Jackson didn't catch the rest of their debate. He maintained his firm grasp* on Cece's hair, her chin pulled upward. He looked at the frail girl: her tiny blue leggings, white sweater, and angry eyes. What did this little thing want? She was nothing but a worm.

"Jackson!" Marley snarled.

Looking at the girl once more, he released his grip. She yelped.

"She'll do, won't she?" He glared viciously at Marley.

The crooked weasel looked back at him. "If you mean that she's pretty for her age and we look great together, then yes, she'll do." Marley smiled. "Cecelia, sweetheart, why don't you take this money and buy yourself a muffin from the bakery? If anyone asks, just tell them your mom is outside waiting for you," he said. The young girl accepted the money and shuffled off to get her snack.

Jackson grimaced as Marley watched her leave.

"What's the matter with you?" He moved forward, ready to attack.

"Wait! I didn't do anything wrong! You gotta believe me!"

He backed off for a moment. "Explain."

"I was out scouting like normal, and I see this little girl watching me. I try to ignore her, but you know how it is when someone just won't look away! Annoying as all get out! I started to leave, but she ran after me and introduced herself. Said she's running away and wanted to come with me."

"Really?" Jackson figured it was a lie, until a few years later when Cece verified the story.

"It's the truth! Why else would I've let her wander off on her own? You think I'd be that dumb? I know the rules—we don't take hostages. She wanted to come with me!"

Slowly stepping away, he kept his eyes locked on Marley.

"Just so long as you aren't getting us in over our heads, Mar," Tommy chimed in. Jackson still hadn't looked away. "She's your worm, isn't she, Marley?"

"What's that supposed to mean?"

"She sure looks like one. Gonna use her to reel in some fish, are ya?" He folded his arms and raised an eyebrow. His cleverness impressed even himself at times.

"She'll fit, won't she?" Marley answered. It was the first believable thing he'd said. Despicable, but believable.

"Does she know?"

Marley turned and walked toward the street in the direction his new toy had gone, obviously avoiding the question.

"She doesn't know." Jackson leaned toward Tommy. "If his plan backfires, we're out of here, you got that?"

Tommy nodded.

Finally, the worm returned with a banana muffin and some change. She handed the coins to Marley and re-entered the alley.

Smiling, Jackson approached the young girl. "Hey, there. I'm terribly sorry about what happened earlier. A little misunderstanding, that's all."

The girl lowered her face and ate.

"We haven't been formally introduced. The name's Jackson."

She raised her eyes to meet his, then turned her head away.

He nodded and straightened as the worm returned to her muffin. He gestured to Tommy, and the two approached Marley at the end of the alley. As Tommy walked out, Jackson thrust his finger in Marley's face.

"She's your responsibility. You hear me? I want nothing to do with her."


Three hours had passed like flowing molasses. Jackson stood, stretched his arms, and proceeded to a window at the side of the house, out of view from the main street. After unlatching the lock, he carefully raised the window, removed the screen, and climbed out. Once outside, he gently laid the screen against the house and lowered the window, keeping it open just enough to get his fingers under on the way back in. He crept toward the front porch.

Bart lived nearby. The memory was still fresh from their meeting early that morning. After he and Tommy went back to the river and realized Cece was gone, they drove to the closest town first: Bomilton. It was still dark out, but Bart was already awake, chopping wood on the outskirts of town. The guy had been so easy to manipulate. Took them back to his house to discuss the particulars, and the rest was history. What a chump. All Jackson had to do now was slip inside, take Cece, and skip town, free from paying the "reward" he'd promised.

Scanning the outline of houses across the street, he stopped. There it was, one block down. Casually, he crossed the road, assuming nobody would be awake to see him—and even if they were, it was too dark for someone to recognize his face. Although he was still careful, he didn't care for unnecessary precautions.

Once across, he sauntered toward the log cabin. Approaching the porch steps, he paused for a moment to evaluate his plan. If the package was inside, as he hoped, things might get a little rocky from here. That girl could maneuver about in the night and certainly would not be sleeping—he was sure of it.

Noticing two first-story windows, he decided to look in. He crouched down and slunk up the steps, then crawled to the first window. He peered inside, using a hand to block the glare from a nearby lantern. It appeared to be a kitchen area. He waited a few seconds. No movement. He continued to the next window, crawling across a mat that read "Welcome." Raising his body, he knelt and peered inside.

There she was, sleeping on a couch with a blanket draped over her body. Grinning, he stood, casting a shadow into the room; but as he reached for the window handle, Cece shot up on the couch. He fell to the ground. If she was right by the door, there's no way he'd get the drop on her. What he needed was the element of surprise, like they had the night before. If he entered now, she'd probably fight back, prompting Bart to come help. The last thing he needed was an eyewitness.

Turning, he hurried down the stairs and ran back across the street. After climbing in the window of his hosts' home, he looked at his filthy shirt. Dirt: the enemy of ignorance, who could rat him out. He turned his shirt inside-out and brushed off his pants into the empty fireplace. Although he thought about going out again, he decided that what he'd planned for tomorrow would be much too fun to pass up. The look on her face would be priceless when she saw him. She'd certainly be surprised, considering that when they interacted with her last night, she was clueless. Sure, she was blindfolded, but Marley's voice disguise was a total joke. This new life had really taken its toll on her mental prowess. She wasn't even a shadow of her former self. Getting caught, being clueless, falling asleep in a stranger's home—going *with* a stranger: she had lost it.

His eyes scanned the mantel and landed on what appeared to be a crystal crescent moon. He laughed. *Oh, Cece,* he thought. *Your fascination with creation plays a hand in your undoing.* Pocketing the small treasure, he slumped on the couch. *You brought this upon yourself.*

***

The town was black, a qualifying factor for each job. Three street lanterns were dimmed by a thick mist hovering about the buildings. All that moved were two thin feet that crept from out of an alley and onto the street. Cece looked about cautiously, assessing her surroundings. She recognized the building beside the alley; it was McGreggor's.

She froze on the side of the street, fear sinking into her body. She glanced right and left, then proceeded forward. She didn't want to go but found herself moving anyway. She trotted across the street, floating like a gazelle. Although it was dark, she knew she must take precautions to avoid detection, which meant moving quickly. Once across the street, she stooped between two buildings and looked up. This was the house. She didn't recognize it, but somehow, she knew that it was her assignment. She had always known, but in previous cases, the knowledge came from pictures she'd been shown.

The darkness weighed upon her as she tip-toed toward a window—she could feel its grip like a hand around her throat. She shivered. Arriving at the window, she peered in and saw the face of a man staring back at her. His sinister eyes and witty smirk made her shriek as she stumbled backward—

Cece's eyes popped open as she awoke, panting furiously. She wiped a tear from her cheek and folded her arms, resting each hand in a moist armpit. There she lay, refusing to sleep again. Thoughts warred in her mind: Would they find her? What would happen if they did? Would she ever get home? Finally, she rolled over on her side. *Will they ever forget?*

In a soft, inaudible whisper, she prayed, "God, please help me. I know that's not my life anymore." She paused. "I want to be free from it all."

## Chapter 10
## No Thank Yous Necessary

Sunday, 9:03 a.m.

Cece fell back asleep. She had been determined not to let her mind wander about loosely in dreams, mixing the present with the past. But against her will, her heavy eyelids eventually closed, only to be pried open again—this time, by the ringing of a telephone.

She blinked a few times; each time, her surroundings became clearer. She rubbed her eyes with her fists and yawned as she sat upright on the sofa. Then, it struck her. A phone! She held still and listened carefully. A soft, muffled voice seeped through the living room wall. Carefully, she arose from the couch and crept toward the sound. She gently touched each floorboard with the ball of her foot, testing its creakiness, before shifting her body weight forward.

When she got to the wall, she placed her ear against it and listened. Still indistinguishable. Pressing her back against the wallpaper, Cece slunk around the corner and down the hallway. She expected to find Bart's room somewhere around there, and sure enough, she did. As she approached the brown, splintered door to her left, the voice became louder. She leaned her head toward the door and froze.

"Now?"

Bart's voice sounded different. It lacked the overconfidence she'd previously observed. Instead, it was like a storeowner at gunpoint:

faking bravery to hide its fear. She'd heard the tone many times before; although this time, she was confused. Why would Bart be scared? There was a long pause, during which she presumed the other person was speaking.

"No, sir. You got me wrong. You wanted a favor—I did you a favor. If you're the guy I thought you were, you can wait until I'm good and ready!" The strength in Bart's voice returned, which made Cece smile until she considered the call's context. Was this the call he was expecting? Possibilities raced through her mind until she heard him say, "Fine, Mr. Connor. I'll meet you then . . . yeah."

Her eyes shifted back and forth in panic. As she went to return to the living room, the floorboard squeaked. Realizing Bart must have heard her, she ran to the sofa and pulled the wool blanket over her head. Mr. Connor: not a name she knew, which was a slight relief.

Bart emerged from his bedroom, walked around the couch where she pretended to sleep, and entered the kitchen. "I sure hope you're fixin' to get up sometime soon, Miss Burbin. You have quite the day ahead of you."

Cece opened her mouth to respond, but nothing came out. Lowering the blanket, she twisted her torso and looked over the side of the sofa. She tried her best to appear as though she'd just awoken.

"I do?" she mouthed.

Bart glanced at her, then rattled around in a kitchen drawer. Seconds later, he emerged with a pencil and paper in hand. "I think you'll be needing these," he said, handing her the items. "Now, what was it you were saying?"

After Bart prepared breakfast, the two went back and forth with their conversation. Cece wrote her questions and comments, while

Bart answered verbally between bites of toast. His sensible responses put most of her nerves at ease. He even explained what the call was about without her directly asking. Apparently, he was in the wood business and had chopped some logs for a friend. He had agreed to deliver the wood today, but that was before he knew he'd have company. He had hoped to reschedule, but it turned out his friend was ungrateful and impatient; so rather than risk losing business, Bart arranged to meet Mr. Connor early as planned.

She smiled, and Bart returned her pleasant expression with one of his own. She was thrilled at the idea of being alone with the phone—if only she could find a way to get her message through to Jason. Hopefully, Bart's absence would allow her plenty of time; and if things went her way, she'd be gone before he returned.

"Thank you," she wrote, drawing a little happy face after. It made perfect sense: Bart's uneasy tone on the phone, the mention of a favor, even his final agreement to meet the man. And yet, there was something still bothering her. She withdrew the paper once more: "Mr. Connor?"

"Yes," Bart confirmed. "Why don't you go get ready? Your dress should be clean . . . A little rip here and there, but it should do all right." He gave her a reassuring nod toward the bathroom.

She hesitated. "Ready for what?"

He read her question. "I figure it's a beautiful day for some fresh air. You can come on with me, and we'll figure out how to get you home. How does that sound?"

Calmly, she stood and walked toward the bathroom door. While this changed things, it still ended in a way home. She thought about Bart. It was silly of her to think he was involved in some scheme.

Maybe the scene at McGreggor's last night was his attempt at humor, although she certainly didn't get it.

Her gown hung from the doorframe. Taking it in her hands, the silky, purple fabric caressed her fingers. She hugged it against her chest, fighting back tears as she inhaled the fresh aroma. She could trust Bart. She must. What other choice was there? He would help her get home—help her escape this living nightmare. It was a dream from which she'd thought she had awoken years ago.

She glanced back at Bart, who remained seated at the coffee table. He didn't seem like the type of person who'd hurt someone. When he looked over, she mouthed the words, "Thank you," before turning and entering the bathroom.

"No thank yous necessary, Miss Burbin," she heard him say. "No thanks necessary."

# Chapter 11
## *Four of a Kind*

June 19, 1986

A cool breeze twisted about the streets, brushing against the gang's vehicle. As Marley sat tapping the black leather steering wheel, Tommy—who had been exiled to the back seat—rambled about where he'd go for breakfast. Unfortunately, Wilson's Waffle House didn't open until 6:00 a.m. Marley knew because Tommy wouldn't shut up about it. Apparently, that restaurant wasn't an option because cry-baby Tommy would be asleep by then.

"Is it too much to ask for an all-night breakfast place? What's a guy gotta do to get some bacon 'round here?"

"You could cook it, you moron," Marley answered as he continued to glance in his right-side mirror.

"Whatever," Tommy mumbled. "Half of what's good about bacon is not having to make it."

Marley grabbed the window crank and jerked it in circles. Slowly, his left window inched down into the door. Placing his forearm on top, he glanced across the street.

"Psst! Jackson!" he whispered. Jackson ignored him. "Jackson!" Still nothing. "Jackson!" He raised his voice and, immediately regretting his error, ducked back into the car.

"He won't respond to you, Mar," Tommy said. "As far as he's concerned, you don't exist. Remember?"

"Yes, yes, I know . . . I'm not stupid!" He looked at his nails, bit off dead skin on his right index finger, spit it out the window, and continued tapping his heel against the floor. His heart was a pounding menace as he watched Jackson stroll down the street.

"There she is!" Tommy pointed.

Marley's eyes responded immediately. Sure enough, there was Cece window shopping. She walked a few steps, looked in a window, walked a few more, bent to tie her shoe, and so forth. He started the car.

Finally, she made it to the door and slid in the back seat beside Tommy.

"Took your good, old time, huh?" Marley began as he drove.

"Excuse me?"

"Walking that slow—what's the matter with you?"

She huffed. "You want me to run out of there, is that it? So if anyone sees me, they'll know? What, are you *trying* to get me caught?" Her attitude angered him more than he could stand.

"You're a spoiled brat. You know that?" He could feel heat rushing to his face. "You get what you want because you're *so* special, because we *need* you. Well, I've about had it!"

As he continued talking, he saw her reflection in the rearview mirror. She was staring out the window, her face blank and cold.

Unimpeded by her silence, he raised his voice until taking a break to breathe.

"Don't worry, Cece. I get you." Tommy laid his hand on her shoulder.

Marley frowned. He swerved to miss a car, then watched as Cece jerked her shoulder away.

"Something wrong?" Tommy questioned.

He jumped back in. "Does nobody listen to anything I say? Tommy, I just told you everything you need to know about her. She's ungrateful."

There was silence in the backseat as he shifted his attention to the road.

***

After the gang had arrived home, Jackson walked through the door. He immediately noticed Marley and Tommy playing video games on the floor. Despite his disgust at the crushed popcorn bits sprawled everywhere, he remained focused. "How'd she do?"

"Fine. We got what we wanted . . . Could have been better. You know how it is." Marley's eyes were glued to the television as he and Tommy played "Speed Racers."

"Well, where is she?"

"Sleeping? Who knows?"

Jackson held his breath as he stepped over the two bodies in front of him and headed to the bedroom. Their place—or "hideout" as Marley liked to call it—was large enough to fit one person comfortably. With four of them, the living-kitchen-dining room was constantly overcrowded with a nasty stench coming from the bathroom.

Pushing the door open, Jackson made his way across the crumb-covered floor to where Cece lay on one of the crammed mattresses.

"How'd you do, Kid?" he asked. Leaning in, he quickly pulled back as she turned her head away, nearly slapping him with her hair.

"I know how to work that ponytail, Kid, and you won't like it."

Cece rolled onto her back and looked up. Her face seemed to doubt his threat. Jackson smirked. Girl had attitude, which was fine, as long as it came with results.

"It's me. How do you think I did?" she responded with an air of cockiness.

He laughed. "Oh, is that how it's gonna be then? In that case, where's my share?"

She sat up and pointed at the door. "With everyone else's . . . except mine." She winked.

"You trying to pull a fast one on me, huh? I'm not buying what you're selling."

"Oh?"

"No. Now I want my fair share," he continued.

Cece frowned. "Since when did you start caring about fair?"

"Okay, since we're not playing fair, give it to me!" In one swift motion, he grabbed the rebellious teenager, held her at his side like a football, and felt under her mattress. Despite her kicking and shrieking, he was able to search thoroughly. The little worm's efforts were no match for him. She had all the strength of a baby field mouse.

Finally, Jackson released her, satisfied with what he found.

"Don't take it all!" she pleaded.

He peered at her as she panted on the floor. "Calm down now . . . I won't. You just be straight with me next time, got it?" He gave a comforting smile.

"But I didn't do anything wrong. I shorted the others, not you. More for us."

"I shouldn't have to ask." Without another word, he left.

***

The gang had a habit of sleeping during the day, so they would be alert at night. Cece pretended to be asleep as Tommy, and eventually Marley, stumbled into the room. She wanted to protest when Marley took the mattress next to her but, instead, determined to make it the worst sleep of his life. After careful consideration, she decided to issue a kick periodically throughout the day as he slept, pretending to have a bad dream. If she tried to punch or slap him, there was a chance he'd wake up and break her arm. Nope, a kick was safer. Besides, the bones in her legs would be more difficult to snap.

Unfortunately, the fun of kicking him was short-lived. He didn't even budge—must have been all that popcorn.

As she struggled to sleep, she heard the front door open and close. She sprang out of bed, made it a point to step on Marley, and hurried out of the room.

"What in the . . . ?" she heard as she closed the door behind her.

"Morning, Jackson," she mumbled, approaching the living room.

He turned his head, winked at her, and plopped down on the couch.

"How was your night—I mean, day?" As she moved into the kitchen to get some water, she paused. She smelled something . . . good. It was the light scent of roses. "What's that smell?" She followed the scent and found herself at the point where Jackson lay.

"What are you, a hound dog?" he mumbled, eyes sealed shut.

She stared at him. Her eyes drifted down his body as she analyzed the pieces of his clothing. She squeezed her hips on the couch beside him and saw it. There, on his neck, was a brownish red mark.

"What's that?" she questioned, rising from her spot on the couch.

He forced one eye open. "What?"

"That mark on your neck?"

"Oh." He smirked. "You really wanna know?"

She bit her lips and watched his eyelids creep open as he quickly added, "I'm kidding. Calm down, Kid. It's nothing. Don't worry about it."

"Aren't I allowed to ask about *anything?*" she questioned sarcastically.

"No, not really. You sound like a nosy sister. You know better than to be acting like that."

"You better hope Marley and Tommy don't find out."

"What?"

"That you've been seeing someone. They might think you're spilling stuff."

"They'll be okay," Jackson stated, eyes now closed.

"Well, next time, before you go on a date or whatever, think of the rest of us. I don't want you putting us in danger."

He chuckled. Cece sighed as she went into the kitchen, unsatisfied with the conversation. Nobody took her seriously. As she prepared some water and a snack, there was a knock at the door. Surprised, she peered out the peephole and turned the knob. In front of her stood a beautiful, dark-haired woman with bright-red lipstick.

"Hello there, sweetheart. Does Robbie Jones live here?" the woman asked as she chomped on a large piece of bubble gum. Her smile revealed hundreds of blinding white teeth.

"Robbie Jones?" Cece looked back at the couch and rolled her eyes. "Yeah, just a minute."

"Tell her to go away!" Jackson's edict arose before she could say a word. Slightly surprised by her friend's order, she couldn't resist the temptation to let whoever it was stay.

"Come on in." She feigned politeness as she extended her hand inward.

Still smiling, the woman moved past her and toward Jackson.

"How'd you get here, Silvy?" he asked, irritation in his voice.

"I followed you."

"You what?" He sat up.

"I followed you. I didn't want to lose you again." The lady put her hand on his face. "Who'd ever wanna lose a slick guy like you?"

Cece grimaced. The woman was so sappy, it was gross. How could Jackson possibly like someone this desperate? She knew the answer to that. There's no way he'd still like the woman after a move like this. She chuckled inside at the thought of his current discomfort. Ready to excuse herself, she began, "Well, I'll be back in my room. You kids have fun."

"Now, wait a second," the woman objected. "Robbie, you haven't introduced me to your friend."

"That's because you were just leaving."

Although he was doing a good job of holding it together, Cece knew "Silvy" would soon hear it if she didn't take a hike.

"Nonsense. What's your name, honey?" Silvy rose and approached her.

Stunned, Cece answered, "Nancy Smith."

"Nice to meet you, Nancy! My name's Silvia Reynolds." The woman extended a hand and immediately withdrew it after Cece waved her full hands. Her pretzels and soda wouldn't carry themselves.

"How old are you, honey?"

She detested all of these questions but answered them anyway. "Eighteen." That's what Jackson would expect her to say. They all thought she was three years older than she really was.

"How about that? You sure do look young for your age. Teenage years can be such fun! And when do you turn nineteen?"

Declining to answer, Cece entered the bedroom and kicked the door closed. As she stumbled over Tommy's obnoxiously large feet, she heard Jackson's demand through the wall.

"Get out," he ordered.

She grinned at the stalker woman's misfortune. Clearly, Jackson had no real attachments to Silvy. Hers was just one of a hundred shades of lipstick that had stained his neck over the years. Did these women really think he'd fall for them? Why—because they were beautiful? Beauty doesn't make someone love you. Cece grimaced. She hated that word. What did it have to do with real life? It was a lie—the master tool of manipulation. It tricked women into an illusion of safety and secured their loyalty while the man did whatever he pleased. Soon, the woman hated the man, and everything fell apart.

She would never believe in the L-word. She was too smart for that. Everyone wants something, and if they find someone who can give it to them, then okay. But they should realize it's convenience, not love. She plopped down on her mattress and threw a pretzel in her mouth. Sipping her soda, she looked toward the door. None of it really mattered. Nobody gets what they want in the end. That's life.

# Chapter 12
## *Real*

March 13, 1994
Sunday, 10:15 a.m.

Shortly after breakfast, Bart and Cece headed out for the day. Cece felt clean again with her fresh hair and washed dress. If she had anything else to wear that wasn't twice her size, she would have worn it. This dress, although gorgeous, was already a sad memory.

"Now then," Bart said with friendliness in his voice, "I got to meet this fella right down at that there corner." Her eyes followed Bart's finger as he pointed down the street. "You can explore wherever you'd like, Miss Banks." He winked. "But I'd start with the other end of town if I was you." He raised his hand as if tipping an invisible hat and walked away.

"But . . ." She tried to object, but it was too late, and her nonexistent voice couldn't muster up a peep, let alone a yell.

She watched as he strolled toward his meeting place. So far, it didn't look like anybody was waiting for him. Sure, there were people passing by, stopping to talk and window shopping, but other than that, nothing. She turned to wander through the other end of town, although she wasn't sure what to make of Bart's directions. She would have been more comfortable sticking with him, which surprised her. Perhaps now she could find a place with a phone. *Rats!* She put a hand gently against her throat. She kept forgetting.

Walking along the left-hand side of the street, she glanced in various windows until she happened upon a ceramics shop. She stopped and looked thoughtfully at a plate displayed in the window. Its surface was smooth, the gloss finish reflecting the sunlight that peered in. Soft blue strokes covered the sky and bright-green hills ran across the background. They were dappled with medium and dark green blades of grass, which made the hills look real. In the foreground of the plate was a town: layers upon layers of brightly-colored buildings. The purples, reds, pinks, yellows, oranges—almost every color was represented on this plate's face. It was gorgeous. She smiled as she pulled open the door and entered.

"May I help you?" a pleasant voice asked from behind the front counter.

She shook her head. Slowly, she browsed the tall aisles of the store, examining the ceramic creations and keeping an eye out for the plate she liked so much. Rounding another row of shelves, she once again approached the end wall that contained what she thought were empty boxes.

"Is this the one you're looking for?"

She turned her head and found herself standing face-to-face with a man who resembled someone all too familiar. Her eyes fluttered as she studied his slicked-back hair. Not as long as Jackson's had been, but equally jet black and just as pristine. She stumbled back and steadied herself against a shelf. Thankfully, nothing spilled. She couldn't afford to be the proverbial bull in a china shop.

Why did she feel so dizzy? She looked back at the man, who was now blurry. Lifting her hand to her face, she saw eight, no, ten fingers. Her eyes scanned the hazy image, stopping at a thick patch of her purple skin. The bruise looked even worse than yesterday, or maybe that was because she was seeing double.

"Excuse me, Miss. Are you okay?"

"I'm fi—" As she stepped toward him, she tripped over her own heel and fell forward. In an instant, everything went dark.

***

Bart turned and walked confidently toward his rendezvous point with Mr. Connor. Although he wasn't quite sure how his client would respond, he determined that this was the best course of action. Why comply so easily to a stranger's demands? If Mr. Connor wanted the girl, he'd have to up his game.

Nodding politely as people passed by, he continued to walk. He tucked his hands casually in his pockets and tried to look natural. Fortunately, he arrived at the meeting place early and had time to duck into McGreggor's for a pack of jerky.

"Hey, how you doin' there, Bart?" McGreggor's cheerful voice filled the store. He walked around the register and gave him a hearty pat on the back, shaking hands in the process. "Was afraid I wouldn't be seeing you for a while—not after what happened last night and all. Miss Banks, was it?"

Bart looked at his comrade with a forced smile. "That's right." Holding a ten-pack of jerky in his hand, he asked, "This the best stuff you got, Big G?"

McGreggor laughed. "You're kidding me, right? Man, you've been eating this stuff for years! You know as well as I do, that there jerky's the best-tasting meat around!" Suddenly, his expression changed. He lowered his eyebrows, a sense of concern in his face. "How's the girl?"

Bart turned his head, staring McGreggor right in the face. He refused to acknowledge what Big G may have been implying. "Fine. Still homesick, but fine," he responded.

"Still homesick," his friend repeated, nodding his head as he returned to his spot behind the counter. "Well, missing family can be a heartache, but at least she ain't that Cesonia, or Stephanie. Eh, what was her name?"

"Couldn't tell you," Bart said, pretending to search the shelves for more product.

McGreggor rubbed his fingers against his temples, squeezing his eyes shut. "Cecelia!" he declared. "At least, she's not Cecelia." He leaned his elbows on the cool countertop and waved his friend closer. Reluctantly, Bart approached him, still holding the pack of jerky. "I got a bad feeling about that fella that came in here real early the other morning, you remember me tellin' ya about 'im. Came tapping on the door before we was even open, looking for that girl." He shook his head. "I wish I'd never opened it. Something strange about that fella."

Bart chuckled awkwardly and stood erect. "You got that right," he responded, tossing his item on the counter for purchase.

"Three ninety-nine."

He laid four dollars on the counter, grabbed the bag, and headed out the door.

"See you around, Bart!"

Bart waved his hand behind his head. "I hope so," he muttered, stepping onto the street. He grabbed a piece of jerky, placed it securely between his molars, and ripped off a chunk. Slowly, he turned his head from one side of town to the other, keeping an eye out for his contact. Grinding the jerky in his teeth, he bit again. That was the stuff.

"Excuse me." He flinched as a recognizable voice came from behind. It was coated in an Italian accent and arrogance. He turned to face the voice. "I believe you have something for me," the man said with a smile.

Bart remained silent. He stuck the jerky back in his mouth and aggressively removed a piece. This "client" was only slightly shorter than he and didn't seem to be easily intimidated. Nonetheless, he rolled his shoulders back and stood tall, counting on his brawny appearance to help in some way.

"Did she talk to anyone? Make any calls?"

He declined to reply.

"You hear me?" The man cocked his head sideways and took a step forward. "Or are you not the sharpest tool in the shed?"

"Talking's kind of hard if you ain't got no voice," he finally responded.

The client smirked, shaking his head as he looked down.

"And I don't see what the big deal is about making a phone call if you're trying to get her back home anyway." He tried to appear apathetic, glancing around and eating his snack.

"Because it was part of the deal," the man insisted. "And if you must know, she lies. She'll do anything to ruin her life, but all we want is what's best for her. She says she's calling her 'boyfriend,' but really, she's off making more plans to get farther away from the people who love her." The client's face softened. "We miss her, okay? Her family misses her. We'll do anything to get her back. It's time for her to come home."

Bart carefully considered what Mr. Connor had said. It certainly explained why Miss Burbin was dressed the way she was and why he found her crossing a river.

"Look, I'm not sure what's going through that head of yours," the client began, moving forward. Instantly, though, he stepped back and started again. "I bet you're a busy guy, and I respect that. Really, I do. So, let's do us all a favor and take care of business. I have to get my cousin home. Her mama's worried sick, like I told you. Now, you hand over my dear Cecelia; I'll give you the reward money; and everybody's happy." He threw his hands up in the air with a smile. "How does that sound?"

Bart continued to chew his beef. "I'm sorry, Mr. Connor, but I don't have your package—" He stared at a point beside the client's head and tried not to make eye contact.

"Excuse me?" the man interjected as he moved closer. "I know you have her!" His voice rose. Instantly, he stopped, cleared his throat, and lowered his voice. "What about our conversation this morning? You found her and decided not to bring her!" He lurched forward and grabbed hold of Bart's shirt. "What happened to respect, huh?"

Bart dropped his jerky and clasped the angry customer's wrists. Clearly, there was a misunderstanding. "Whoa, relax. I meant I don't have her here . . . with me. She's out shopping, but I bet she'll be glad to see you. You have the money?" Looking around, he noticed a small crowd that had gathered, whispering to each other as they watched.

Mr. Connor had noticed, too, and a well-formed tear was already in his eye. "You want me to pay you for my own family?" He snuck a peek at the captivated audience. "I don't have any money. My cousin is all I have!" More tears appeared, and the women were eating it up.

"What?" Bart huffed, throwing his hands in the air. "This is ridiculous! Y'all aren't buying this, are you?"

"Oh, Mister." Barbara emerged from the crowd. She was a middle-aged woman who always butted in. She was one of those few women who could die if she didn't interfere, so keeping her opinions to herself was not an option. "There, there. It'll be all right. We'll straighten this whole thing out. You'll get your cousin back; you best believe me, you will."

The man sniffled. "Thank you, Miss. I usually don't get emotional like this . . ."

Bart rolled his eyes.

"It's just, I reckon this man knows where my lost cousin is and for some reason . . . I can't . . ." He turned his head away. The women were practically melting, elbowing each other and making eyes at him.

"Yes, go on," Barbara urged.

"For some reason, he's trying to keep her from me unless I pay him."

Simultaneously, as if on cue, the small crowd of people broke into chaos.

"Oh, now that's ridiculous!"

"Really now, Bart, how could you?"

"What in the world?"

Placing her hands on her round hips, Barbara looked at him.

In his own defense, he spoke up. "You can't possibly believe this guy! He . . . he . . ." Words escaped him. There was no way they would understand. Whatever he said would make him sound like a bad guy, which he wasn't.

Barbara tilted her head down and gave him the eyebrow. "I think you best be giving this man what he wants, so he can be on his way."

"But, Barbara!"

"Don't 'But, Barbara' me!" She shook her finger. "You got no business standing between this man and his family!"

He glared at Mr. Connor and slowly backed away. "Fine," he agreed. "I'll go get her. You people just hold your horses."

"Just go!" the woman demanded. "This man is waiting for a family member. Now, hurry! We'll keep him company 'til you get back."

Mr. Connor's black eyes followed him closely. He was sure they'd pierce a hole in his back once he turned around. After tripping over McGreggor's steps, he had no choice but to face forward. Miss Burbin should be around here somewhere. It's no wonder she ran away. With a family like that, he'd run away, too. Looking in the windows of storefronts as he passed, he reassured himself that this was a good thing. She would be taken home to receive the care and help she deserved. She seemed like a nice girl, aside from the scene at McGreggor's last night.

He glanced at the sun and took a deep breath. It was a beautiful day, perfect for a special occasion. Reunification of a family was special. Perhaps this was meant to be. He kept walking, each step feeling heavier than the last. If it was all so right, why did something feel . . . wrong?

# Chapter 13
## *Ceramic Creativity*

10:45 a.m.

A small bell shook as Bart entered the ceramic store. He'd been glancing in windows and searching through shops along the left side of the street. His plan was to walk up one side and down the other until he found Miss Burbin. At this point, his stomach was in knots. On the bright side, so many thoughts dashed about his head that he found it difficult to get overwhelmed by any one thing. It helped that he wasn't quite sure what he'd gotten himself into. Yes, he knew Mr. Connor was shady the moment he agreed to work with him, but he needed the money. Besides, he had done a few under-the-table deals in the past and thought he was plenty prepared to handle whatever this shady character threw his way. Unfortunately, he had been unacquainted with Mr. Connor's superb acting skills. Plus, the ladies of the town probably thought the new guy was handsome, which made Bart yesterday's news.

*Can't those people see past the tips of their noses?* he thought as he passed quickly through the shop aisles. *He'll get them hooked and yank back on their chains so hard, they'll break in two.* While grumbling to himself, he finally found the place where a few people were caring for someone. He stopped and moved his head around, trying to see what had happened, but the shopkeeper's body blocked his view.

"Excuse me, Ms. Nutmegen," he began. "Who is it you got there?"

The shopkeeper looked back, although she already knew the voice. "Morning! I'm sorry, I didn't hear you come in." She returned her attention to the person in front of her. "Not quite sure, to tell you the truth. Gal looks like she's sixteen!"

He approached the small group of people. The first thing he noticed was the flowing, blonde hair that was sprawled across the floor. Moving closer, he saw the fair skin and delicate frame: it was Miss Burbin all right. Casually, he informed the concerned audience: "That there's Miss . . . Banks. She's with me." Ms. Nutmegen and the two others raised their eyebrows at him, almost in unison.

"Don't y'all give me those looks! We're not 'together' together! And even if we were, she's no sixteen-year-old, so it'd be fine and dandy."

One of the guys, a fellow named Riley, chuckled. He was one of the men who attended McGreggor's weekly card game. "All right, Bart! The ladies' man is finally settling down, huh?" He raised a hand to give Bart a high-five, but Bart ignored it.

"Since when did I become a 'ladies' man?'" He was beginning to sound defensive. It didn't help that he was in a hurry.

"Oh, Bart," another woman chimed in, "don't play that game with us! You've been a bachelor around here for years. You're still young and healthy. The fact that you got that muscle and those eyes are just a perk for them pretty gals that been looking at you!" The trio laughed, looking up at him to gauge his reaction.

"I don't see why it's any of y'alls business anyway," he snapped. "If you wanna say I'm a lady's dream, then fine. Say it. But don't you be putting around town that I'm a player because it ain't true. I'll settle down when I'm good and ready!" He moved toward Miss Burbin and bent down to pick her up.

"Simmer down there, Bart," Riley started. "Any other fella might consider it a compliment. Pssh, it'd be nice to have the ladies fighting over me every now and then." He tried not to make eye contact with any of the women around him.

Bart raised his eyes, slightly frustrated by the whole situation. Although he liked these people, they didn't pick the best time to start teasing him about things like this.

"Well, Riley . . . " He knew he was gonna say somethin' that might make people uncomfortable, but he didn't filter it the way he would have had he been in a better mood. "I'm sure Loretta would gladly fight for you."

Loretta—the woman at Cecelia's feet—blushed fiercely at his comment.

Standing to his feet, he lifted the limp body and held her in his arm. As he made his way to the door, Ms. Nutmegen followed.

"Ms. Nutmegen?" He stopped.

"Oh, Bart." She slapped his arm playfully. "You know better than that! Call me Lucy." She smiled at him.

"Very well. What happened here?"

She looked in his eyes and glanced back at the place where Riley and Loretta sat awkwardly. "You mean, besides you calling out poor Loretta in front of Riley?" she responded sarcastically.

"Yes." *Obviously.*

"I don't quite know. All I heard was a thump. Riley says she walked around the corner of that there aisle, saw his face, and boom! Fell flat over!"

Bart laughed briefly before recomposing himself. "No, really, what happened?"

"Exactly that. Now *why* she fainted, I don't know. We've been trying to figure that out ourselves."

He squinted his eyes and thought for a moment. He looked back toward Riley, who was busy tying his hair back, and returned his attention to Lucy. "All righty then, thank you. I best be going." He turned to walk out the door. "Do me a favor, will you?"

"Of course."

"If a strange man who looks—well, a bit like Riley, only a little greasier—comes in here asking about a woman, please don't tell him anything."

Although the silence wasn't long, it felt like waiting on a slug race to finish. He knew Ms. Nutmegen was probably perplexed by the request, but she'd known him for a long time. She had no reason not to trust him.

"Okay," she said calmly.

"Oh, and Riley!" Bart called. "Try not to scare any more ladies today! One's quite enough!"

As Bart stepped out of the ceramic shop, cradling Miss Burbin in his arms, he looked down the street toward the small crowd that remained with Mr. Connor. At that moment, his internal conflict reached an unbearable intensity. Now that money was off the table, there was one less thing in the client's corner. What a shame. He could definitely use the money; not only could he use it, he needed it. Regular business was slow, and he had to pay the bills somehow. Who knows? Perhaps, in some way, this man really *was* related to Miss Burbin. Perhaps her mother *did* miss her, and Bart was standing in the way. If he didn't hand her over, he would be doing a disservice to everyone. Besides, people who run away are typically driven by something unreasonable, right? After convincing himself that his thoughts were true, he proceeded toward the crowd.

Each step was taken with slow calculation as he shifted his eyes about the town, searching for any unknown faces and unpopulated alleyways. As he slowly approached the bundle of ants crowded around as though salivating over a stale crumb, he noticed Mr. Connor's head emerge from the pack. The dark, threatening eyes of Miss Burbin's "relative" shifted to display a disturbing pleasure at the sight of the body in his arms.

Bart stepped closer. He was now twenty feet and one valuable exchange away from bringing joy to a grieving family. It was a good thing—very good. He might even be called a hero. His heart beat against his insides. He took deep breaths, trying to calm the chaos that twisted about his chest. *You can do it, Bart. You can do it. Her family misses her. Mr. Connor's going to take her back to people who'll love and care for her.* He moved closer, one foot in front of the other. He was now fifteen feet away.

Keeping his eyes on the final target, he caught a glimpse of Mr. Connor's head peeking through the crowd again. This time, they made eye contact. He watched as the corners of the client's lips rose to unveil a sinister grin. Something wasn't right.

At that moment, Bart bolted to his left and darted across the street. He ran through a crack between houses, sure he was being chased.

"There he goes!" he heard the con artist cry. "He's kidnapping my cousin!"

He couldn't distinguish what happened next. All he heard were outcries and rampaging feet that he assumed were heading his way. While he wasn't the fastest man in town, he'd grown up here and knew everywhere a person could hide. There was a good place behind an old shop uptown.

Ducking between buildings and behind hedges, he fled. With each stride, Miss Burbin flopped in his arms. He ran until his lungs ached, at which point he ducked into a woodshed behind Carper's Furniture Store. There, he laid her down. He'd begin his efforts to bring her back to consciousness once he could breathe again.

## Chapter 14
### *Future Hopes*

1:30 p.m.

Jason stood still, staring at the door in front of him. Because Cece had no close family or relatives in the area, her apartment had remained untouched since she left. Even if she had family nearby, they probably wouldn't have rushed to change things. After all, she had only just left yesterday, though the hours passed like an eternity. Still, he wasn't sure why her landlady, Miss Horner, had stopped by after church to insist that Cece wasn't returning and that he retrieve her belongings as soon as possible. He hadn't gone to church that morning. Maybe he should have. His decision to stay home had caused concern amongst two of his buddies who had called to check up on him. Somehow, he had managed to fumble his way through the conversations without revealing the reason for his absence: he refused to tolerate the gossip. Who knew what he might have done if confronted with the overt celebration of his fiancée's ... betrayal? Was that the word? Nevertheless, he hadn't wanted to start an argument with his buddies, or Miss Horner, so here he was.

Cece's door was made of wood. There were a few cracks running down the front but nothing that demanded immediate attention. Jason looked at the silver handle—although a bit tarnished, it was still eye-catching. Finally, he took a deep breath and inserted the spare key Miss Horner had given him.

"You take what you want," she had said. "Anything else I'll be giving to charity."

He jiggled the key, twisted the knob, and gave a little extra nudge to open the door. The fresh scent of flowers wafted into the hall as he entered, encircling him and drawing him in. As he shifted his eyes about the apartment, the pastel yellows and greens on the walls filled his mind with memories. The rooms used to be white, but Cece somehow managed to convince Miss Horner to let her paint. He lowered himself onto the paisley couch as he remembered.

*"So, what colors you gonna paint?" He playfully grabbed the color swatches from Cece's hands. She rose onto one knee and leaned over him to retrieve her valuable squares. After a moment of struggling—just long enough to get a cute rise out of her—he relented and let his girlfriend win. She smiled victoriously as she sat back on the couch beside him.*

*"I think I'll go with Easter Egg Yellow for the living room and Sea Green for my bedroom," she answered as she analyzed the colors in front of her.*

*"Why those two?" he asked, reaching his right arm around her shoulders.*

*"Well, yellow seems like such a happy color, you know?" She glanced over at him, an inquisitive look on her face. She turned her head back and smiled. "It seems so . . . "*

*"Hopeful?" he offered.*

*Her eyes met his. "Exactly," she proclaimed joyfully. "And green reminds me of grass and plants and things . . . life." She went on to explain: "I didn't choose regular green because it'd make the room too dark. I want light, fresh colors."*

Awaking from his daydream, he rose from the couch and moved toward Cece's bedroom. Although he didn't want to take things, he couldn't stand someone else having them. He wanted everything to stay exactly as it was. They both had decided to move her belongings to his home after they returned from their honeymoon. She was so excited to decorate. If she did come back, she'd want her things to be here.

The green bedroom was a little messy, but Cece insisted it was clean. "Organized chaos," they had agreed to call it. She knew where everything was, and that's what mattered. He smirked, allowing his eyes to scan the room. Suddenly, he froze. On the closet door hung a white, satin dress. Shiny glass beads danced about the fabric in swirls reminiscent of flowers. He turned his face away, almost instinctively. He wasn't supposed to see the dress before the wedding; and although the day had passed, he still couldn't do it. It felt like walking in on someone while they're changing. He moved past the closet.

Below her bed were sparkly, silver shoes. He smiled. They must have been the ones she mentioned, wanting so badly to show him, yet trying so hard not to give too much away. As he circled the room, he came to her nightstand. A Bible lay open on the surface, right in front of a wooden cross. He reached his hand toward the cross and slowly lifted it up. *Cecelia.* He remembered how important it was to her, how it reminded her of the night that God changed her life.

"Why would she leave?" he whispered. He squeezed his eyelids shut and held the cross against his chest. "I thought we had something special, God. Why would she leave me?"

After several minutes had passed, Jason put the cross in his back pocket, exited the apartment, locked the front door, and proceeded down to Miss Horner's office.

"Jason!" The chipper woman called as though they hadn't just spoken. "Going home for boxes?"

"I don't mean to be rude," he began. "But how do you know she won't come back?"

Her eyes widened. In seconds, her expression changed as though a light bulb turned on inside her head. "Oh, my dear boy! Don't you know?"

"Know what?" He stepped into the tiny office. It contained more bookshelves and filing cabinets than the contractors had allowed space for.

Miss Horner opened a drawer in the upper section of her desk and retrieved a piece of dirty paper. "I found this under my door yesterday morning, right after . . . you know . . . after she didn't show. I came in to open my office, and there it was!" She handed the document to Jason. "Apparently, she planned to leave."

He stretched out a hand and took the letter. There were no words. He wanted to say something—anything—but nothing came out.

"You keep it, honey. I don't need it."

He left the office, closing the door behind him; he heard faint sobs through the wooden barrier. Perhaps Cece did mean something to someone else in this town. Slowly, he made his way home, contemplating what he just learned. Why would Cece leave her note with Miss Horner instead of him? He tried not to let his embarrassment convolute the issue. Instead, he slid his fingers along the folded edges and considered what it might say. How she needed more time, perhaps? Maybe . . . His heart raced as a new thought emerged. Maybe she had gone to make amends with her mother—invite her to the wedding after all. He started walking faster. If there was a reason for Cece to postpone the wedding, that was it. Perhaps she did still love him after all.

Though he was almost certain of the letter's contents, he couldn't risk reading it in public. This was much too personal for that. Fixing his eyes on the picket fence that lined their grassy yard, he hurried across the street and made his way toward the sidewalk.

He was just about there when he felt a thud against his shoulder. "Oh, excuse me!"

He turned to see the woman he had evidently bumped into. Her polka-dotted purse lay on the ground, its contents strewn about.

"I am sorry, ma'am," he said. Sliding the letter into his back pocket, he scooped to help collect her scattered things. "I must have been distracted."

She smiled, her teeth white enough to be on a toothpaste commercial. "Call me Wendy," she began. "And that's all right. Guy like you must have a bunch of important things on his mind."

"Something like that." He handed her a tube of red lip gloss that had rolled to the edge of the curb.

Taking it, her fingers touched his. They were cold, like Cece's. He glanced at their hands and pulled away.

"Have a nice day." He turned to leave, reaching back to retrieve the letter from his pocket. But before he was home-free, the voice returned.

"You know, I just arrived in town," she began, "and could use a nice fella to show me around. You interested?"

"No, but welcome to Ichacar." Turning, he leapt onto the sidewalk and hurried inside. He knew he was being rude, but he had no intention of showing a woman around town the day after his scheduled wedding. Some guy would be tickled to show her around, but that guy wasn't him. After all, Cece's letter had set fire to his hand. He had to know what it said.

Although he had every intention of reading it right away, it took him a while. Instead, he lay sideways atop his bed, squeezing a tennis ball. What if Miss Horner was right? What if Cece *did* want to leave him? As much as he wanted to know the truth, there was a strange ease that came with not knowing. Not knowing meant that she could still love him, that there was hope. If he were to know something for sure, he wanted it to be that his bride was forced to leave town for an issue she had to take care of—like bringing a distant relative back for the wedding. Under no circumstances did he want to hear that the woman he loved chose to leave him.

He eventually determined that no matter how much it hurt, he could not live his whole life in a place of uncertainty. Slowly, he stood, approached his desk, and unfolded the dirt-stained paper. Hesitantly, he read:

*Dear Miss & Others,*

*I won't be returning to Ichacar. The pressure of getting married is too much, and I can't stick around. I'm going to start a different life far away from here. It will be better this way.*

*Tell Jason I never really loved him and that my heart belongs to someone else. This guy is more of a man than he'll ever be. Also tell him not to bother searching for me. As part of my new start, I will change my name, so finding me will be impossible.*

*Cece*

He examined the typed words, his moist fingers dampening the paper's crinkled edges. Cece had always hated her handwriting and would turn away red-cheeked anytime Jason caught her jotting notes.

Notes.

This note was different. Its words carried more weight than the list of items Cece needed from the store or remembering to meet Auntie May for breakfast; yet somehow, they took a moment to sink in. Like a person sprawled across quicksand, he resisted the recognition that threatened to bring him under.

Turning his head sideways, he looked out toward the sky. It was somewhat cloudy today with the sun peeking through sporadic holes, trying to break free. Rising to his feet, he approached the window and rested his hands upon the white sill. People passed on the road below, going about their usual Sunday business. Some were visiting with neighbors, others out for a stroll, but in all cases, the general feel of the town seemed positive. Maybe people had already forgotten. He hoped they had. The last thing he needed was pity.

*Tell Jason I never really loved him and that my heart belongs to someone else.* Now, the words were sinking in. Wiping sweat from his forehead, he grabbed his twisting stomach and looked at the trashcan. It was close enough that he'd make it if he threw up. Another man? The only other guy she had ever dated was terrible to her. She had told him all about it. It was some goon, who she claimed was in prison. Apparently, they were engaged for a while, but it ended badly. She said she was so ashamed of her past and that she wanted to forget all about it—including her ex—forever. Jason had believed her. He had believed that she was the one for him, a treasure from God. Was it all a lie? In her words, she had been a "master of deception" in her old life.

Feeling his stomach churn, his eyes rolled back as he reached for the trashcan. He felt his hands clench. Fury spread from his fists, through his veins, and into his heart. It filled his face and attacked his brain. He didn't understand. *I can't comprehend it, Lord! I can't . . . I don't . . .* He fought to put his emotions into words, but every word in the English language seemed to elude him. It was as if they were playing a taunting game with his mind, telling him to assemble a puzzle of a thousand pieces. As he reached for a piece to use, he realized all the pieces were from separate puzzles. He could force the pieces together but feared what that picture would be. The quicksand had got him, and he was sinking . . . fast.

## Chapter 15
## Why, Hello

September 15, 1990

The wind caressed the surface of Cece's skin. She heard the rustling of leaves above and the crisp crunch of those being trampled by pedestrians below. Although the cool temperature made her wish she had worn long sleeves, she refused to move from her spot. There she sat, eyes closed and knees folded on the park bench, listening to the joyful sounds of children playing with their friends. She heard giggles, racing feet, the rubbing of bare hands against the plastic surfaces of sliding boards, and occasional shrieks. In the latter case, an adult's voice would firmly respond with something like, "Suzy!" or "Billy, no!"

Gradually, she released her legs, letting the soles of her white tennis shoes casually rest upon the ground. She sank down on the bench and relaxed her neck, arching it over the wooden ledge until her head rested on nothing but air. Peace. Almost anything would feel peaceful compared to the lifestyle she had recently left. She didn't even want to think about it. She was determined to start anew and forget what transpired just three months ago.

"Anyone sitting here?" a masculine voice broke her relaxation. Startled, her eyes shot open, and she lifted her head to see the face of her interrupter. Surprised, and somewhat tickled by the man's agreeable appearance, she calmly laid her neck back and resumed her prior position.

"Don't think so," she replied politely, although careful not to convey any emotions about his sitting there.

The man sat, and her heart began beating a little faster. She took a deep breath and let out a sigh, hoping it would help her relax once again. She knew better than to get caught up in appearances, even one as appealing as his—especially not one like that.

"Well, if I knew my sitting here would make you that upset, I might have come earlier." The man's voice seemed confident. She opened her eyes, squinted to protect them from the sun, and looked at the man sitting next to her. He winked.

"I'm kidding," he said with a smile. "So, what's your name?"

She lay back again. What was her name today? Sally Clearwater? Nancy Smith? Rebecca . . . Wait. Why not use her real name? She wasn't on a job, and besides, that old life was behind her now. The instinct to deceive was so frustrating. That wasn't her anymore. Things were different.

The man chuckled uncomfortably. "All right, I get it." He rose and began walking away. "I didn't mean to disturb you. Enjoy your afternoon."

"Cece," she politely declared, still relaxing on the bench. "Cecelia Burbin." While she internally resisted a continued conversation with the man, she didn't want to be rude. She would answer his questions, but that was it.

The man turned toward her and replied with a smile, "Wow." He strolled back to the bench and sat down. "I must say, for the wait, I was kind of expecting a better name."

Her eyes rolled as she laid her right hand on his shoulder. Slowly, she slid her palm a couple inches down and stopped. The man's eyes followed her hand. In an instant, she sat up and thrust her palm into his upper arm, pushing him over.

The man chuckled. "You've got some strength in that arm! Is that your way of asking my name?"

"That's my way of doing a lot of things," she retorted. "Best be leaving me alone." She grabbed her bag, rose from the bench, and began walking away.

"Come on! I was kidding. Cece's a pretty name!"

She kept walking.

"Hey!" he called out, catching up to her. "I'm sorry. Here I am kidding around, and we don't even know each other." He moved in front and walked backward as she continued on her path. "Let me introduce myself."

She stopped and looked into his deep, brown eyes. "Trust me, you don't really want to know me. You just think you do. I'm doing you a favor." She passed him and continued walking. Brushing off someone who's incredibly attractive wasn't easy, but she had years of practice. *God, I can't do this again. If this guy is anything like Marley, I want nothing to do with him.* Although she meant it, she knew that not all men were like that, but it was easier just to say they were and move on.

"That's where you're wrong," the man responded.

She turned around. "Excuse me?"

"Look, I know it's dangerous to disagree with women . . ."

Cece smirked.

" . . . but I've never had a stronger desire to meet a woman in my life."

"So, you don't wander around parks and pick someone up every weekend?" she asked sarcastically.

"No, not usually. I mean, maybe when things get busy; but in a town this size, I'd have to start cycling back through after the first month. You don't gotta be an expert to see why that wouldn't work out too well!"

Against her will, she laughed.

The man continued as he moved closer. "Then there'd be awkward moments when I'd be out with one woman and see another from the week before." He locked his gaze with hers. "It's really hard to be so smooth." Before she knew it, he was standing right in front of her. "I'm sorry. I shouldn't have joked around like that before I knew you. The truth is, I'm not quite used to initiating conversations with beautiful women."

She felt her heart leap inside her chest. As much as she wanted to maintain her tough appearance, his playful persistence made it difficult. "Oh?" she questioned, hoping her cheeks weren't turning red.

"Yeah," the man confirmed with a smile. "Apparently, you make me nervous."

Nervous? He didn't seem nervous. Her heart began to race; it was beating so hard that she was afraid the man might hear. She wasn't quite sure what to say. If only there was a way to test whether or not he was being real. She hoped he was but knew better than that. He appeared genuine, but from her experience, the people who seem the most trustworthy are the ones to watch. Still, there was something in his countenance and tone of voice that made her feel okay.

"Really?" She could have kicked herself. What a cheesy thing to say.

The man smiled. He looked down at the ground and then raised his eyes to meet hers again. "Yeah, really," he repeated. "I'd like to get to know you. Despite what must have been a terrible first impression, I'm really a stand-up guy. Look, I'm standing now!" His smile practically made her ankles quiver. Something about this guy was rather charming. She did, however, know other people skilled in the art of "charming." Instead of people charming snakes, they were snakes charming people. She knew.

Despite her wandering thoughts, she forced a pleasant look. She needed to move on and let someone else in. What could be the harm? Pain? Heartache? Self-loathing? But what about the good? Was good even possible?

"Okay."

"Yeah?"

"Yeah. Just don't be saying bad things about my name." She winked at him and turned to walk away. She paused. "I almost forgot. What *is* your name?"

"Jason. Jason Porter."

## Chapter 16
### *Truth Be Told*

March 13, 1994
Sunday, 1:15 p.m.

"Miss Burbin, you okay?" Bart tapped Cece's check.

She slowly opened her eyes to a blurry haze. She couldn't remember where she was or why she was there. Suddenly, becoming aware of her surroundings, she bolted upright and frantically struggled to get away.

"Get back!" she gasped, clutching her throat. "My voice! What did you do to me?" Her eyes widened as adrenaline rushed through her body.

"It's okay; it's okay! Shh . . . calm down now. Miss Burbin! It's me, Bart." He spoke quietly while holding her wrists.

She glanced down at the large hands restraining her—they might as well have been shackles. Raising her eyes, she stared at her captor's face. "You," she whispered. "You look familiar . . . "

"That's right," he smiled. "I'm your friend. It's gonna be okay."

Her eyes penetrated through the façade of the man in front of her and determined the truth: "No . . . you're one of them!" Her throat ached, but she pushed through it despite the constant throbbing. This time, she swung her elbows as though fighting for her life.

"Them?" His eyebrow shot up.

"The men from last night! You ruined my life!"

"Last night? You slept on my couch last night. It's Sunday, Miss Burbin. Don't you remember?"

"Get away from me!" she wailed, giving the thug a fierce kick to the groin. Her hands shook violently as she stumbled through the woodshed and toward the door. Glancing back, she saw her captor hunched over on the floor. This was her chance to escape.

Once outside the shed, she ran. She kept running as fast as she could for as long as she could, until she finally collapsed in the middle of a field. Long blades of grass swallowed her in their bed as she fought for breath.

"Can I help you?"

***

After taking a moment to nurse his injury, Bart took a deep breath. Frustrated with what had just transpired, he threw his back against the shed wall and allowed himself to slide down. There he sat—alone with his thoughts and a throbbing groin. Who in their right mind would ever want to be around this girl? So far, she'd been nothing but confusion and trouble. He had tried to help, but it was all in Miss Burbin's hands now. She had made her decision and would have to face whatever happened with the recognition that her actions have consequences. Why would she treat him like this, anyway? He'd done nothing but try to help her. His chin fell. He knew that wasn't true. What if something traumatic had happened? He shook his head. Of course, something must have happened. Why else would she have attacked him like that? He looked at the door swinging in the breeze. Grinding his teeth, he rose to his feet.

***

She knew that voice. It was dark, sarcastic, and smug. Instant panic gripped her heart. She spun around. "Jackson?"

"Oh, little one," he began as he squatted down. "What happened to your voice?" Mockingly, he cocked his head. "Having a bad weekend?"

She was instantly fed up with his arrogant smile. Before he could say another word, she whipped her hand toward his face. He clasped it and held tight to her wrist.

"Ahh, I see you missed me." He smirked, throwing her hand down.

"What do you want?"

Jackson was one of the last people she expected to see in this field. While she suspected he might come looking for her someday, she'd hoped he wouldn't. She figured he'd wait until his boss was out of jail. It had been only four years since she left, which meant he was still incarcerated.

As thoughts flashed through her mind, the memory of yesterday started coming back. She shook her head. If she had remembered who Bart was, she wouldn't have run from him like that—at least, not without learning more about . . .

"*You're* Mr. Connor." Her lips moved without sound, though it was clear Jackson knew exactly what she said.

Confirming her suspicion with a mischievous grin, he rose and moseyed around her. "You know . . . aside from those dirty feet and bent-up arms, you didn't turn out half-bad. Your parents would be proud."

She watched her predator closely as he circled.

"Oh, wait, no, they wouldn't. What did you do for a living again? No wonder they didn't want you back." He stopped and puffed out his bottom lip. "So sad."

She gritted her teeth and stood. "At least, I'm not a coward."

"Oh?" he questioned. "Please, enlighten me."

"If you missed me so much—"

"Oh, now, wait just a moment there. You're already jumping to conclusions; you see, I didn't miss you . . . Now, go on."

"I said," she spoke as firmly as she could in a whisper, maintaining eye contact. She wouldn't give him the satisfaction of making her look away. "If you missed me so much, why didn't you come and get me yourself? Had to hire a goon squad, huh? What's the matter? Scared?"

"Ha ha. You're cute, Kid, but no. No squad necessary. I wouldn't have given someone else the satisfaction of roughing you up. Not after what you did."

She stood breathless, stunned at what she heard. Perhaps it should have seemed obvious, but she had no idea that he was behind all of this. Besides, she distinctly remembered four people being involved in the kidnapping. If Jackson were one of them, Tommy must have been there, too. That left two others.

"Who else?" she questioned. "You, Tommy, and?"

He grinned. "Ah, yes. You haven't met our newest recruit. She's good. Not quite as feisty as you were, but definitely more of a team player."

She hated that wink. He had always thought he was the best thing since colored television, but he was sorely mistaken. Wait a minute . . .

"A woman? You got someone else?" Her head spun as a bead of sweat dripped down her face. She couldn't faint now. Spreading her feet apart, she attempted to steady herself. "Leave her alone, Jackson!"

He laughed. "Don't get your socks in a bunch."

She followed his eyes as he glanced at her bare feet. Bart's shoes were huge. There's no way a pair of his would have fit.

"You think we're out to get everyone," he continued. "But not everyone—just you. What's the word he used? That's right—your sentence."

"And who is *he*? I know there was someone else there that night." Her gut wrenched, but she had to know. "Was it Bart?"

Jackson raised his eyebrows.

"Don't give me that look." Dark emotions stirred in her gut like an awakened volcano. She felt pressure as they continued building inside of her. "Marley's still in prison, so who is it?" *Please, God, help me.* It was all she could do not to attack, and she didn't want blood on her hands.

Jackson sighed. "Hmm . . . that's quite a question you got there. How about I give you a hint?"

"Don't toy with me."

"Would I do that? Really, Cecelia? That hurts."

"Jackson!" She grabbed her throat. It took everything she had to speak through the invisible needles stabbing it like a pincushion.

"Okay, okay. Here's your clue: you know him, but that's all I'm going to say."

She struggled to make sense of the information. Of course, he could be lying, but she knew him too well for that. He fooled many people, but she could read him like no one else could. Unfortunately, that's what happened when a student grew to rival their teacher.

"Now, let's go. We've got places to be." He extended a hand.

"Why would you think that I'd go with you?" The thought disgusted her. How could a man who was once like family be so repulsive?

Instantly, he stopped smiling. "You want a reason? Because I said so."

She stared at him but said nothing.

"Come on, Cece. It's me," he said, nodding toward the river. "We'll head that way, turn right, and get to the road by nightfall. Maybe we can have a campout!"

Though sarcasm befit him, she detested it. "I'm not going anywhere with you." Her eyelids fluttered as she fought to stay focused.

"There's no time for this," he insisted. "Let's go."

***

Bart had been watching carefully as Miss Burbin attempted to speak with Mr. Connor. He could imagine her frustration at being unable to fully communicate. Part of him expected her to knock the guy out—a part of him which was silenced as he continued to watch the two, stone-faced mimes interact from a distance.

As he crept forward through the long grass, he somehow managed to get close enough to make his move. Impatiently, he waited for the right moment. Then, he saw Mr. Connor stretch out his hand toward Miss Burbin; and to his surprise, it looked like she might take it. At that moment, he rose from where he'd been crawling in the field and revealed himself. He yelled out as he raced toward a wide-eyed Mr. Connor and punched him with full force square in the jaw.

"Come on, Burbin!" He grabbed Cece's hand, and they ran, leaving Mr. Connor alone on the ground.

"We've got to go back!" she pleaded, lifting her knees as they ran.

"Can't. We ain't got no time!" He panted as they headed toward town.

"But he knows who's involved! We can't let him get away. He'll just keep coming!"

He could hardly believe her words. "There ain't nothin' we can do 'bout that right now."

## Chapter 17
# What You Don't Know

2:30 p.m.

The two escapees continued until they arrived back at Bart's house. It took a little longer than usual, considering the added necessity of hiding from the townspeople. After slipping through the back door, they grabbed some money and food before he led her back toward the riverbank. They couldn't take his vehicle. It was parked in front of his house, and people would see them leave on a Sunday afternoon. It was longer but safer to go on foot. They would head to the river and down to the main road. The trees and bushes along the bank could provide adequate cover. Once at the road, they would hitchhike to another town—far away—where Mr. Connor couldn't find her.

When it grew dark, they settled down by a group of bushes. Bart wanted to cook some fish over a fire, but Cece cautioned him against the idea. She still wasn't sure who helped Jackson in her kidnapping, although she also didn't know why he needed help in the first place. Her only conclusion was that somebody else wanted her, but who? Someone needing her for a job? That was the last thing she wanted to do. She was happy to be out of the crime scene. Nothing could make her go back.

"So, Cece—that's what they call you, right?"

She nodded.

"I thought that's what you told that fella on the phone yesterday."

The phone—such a useful tool, but without her voice, it had failed her. Or was it Bart who failed her? He was the one who viciously interrupted her call and lied about the reason why. Could he be the mastermind behind this nonsense? She glared at him. His green eyes were coated in darkness like damp leaves at midnight. She wanted to know why he did it. What were his secrets? Ugh, secrets. Her stomach was a sponge being wrung out to dry, although it never dried, so it just kept wringing. She had the worst secrets of anyone. Why must she keep staring at them? She didn't want to acknowledge that her past existed, let alone look at it.

Gazing up at the sky, she sought to escape into the breathtaking expanse. Maybe if she ignored Bart, he would take the hint and let her be. She wasn't ready to talk to him like a civilized person.

"Look, I know your voice ain't so good, but could you *try* talking to me?"

She pretended not to hear.

"Cece."

Feeling a hand on her shoulder, she jerked her body away and scowled at him. "Don't touch me."

"My apologies, Miss Burbin, but I think you owe me an explanation for why you ran away," he said, looking down at his crotch and wincing at the memory.

Normally, she would laugh, but today, that wasn't funny. "Who's to say you didn't deserve it?" Her voice was still sparse, and after the troublesome events of the day, her throat ached.

"Hold on just a minute. Didn't I rescue you from that Connor fella? Haven't we spent the last million hours together, hiking this forsaken riverbank?"

She watched his face as he spoke, searching for lies.

"Why am *I* the bad guy?"

That was it. He asked for it. Struggling to her feet, she fumed. "Really?" Pins slashed the back of her throat, but she persisted. "Four people attacked me the other night and ruined what was supposed to be the happiest day of my life, and you were part of it!"

Bart's face fell as his bottom lip hung open. She waited as he cracked his neck and rolled his shoulders back. Her eyes had adjusted to the night, and she could see his clenched knuckles pressed against the dirt. Finally, he responded.

"They did *what?*" His tone was sharp, and his eyes found hers. There was a sorrow to his gaze that softened her.

Carefully, she lowered herself to the ground and sat across from him. "You didn't know?"

"Cross my heart, Cece. That Connor guy told me you ran away from home, and he was tryin' to bring you back. Said there was a rewar . . ."

She clenched her teeth. "A *what?*"

Bart winced.

"A *reward?*" Now *her* fists were folded, although she didn't have the strength to swat a fly at the moment, let alone take on someone twice her size. "You helped them for money?"

He threw his hands in the air. "I thought he was your cousin! Your mama was worried sick! I thought I was doing something good. Please, you have to understand—"

"Oh, I do," she declared, her words a whispery breath.

"—that I'm sorry, Miss Burbin. I made a mistake. I was a terrible judge of character. I guess . . . I guess maybe I didn't want to know, so I chose to believe what he told me, and that was wrong."

Her gut writhed again. How could he believe something so ridiculous? She didn't want to forgive him. Lifting her face to the sky, she closed her eyes and sighed. The mistakes she'd made over the years were countless, but God had forgiven them all. She knew that. God was a much better forgiver than she was, although she still struggled with feeling worthy of His mercy. She had been the worst. Why did she deserve forgiveness? Why did Bart? She knew the right thing to do, but that didn't make it easy.

"I wanna help you, Cece," he continued. "Let me make things right—get you back to that fella of yours."

Looking back at him, she saw desperation painted across his face. She knew that feeling all too well.

"Fine," she said.

With the fatigue that engulfed her, there was no telling how far she could make it alone before Jackson caught up. Perhaps staying with Bart was a risk worth taking. Besides, she was in no condition to outrun him.

"Good." Scooting toward the nearest willow tree, Bart rested his back against its bark. "I'll stay up and keep watch. You'll be safe here."

Her eyes narrowed.

"I promise. Now, get some sleep."

She wanted to, but memories haunted her. There was this one in particular: the muffin incident. She had stolen a muffin from a little girl. It was so easy. The girl's mama hadn't even noticed. She was busy talking with someone a few tables away. While she was distracted, Cece walked by, snatched it, and continued out the door while the little girl was in the restroom.

Cece cringed. She wanted to turn it off, but the play button was stuck. The memory was surprisingly vivid, like it happened yesterday, and it enveloped her. Never again did she want to see another person take the blame for something she'd done like the innocent, little girl did that day.

She had watched the girl's tears from outside the bakery window. After the girl returned from the bathroom, she cried to her mama and pointed to the muffin case. When they left the bakery, she heard the little girl pleading for another as her mama lectured her on the consequences of fibbing. At the time, Cece smirked. Somehow, it had made her feel like her life was normal. As a twelve-year-old who had just become an adult, she considered it her duty to teach others the harsh realities of life. You couldn't count on anyone—not even your mother.

*Mama.* She took a deep breath and released it to Heaven. She hadn't seen her mother in . . . eleven years. Had it been that long? She had thought about going back several times since she accepted Jesus, but every time, she couldn't bring herself to do it. Thankfully, Jason had been patient with her. He said he understood how difficult it was and explained that God would give her strength, even if she felt she had none. In their weakness, God was strong.

Her eyes grew glossy as she thought of the man she loved. A man so perfect, of whom she was completely undeserving.

*God,* she began. *I know You do miracles. Please, help me get home . . . and give me strength to make it through. I miss Jason, and Auntie May.* She paused. *I want a family. I feel so weak right now, but I know You are strong. Please be strong in me.* She squeezed her eyes shut, keeping the tears suppressed behind her eyes.

Laying down, she felt the dirt agitate a brush burn on the back of her arm. Physical wounds would heal, but she wondered if her heart ever would. When she had told Jason about her past, it felt as though someone had pulled open the changing room curtain while she was undressed, exposing a part of her that wasn't meant to be seen. She had wanted so desperately to forget, that to talk about it was like unraveling the meticulous stitches she had sewn in her heart—work meant to hide who she feared she still was.

## Chapter 18
# Do Me the Honor

Monday, 2:45 a.m.

Cece lay still under the night sky, hands resting beneath her head as thoughts flooded her mind. Although she wanted so badly to be at home in Ichacar, resting in Jason's arms, she had concluded that dwelling on the situation would do no good. She must try to relax. Glancing to the left, she saw Bart's chest rising up and down as he slept. His intention to keep watch clearly didn't go as planned.

As she gazed at the starry sky, she reflected upon the moment Jason asked her to be his wife. It was exactly five months, one-and-a-half days ago. He had arranged for them to take a carriage ride through town, ending at the park where they first met. She remembered feeling excited as he took her hand and led her outside.

*There it was: a horse-drawn carriage. She had never been on a carriage before and began bursting with enthusiasm.*

*"A carriage? Is it for us?" she questioned.*

*"You bet it is. Are you ready?" he asked with a beaming smile, though maintaining his composure.*

*Together, they rode hand-in-hand, not minding occasional bumps along the way. Jason, with such tenderness, wrapped his strong arm around her.*

*She, accepting the touch, moved in to lay her head upon his shoulder. They sat peacefully, and she was delighted by how secure she felt.*

*Upon arriving at the park, Jason dismounted first. He offered her his hand as she descended the carriage steps and hopped down on the gravel pathway. Together they strolled, her fingers intertwined with his.*

*"You remember this bench?" he had asked.*

*She chuckled with a coy smile. "How could I forget?"*

*"That's where it all began," he declared, pulling her in for a hug. He was so romantic that it was borderline cheesy, but she didn't mind. She actually liked it, which was a relief to Jason. He had told her before that his true feelings would sound gooey to almost anyone. He couldn't help it. Apparently, she brought it out of him.*

*She moved toward the bench and sat down as his eyes followed her. Swallowing hard, he moved closer and knelt down on one knee. She was filled with momentary panic.*

*"What are you doing?" she asked.*

*Without answering, he began, "From the moment I saw you, I thought you were different. Then I talked to you and knew it was true. You're more than I expected to ever find in a girlfriend: you're sweet and strong . . . "*

*Her heart raced.*

*" . . . and have the most beautiful eyes I've ever seen. Your passion for God and excitement over the small things in life inspire me." At that moment, he reached in his jacket pocket and pulled out a small, green, velvet box. "I love you, Cecelia Karen Burbin, and will be forever thankful that God blessed me with the opportunity to know you. Will you do me the honor of becoming my wife?"*

As she recalled the details of that wonderful evening, a cool breeze brushed against her tangled hair. He was so wonderful, and she had been so excited to marry him—scared, but excited. This whole issue with Jackson, Tommy, and whomever else had her questioning whether she deserved a man like that. God had forgiven her of her past, and she had started a new life in Christ. Why, then, was it so hard to forget? Why was she feeling such shame and remorse? Two nights ago, all she had wanted was to return home and become Mrs. Jason Porter, but what if she really was undeserving? He was the most remarkable man she had ever met, and he deserved someone who was as special as he was—someone untainted, someone pure. He should have the very best life, even if it wasn't with her. Her heart ached as she squeezed her eyes shut. She'd never imagined she could love someone this much.

## Chapter 19

### *Outsider*

6:10 a.m.

The outskirts of Bomilton were beautiful that Monday morning. Cece extended a hand toward the sky as she yawned, rising from her place on the ground. Her body ached. It was as though her emotions had infiltrated her limbs, reminding them of the unrelenting turmoil within her heart. The sound of birds chirping drew her attention to a nearby tree. She assumed it was early, judging by the position of the sun. That, and Bart was still sound asleep in the grass only a few feet away. As she looked out toward the hazy, orange sphere peering over a grassy horizon, she felt compelled to go for a walk. She glanced back at Bart. The corner of his mouth was cracked open, and a small stream of saliva crept out. He would be sleeping for a while.

Before leaving, she noticed a patch of flattened grass where she'd slept. Calmly, she squatted down and gently pulled at the blades. After ruffling the area, she was content that her spot was sufficiently concealed. Turning toward an open field that lay past the tree line, she lifted her knees and high-stepped through the tall grass toward the stunning sunrise.

A cool, dry breeze fluttered through her hair, sending goose bumps down her exposed arms. The back of her gown flapped softly. She wanted to open her arms and run toward the light, letting her hair and dress dance wildly behind her, but she knew she shouldn't wander far.

As she walked, memories of life in Ichacar flashed through her mind. When she had first arrived, she struggled with the thought of finding a job. Having ended her education at the age of twelve, she was an unqualified nineteen-year-old whose only job experience was theft. The gang had tried to educate her to an extent, but their range of knowledge didn't seem very broad. All they appeared to care about teaching her were tricks that would help break into homes, cars, offices—anywhere she didn't belong.

She remembered the heavy feeling of walking down the streets of Ichacar that first day. Although she prayed to God, she wasn't sure what to do next. She tried to forget what she'd done, convince herself that she was starting fresh, but couldn't seem to shake the memories. She hadn't known much about God, just that she believed He existed. She didn't know what believing in Him really meant in terms of her life—past and future.

*People stared at her. Some squinted and frowned; others would pretend not to look and then peer critically after she passed—she had felt their eyes. There was one man with abnormally bright hair—one of the main reasons he stuck out in her mind. His hair was so blond that it appeared white. He wore a navy blue shirt with light, ripped jeans; and as she walked by, he shook his head. She wasn't sure what it meant. All she knew was that she was a stranger, and the people of Ichacar cared in a bad way. It was almost as though they knew about her past.*

*The soles of her thin, black tennis shoes lightly brushed the pavement as she walked along the right side of the street. Where the ground dipped, dust* particles rose in puffs of smoke as she stepped. Carefully, she began reading the shop signs: "Betty's Bakery," "Coats and Tails," and "Step by Step." She determined them to be a bakery, suit store, and shoe shop respectively.

Finally, she found something that could work. The sign was simple and appeared to be made of stained wood. Painted in dark red was the word, "Locks." If her experience would qualify her for anything, aside from organized crime, it would be working with a locksmith. She entered through the open door and cringed at the loud noise within. Making her way around two aisles of blank keys and sample locks, she approached the owner. The man standing there was the only person in the store and was positioned behind a machine that sounded like it was used to cut keys.

Mr. Jones, the locksmith, reluctantly stepped away from his machine and didn't believe her when she mentioned having worked with locks. Of course, she wasn't very specific. She basically told him that she had experience in security testing, especially in the area of locks and keys. Mr. Jones looked her up and down, probably scrutinizing her just like the others had.

"You can work with locks, huh?"

"I think so," she responded hesitantly.

"What's that mean?" He grabbed a damp cloth and wiped his hands. "Can ya carve keys? Build locks?"

"I don't know, but I can test them. Make sure they are difficult to open without the right key."

He raised an eyebrow. "Oh, yeah? Why would I care about that? I make locks secure enough. It's the customer's responsibility to take other necessary precautions to prevent break-ins, if that's what you're getting at. Now, if you'd excuse me," he started with a nod, "I'll be getting back to work." Without awaiting her response, he lowered his face-shield and walked back toward the key-cutting machine.

*After his rebuttal, Cece was filled with a renewed sense of confidence. She was sure her skills could help him and his clients. Following him at a distance, she began: "Security, Mr. Jones."*

*He continued walking.*

*Far from discouraged, she was determined to defend herself. She had previously taken pride in her quick tongue and its ability to talk her out of questionable situations. Today, she hoped it would talk her into something.*

*"Don't you think your clients would like a guarantee that your locks are better than others in guarding against petty theft?"*

*This got his attention, and after he offered her a meager salary to start, it was official. She worked at Locks for one year, despite Mr. Jones' constant skeptical expressions. He always seemed to have an eye on her. Whenever she'd turn around, he was there, ready to offer input or make suggestions. Thankfully, he liked her work. She could tell by the way he talked about it with customers. Mr. Jones installed quite a few locks that year, and she figured her efforts had something to do with that.*

*Throughout her time there, she'd occasionally find Mrs. Jones watching her, too. She guessed her to be around fifty years old, due to the woman's leathery skin and strands of gray hair in her bun. After a year of odd looks and watching, Mrs. Jones finally offered Cece a job in a part-time quilting business. She had always wanted to begin one but didn't have the help needed. Cece seemed to learn quickly and work well; so, despite the opposition of Mr. Jones, Mrs. Jones spoke with her.*

*"Besides," she had said, "a locksmith's is no place for a woman. Come, I'll teach you."*

*Cece was thrilled about the idea of learning a new skill, although surprised that the opportunity arose through Mrs. Jones. She had previously been under the impression that the boss' wife questioned her presence in the* shop for reasons other than those mentioned in their conversation. Through the rest of her shift that day, she was joyfully lost in visions of her future. She watched herself lift a needle and effortlessly weave it through a magnificent blanket, smiling and laughing as she worked. Although a lack of quilting knowledge hindered the accuracy of her imagined technical prowess, she continued in her daydream with delight.

As she worked, she overheard Mr. Jones object again to his wife's plan.

"You're really gonna take her, Annie?"

Mrs. Jones replied, "You've been suspicious since she got here, George. Best let her try something different. If she don't like it, she can come back and work with you."

"Well, seeing as how I don't got a say, perhaps you could teach her some reading, too. The girl's a little slow in that."

There was silence for a while. Cece had no idea Mr. Jones thought that way about her reading and was curious to hear what his wife would say. Finally, she responded.

"What do I got for someone her age to read?"

"I don't know. You at least got a magazine, newspaper—why, even a Bible would do."

Cece's heart leapt. A Bible. Although she had heard about it before, she never had a chance to read one. Perhaps it contained a key that would unlock the door of answers.

A large gust of wind brought Cece back to the present by knocking her a few steps back. Startled, she braced herself and held her position. She couldn't help but think that this moment, this field would be more beautiful without the burden that presently weighed on her heart. When would it end? She knew that God forgave her for the actions of her past—He did that years ago. So why were Jackson and Tommy showing up now? *I thought being forgiven meant this was supposed to be over.* She collapsed and sat with her legs folded in the grass. She laid her forehead against her palms and rested her elbows against her knees.

***

Jackson watched from a distance as Cece sat on the ground. Her shoulders, head, and neck were visible above the ridiculous safari grass. As he waited, he pondered the situation. It'd take about five minutes to reach her crawling. There'd be no chase, no argument. He would grab her from behind—no, the side. He smirked when picturing the look of terror on her face. Or he could save himself the time and run. It'd take less than a minute to get to her and another thirty seconds of chasing. He rolled his eyes. He was sick of wasting time.

When he had set out after her yesterday, he pondered the idea of taking her somewhere safe. Truth be told, he hadn't known Marley's real intentions with Cece until last Friday night. The man had managed to convince them that they'd kidnap her, give her a good scare, teach her "a lesson"—so to speak—then let her go. Honestly, he wasn't convinced Marley had originally planned to kill her, but something that night unleashed a darkness within him—something about looking at the woman he once claimed to love.

Now, Jackson had options. He could give her a friendly punch in the face, rip some fabric from her dress, wipe the blood with it, and return it to Marley. But as he continued to wait, he remembered her defiance, and his own frustration began taking hold of his common sense. There was also the fact that Marley had been whining about her for weeks. Ever since they busted him out of the joint, "justice" was all he could talk about. Although Jackson was never one to give into Marley's fits, the girl had brought this upon herself, so he allowed some leeway for his comrade's behavior. You never betray family without suffering the consequences. For now, he'd enjoy the game. He could decide later what the real consequences should be. Smirking, he crouched like a tiger watching its prey.

Before he could make his move, Cece rose and began walking away. The wind was at her back, pushing her along as she leaned against it. Without hesitation, he sprang to his feet and ran after her. She turned, her eyes widening as he sprinted forward. In an instant, she made a beeline toward the trees. Though it looked like she was calling for help, all he heard was a faint yelp that sounded like a wounded mouse. When he was close enough, he leaped and tackled her.

"Hey there, Kid," he declared with a grin. "You miss me?"

# Chapter 20
## Short on Time

8:30 a.m.

Moist morning air lingered about the town. Unwilling to provide release, the humidity was so dense that it was almost hard to breathe. The conditions would have seemed unbearable had it not been for the cool temperatures that early spring provided. At 8:30 a.m., the streets were bustling with people off to their morning activities.

Veering from their typical Monday schedule, Tommy and Marley walked the main street of Ichacar. Had they not been in the middle of a mission, the town would have felt comfortable—not too big, not too small. Tommy was doing his best to keep Marley's mind at ease, although the effort seemed futile. It was nearing two days since they went back to the river. Cece's body had not been found, and Tommy assured Marley that Jackson would straighten things out—although he wasn't quite sure how.

The soles of Tommy's boots scuffed the ground as they walked. They both wore casual clothing and hats, trying to hide the fact that they were outsiders. Despite Tommy's efforts to appease the boss, Marley was already in one of his moods.

"I can't believe we're doing this!" he said, shoving his hands in his pockets.

Tommy took a bite of cold pizza and stuffed it in his cheek. "You can't? But it was your idea." Although he attempted to conceal the food in his mouth, specks of pizza shot out as he spoke.

Marley stopped walking. He frowned and contorted his mouth. "You think you could finish chewing before ya open your trap?" He continued walking, mumbling as he went. "Disgusting—a grown man spitting his food at people! Must we act like animals?"

Tommy quickly shoved the rest of the pizza in his mouth, chomped on it, and jogged to catch up. He wasn't surprised that Marley flipped over his eating—it wasn't the first time. For some reason, the boss had a thing about appearing uncivilized. Spitting, open-mouthed chewing, loud burping in public, urinating behind buildings—things Tommy wouldn't have given a second thought, Marley detested. After so many years of partnership, he had learned to do his best to appease Marley's strange expectations, however warped they were.

In the present case, he could tell the boss was nervous. He did his best to follow his lead as they walked, but it wasn't easy. Marley would saunter a bit, notice something—or forget what he was doing—and speed up to a quick walk, stop, retrace his steps pretending to look for something, mosey slowly, kick his feet, and stop abruptly. One time, he stopped so suddenly that Tommy bumped into him, sending the already-agitated boss stumbling forward.

After finishing his pizza, Tommy caught up and continued the conversation. "Why we here then, boss?"

"We've been over this, you nut!" Marley sighed. "If Cece's alive, she's gonna try to come back home. If we're here, we can get her before that happens."

"But how? Won't people see us?"

Marley huffed. "We won't do it here in the street! When I say it's time, we'll stake out a spot near that guy's house and get her before he does."

"You mean her fiancé?" Tommy asked teasingly. Marley's face grew red. "I hear he's popular with the ladies." He knew he was pushing it, but he couldn't help himself. "Probably a real man—someone who's tougher than any guy she's ever known."

Marley grabbed the front of his shirt and pursed his lips.

Instantly, Tommy changed his tune. "Easy now, boss," he said. "I was only fooling. Nobody's tough as you."

Marley released his grip. "Jerk."

Tommy lied; and although it typically made him uncomfortable to lie to his friends, the boss didn't count. Marley was one of those people who could always be appeased by hearing what he wanted to hear as long as he believed it. Right now, Tommy knew what he wanted. Rolling with that thought, he continued, "I thought Jackson told you he took care of her."

Marley raised an eyebrow. "He?" There was a short pause.

"Well, I wasn't the one who did the deed myself—just helped," he replied nervously. He looked in different directions and began walking quickly, hoping Marley wouldn't notice his discomfort.

"Yes . . . yes, he did. But considering we didn't find the body, I wanna be sure. You understand." Marley spoke with a sly expression, probably proud of his own intelligence. "Where is that fool, anyway?"

"Cece?"

"No, Jackson."

"Probably taking care of things. I bet he's gonna get the body to show you." He wasn't sure whether or not he believed that himself. He was reasonably sure that Jackson, clever as he was, would think of something. But what he'd come up with was beyond him. Perhaps Jackson *would* bring the body back.

Marley rolled his eyes; but before he responded, a tan, sturdy man with dark hair came out of a yellow house across the street.

"Isn't that him?" Tommy questioned, happy to be the one to make such an important discovery. He pointed toward the man.

Marley snapped his head in that direction. "Yeah, must be." He lowered the brim of his hat.

"You've seen him before, right?"

"Sort of," Marley explained. "Only from far away, that day before the . . . incident. Anyway, it looks like him."

"So, whatcha planning to do?" He hoped it wouldn't involve another kidnapping. He'd be relieved when this was all over.

"*We* are gonna keep our distance and watch. If she comes back, we'll be ready. Got it?"

"You think he'll still want her after that note?"

Marley grinned. "I think if the note doesn't work, Wendy will. If the traitor comes back, she'll find her man has moved on; then she can die with a broken heart."

He nodded and shifted his attention back toward the fiancé. "Boy, he don't look too happy, boss. You sure Wendy can change his mind about Cece?"

He got another look from Marley. "Do I question your ideas?"

"Well—"

"Just calm down and keep your trap shut!"

Sticking out his tongue, Tommy crossed his arms and plopped on a nearby bench. He watched as the fiancé slumped down the sidewalk. "Don't you think he looks down, though?" Tommy asked.

"Appearances can be deceiving," the boss responded. The crazed look in his eyes made Tommy wonder exactly what he was planning. "You can't always believe what you see."

## Chapter 21
# Driving Nails

8:55 a.m.

On a typical Monday, Jason would rise early and head to work. As owner of the only wood workshop in town, he had enough tables to make and chairs to fix to last several weeks. After that, he'd have a whole new list of requests. Today, he hadn't planned to work; he had taken off for his honeymoon with Cece. Part of him had wanted to work and save the vacation time for when she returned, although now, he doubted that day would ever come.

As he walked to his workshop, the few people and noises were nothing but blurs. He determined that the easiest way to make it through the day was to avoid anything that would remind him of Cece. Thus far, the plan was failing miserably. Even his cool mint mouthwash brought back memories. It was Cece's favorite, and she'd commented more than once about the enticing flavor it left on his lips.

Rounding the corner of Elm Street, the workshop came into view. It was inside a two-car, standalone garage. The large white door was still closed, as it was every morning. Derek covered the late shift, which meant that Jason had roughly four hours of alone time before he had to be at least somewhat congenial.

Unhooking the garage door opener from his back jean pocket, he pressed the button and waited as the door slowly rose. Clearly, Derek had been here since Jason cleaned and closed up shop last Thursday. Wooden boards of various sizes were stacked against the steel counter that lined the far wall. Sawdust coated the floor as though mixed into the gray epoxy paint that coated it.

Shaking his head, he stepped over a stray two-by-four and veered right toward his workbench. Stopping at the table's center, he reached for his work gloves, then froze. How many times had he chosen not to wear them, preferring the feeling of boards and tools against his bare hands? He was more comfortable working that way, despite the occasional splinters and permanent callouses that covered his hands. It made him feel more in control over his work. More grounded. The gloves seemed like an unnecessary barrier, and while working alone, he usually kept them off. Besides, Cece loved his rough hands.

Cece.

There she was again, creeping into his thoughts. Truth be told, she never really left. Try as he may to change the disk, the same songs kept interfering with his decision to distract himself. He clenched his teeth. Why did this happen? Although he knew that God was still there, he found it difficult to walk by faith—it meant letting go of the anger, and he wasn't sure he could do that.

"Why, God?" he questioned as he lifted a board onto the worktable. "Why did you bring her into my life if she was just going to leave like this?" He felt like his heart was disintegrating within him. He didn't realize it was possible to have real, physical pain from an emotional wound. Before he said another word, he stood upright and took some deep breaths.

*Choose Me.*

"What?" He was still battling frustration. "But I've already chosen You, God. What about her?"

*Choose to trust Me. Trust Me with your heart, and trust Me with hers. Am I not big enough?*

"Of course, You are. I *know* You are, but it's hard, Lord. I want to fix this. I *need* to."

That was one thing he liked about building things: he could measure, cut, and assemble masterpieces. When the edges were rough, he'd sand them. If a section came loose, he'd fix it. Then, before a piece was completed, he'd apply varnish to protect it. He could control every aspect of the process and correct the things that went wrong. Now, he had no control. The vision he'd had for the future was stripped raw. His life was broken, and no number of nails could piece together what he'd lost.

The time slipped away as he measured, sawed, hammered, and sanded. He was constructing the second of two picnic benches when the sound of Derek's Harley announced the night owl's arrival. Was it one o'clock already? He glanced at the clock to his right: *10:30*. Odd. His friend was one of those guys who ate breakfast at noon and believed the sunrise was beautiful as an act of faith because he'd certainly never seen it. That's why Derek covered the late shift, wrapping up work by eight o'clock and tinkering with personal projects until the wee morning hours—that is, unless something more exciting came along.

He glanced at his friend entering the garage, a shiny black helmet tucked securely under his arm.

"Dude, I didn't think you'd be here," Derek began. He lifted his blue reflective sunglasses onto the top of his head—glasses he preferred to use in lieu of safety goggles. "After our call yesterday, I figured you'd take the week off. Good to see you, Man." Stepping toward him, Derek extended a fist and waited for Jason to bump it, which he did.

"Up before noon? This has to be some kind of record." Jason folded his arms and leaned back against the wall, watching as Derek strutted toward the workbench that ran parallel to his.

Derek tossed a pair of keys on the cluttered surface as though he'd never need to find them again. "Eh, well, I figured you wouldn't be here today—thought I'd see what morning looks like." He winked. "Don't take this the wrong way, Man, but what *are* you doing here?"

There it was. The topic he'd hoped to avoid. "What do you mean?" he asked, knowing the answer. He stepped up to resume his work, hoping his body language would be enough to deter further lecturing.

"Bro, you just got dumped."

Tactfulness had never been Derek's strong suit. Nevertheless, Jason could sense the concern in his best friend's tone.

"Go home. Decompress. Punch something. Watch a romcom and cry."

"A romcom?" His left eyebrow spiked.

Derek smiled. "Hey, I had to be sure you were listening."

Realizing his gloves were still off, Jason reached across the bench and slipped them on. Thankfully, his safety goggles were still in place—he didn't want to risk a scrap of wood to the eye.

"I know you don't wear them, ya know." Derek laughed. "You don't gotta be Mr. Safety for my sake."

Jason was going to offer a response but refrained. He should be wearing the gloves anyway. Maybe it was time to try something different. Perhaps, soft hands would suit him. Anything to get his mind off—

"It's okay, you know." His friend's hand landed hard on his shoulder. He had moved around the room like a ninja, emerging next to Jason undetected. "You don't always need to have it all together."

"I don't," he protested. "I'm the first one to say I'm not perfect. I need grace just as much as anybody." Right now, he needed more. Way more. His stomach started spinning like the buzzsaw he'd abandoned.

"Dude, I know. You're a good guy, but you act like everything's fine and dandy, even when it's not. You don't let anyone see when that big heart of yours is rubbed raw."

He felt Derek's stare beating against the side of his head. Pulling away, Jason pretended to search for something in the toolbox.

"Don't be like that."

"Like what? I'm fine." The words slipped out before he could filter them. Glancing over, he caught Derek's "see?" face. "So maybe I'm not fine, but I will be," he continued. "Besides, I want to be a light, not a stick in the mud. Nobody wants to hear me moan about what happened."

"I do." Derek went back to his workbench and hoisted himself up on the only open space available. "I've been worried about you ever since you told us to leave the church without you Saturday. Tim, Nick, me—we would have waited all day with you, Man. You know that, right?"

For a split second, a faint grin threatened Jason's mellow mood. "I know. I had quite the friends."

"*Have*," Derek corrected. "You *have* quite the friends, and we're still with you, Bro. You don't need to keep it together all the time. It's okay to be vulnerable. Just let people help you. There are some things we can't do on our own."

"I know I can't do it on my own, but God can."

"True." Derek's boots swung back and forth as he spoke, dangling in the thick air. "But God sends people, too, right? We aren't created to walk alone."

Jason recognized the words spoken back to him that he had shared with Derek on numerous occasions. It was certainly easier to give advice than to receive it. Sighing, he turned and pulled a nail from the massive toolbox. Not the best selection to make his search look real. No matter. There's no way Derek was paying attention that closely. Although trying to appear inconspicuous, he glanced up to catch Derek's toothy grin.

"Find what you were looking for?"

There was that sinking feeling again. "I thought so." Exhaling, he reached for a hammer. He had a hundred ways he could make this nail productive, but none of them involved fixing what was most broken: his heart. He squeezed his eyes shut. No matter what Derek said, there was no way he was going to cry at work.

"Go home, Man." Hopping off the bench, Derek circled around to the side nearest the concrete wall and lowered his sunglasses to shield his eyes. "And let people help you, starting with me. I've got the shop covered."

## Chapter 22
# Nothing if Not Cautious

10:35 a.m.

The clouds moved differently that morning in Youngsburg City. Nanna Moore, a town elder and noble citizen, noticed the obscurity while drinking her morning coffee. Slowly, she rocked back and forth, analyzing the sky like a rabbit would a fox. Despite her impressive mobility for a woman of eighty-three, she was nothing if not cautious. At least, that's what she told people.

"You know me," her shaky voice would begin. "I'm nothing if not cautious!"

A polite nod was always the response.

"You know, I got one of them crank calls the other day—someone tryin' ta tell me I owned one thousand dollars for something or other. A thousand dollars! I wouldn't spend that on a golden couch with wings! Know what I did? I said they're mistaken and hung up the phone. I'm nothing if not cautious."

"That's smart, Nanna," the listener would offer politely as they tried to inch away.

Nanna returned the sentiment with a gentle grin. "Thank you, darling." As soon as the individual thought they were free, she added, "That's the problem these days. Folks are in such a hurry to make a dishonest dollar. Nobody appreciates the value of hard work, let alone a good deed! Did you know that I saw a cat roaming Main Street yesterday? Roaming. No leash, no collar, nothing. It was a miracle the poor thing didn't go hungry!"

The listener would nod, finding themselves suddenly curious to hear more. "What'd you do? Did you keep the cat?"

"After watching as people passed by, I got up from my table at The Cozy Café—you know, the place across from Bobs and Barbers. That's where my brother used to get his hair cut. Are you familiar with the place? Bob's a classy fellow—been in business for years. I imagine if he weren't busy, he would've helped the cat. Do you know Bob? Before they meet him, most folks don't know the store name is a play on words."

"Interesting, but what about the cat?" Something about Nanna's passion and stories eventually drew people in. She cared about things, and she cared about people, too, leading many to consider her their third grandmother.

With a satisfied smile, Nanna gladly proceeded: "People passed by, and nobody did a thing. Eventually, five more minutes elapsed, and I had to act. I rescued the little guy and everything!"

"Really? You rescued it?" The listener was now seated in a chair next to Nanna, leaning in with their elbow perched atop the armrest, chin resting in their open palm.

"Don't let appearances fool you. I might not be the first to jump, but I jump if needed. Remember, I'm nothing if not cautious!"

\*\*\*

Nanna continued watching the clouds drift mysteriously across the sky. She waited, thought, and looked at her watch. She still had time before meeting Veronica Jones for early afternoon tea at The Cozy

Café. If she wanted to be on time, she ought to begin preparations now. A mile's walk separated her townhouse from the café she liked so much, and she loathed the idea of driving. She determined several years back that anywhere worth going was worth the walk.

Curiously, she lowered the cup of coffee and leaned forward in her rocking chair. With a breath, she thrust herself up and began scooting her way to the door. Before entering her home, she turned to look at the clouds one last time. Come to think of it, they looked like a rat chasing a lion. She shook her head. Not likely.

## Chapter 23
# We Meet Again

A dreary morning led to a dreary afternoon. After the conversation with Derek, Jason took his advice and went home. He could take a day off. Besides, a piece of Auntie May's apple pie was just what he needed to silence his grumbling stomach, which he hoped was a result of hunger and nothing more.

"Hey, Jason!" Uncle Ed called cheerfully from the kitchen as the front door closed.

"Hey," he responded sullenly, although trying to conceal his feelings.

"Come on in here, Buddy. I've got someone I'd like you to meet!"

He made his way through the living room and into the kitchen. There, sitting at the table, was the woman from yesterday with an oversized bow in her hair. She smiled as Auntie May handed her a white mug, steam rolling towards the ceiling.

"My lands, May!" Ed shook his head. "Is there a fire in that cup? Gal could send smoke signals with that thing."

"It's fine." She nodded at their guest, whose toothy grin remained unaffected by Uncle Ed's remarks. "Just blow on it, honey." Turning, she glanced at Jason, her face scrunched. Evidently, she wasn't pleased with what was happening.

"This is Wendy." Uncle Ed beamed as he looked back and forth between the two of them.

Jason forced a smile. "How do you know my uncle?" He watched as she brushed a strand of curly brown hair back behind her shoulder. It was long, like Cece's, though Cece had often worn hers pulled back.

Uncle Ed laughed. "Not quite. It's a funny story, actually." He motioned to Wendy. "Why don't you tell him, darlin'?"

She finished the sip of tea she'd been taking and gracefully rested the mug on a saucer. "I bumped into your uncle at the hardware store this morning. I was looking for some parts to fix an old dresser my grandma gave me . . . " She glanced at Auntie May, whose back shook as she scrubbed the side of the refrigerator.

Was his aunt so distraught that she'd run out of normal things to clean? Realizing his face was contorted, he relaxed his eyebrows and tried to not jump to any conclusions.

" . . . it's an antique," Wendy continued. "Anyway, I had no idea what I was doing!" She giggled. "Thankfully, your uncle said you're great at fixing things." She turned her attention to Uncle Ed. "How'd you put it?"

The man straightened his shoulders. "He's the greatest of the great in this here state!"

She giggled again. "That's right!" Fixing her eyes on Jason, she continued, "I could certainly use a man who's good with his hands."

He felt blood rush to his face. It was hot in here. Auntie May preferred to have the windows open and let fresh air flow through the kitchen, especially in spring, but it was much too hot for that today. He turned toward the three windows that neighbored their kitchen table and glanced out at the thermometer. Fifty-five degrees. Was that it? The room felt like a furnace!

"We'll leave you two to discuss business." It was Uncle Ed's voice. Sure, he'd referred clients to him in the past, but this was different. They were typically men who needed a little guidance, store owners, or married women looking to remodel, not overly flirtatious young ladies in their early twenties.

"But, Ed, don't you think—"

"Come now, May. How's about you and me go for a nice, long walk?"

Jason turned to see his aunt's face soften as Uncle Ed offered her his arm. Before he could object, they were out the door—a place he wished to be. He looked over at Wendy. She sat calmly, her gaze directed out the window. The sun shone through the glass panes and glistened against her cheeks. They sparkled, almost the way Cece's had. Cece liked to wear something on her cheeks that made them look like they were dusted with flecks of gold.

"You have a nice smile."

The voice startled him. He hadn't realized he'd been smiling. Leaning back against a wall, he straightened his lips. "Small world."

Her eye lashes fluttered as she took another sip of tea. "Yeah. How about that?"

"So, you need a dresser fixed?" Crossing his arms, he stared at a spot just above her head. It was a sunflower. Auntie May loved that wallpaper—said it reminded her of Cece. *Cecelia.* He still couldn't get her out of his head.

"That's right. Can you help me?" Wendy's voice was deep and soft.

"I don't think so," he responded, still uninterested in looking at her. If Uncle Ed was trying to set him up, his efforts were futile.

"Oh?" The floor creaked as she scooted her chair back and stood. "May I ask why?"

His eyes slipped, catching a glimpse of her bright red nails resting against her hips. Cece painted her nails sometimes, but she used a clear polish. It was like furniture varnish, preserving the beauty that was already there.

"Jason?"

He never knew his own name could sound so . . . weird. "Oh, right." What was the answer again? Why couldn't he help her? "I'm engaged."

The woman's eyes widened. "And?"

And what? Was he being ridiculous? It wasn't Wendy's fault that Uncle Ed brought her to their home instead of his workshop. Perhaps he was overthinking this. There was no reason why he couldn't help a client. He wasn't short on time. His whole week had recently opened up. He could spare a half-hour. For a quick job like this, that should be all it took.

"I mean, yes, I can fix your dresser. Just bring it by my workshop tomorrow morning, and I'll call you when it's finished." Pushing himself from the wall, he moved toward the entryway and waited for her to follow.

"Are you always so kind?" She smiled. As she stepped around the table, a breeze swept through the kitchen and blew her sundress to the side.

"No," he offered, placing his hands in tattered jean pockets. "I'm usually much worse—awful, really."

She moved closer. "I see you wore your Sunday best. You must have been eager to meet me." Arriving at the place where he stood, she followed him through the living room.

"Ah, my work pants. Gotta save the best for actual Sundays." And his wedding day. His stomach fell to his feet, like a rock cascading down the walls of a hollow canyon.

As they reached the doorway, she looked at him. Her gaze was penetrating, as though trying to unlock his secrets.

"Good day, Miss—"

"You know, I was engaged once, but not anymore," she interrupted. Her comment caught him off guard. She turned away.

Silence lingered as he thought. "I'm sorry. Are you okay?" He could have kicked himself. He had just asked her the one question he hated to hear.

"I am now," she said through a whisper. She folded her arms across her stomach.

"Do you want to talk about it?"

She whipped around, locking eyes. "He was . . . unpredictable—a loose cannon, really. He always wanted to do things his way, and one day, I just wasn't part of his way anymore." Her thick, black lashes dipped over glossy eyes. "It hurt back then, but I'm happy now. I'm finally where I want to be."

"Is that right?"

"Well, almost." She bit her bottom lip and tipped her chin away. "There's still the matter of finding Mr. Right." Her teeth flashed as she smiled up at him.

Did she mean him? She couldn't possibly. They'd only just met. Besides, for all she knew, he was engaged. Unavailable. Taken—that couldn't be truer. His heart belonged to someone who had taken it far away. If only he knew where that might be.

Reaching for the door, he opened it and extended an arm outward.

"I hope you find him," he offered politely.

Without adverting her gaze, she walked onto the porch, then spun around so her body faced him. "Say, would it be all right if I brought the dresser over here today? You're here. I'm here. It's just that this heirloom is so precious to me, and I'll be leaving town soon, so it really has to be now."

"Why not?" There really wasn't a reason, except for all the little ways she reminded him of Cece. How was that possible? They looked nothing alike, yet somehow, his brain managed to find similarities. It was torture. His heart ached enough already. He didn't need more reminders of the woman he missed so much.

"Thank you."

He nodded. "Glad I can help."

"You have no idea!" She grinned, descending the wooden steps. "And Jason? I learned that people like my ex need to be free—people who think only about themselves. You can't make them become something they're not. Just a thought."

Leaving no time for his rebuttal, she walked down the sidewalk to a vehicle parked across the street. What did she mean? He would never try to make Cece something that she was not. He knew exactly who she was, and he loved her for it. From the looks of things, that was never going to change.

## Chapter 24
### To Get Things Straight

11:35 a.m.

After hours of carrying a limp body, Jackson was ready to drive. Immediately after tackling Cece, he had knocked her over the head, rendering her unconscious and transportable. Although carrying her slowed him down, he figured it was still faster than the time he would otherwise spend in dragging her along against her will. Her body didn't weigh much, but it was enough to make a person's back cramp. He had taken several breaks to stretch and cover their tracks along with way. He figured he couldn't go back to Bomilton after the scene he caused yesterday. Besides, when Bart found out that Cece was gone, he might very well return there. Instead, he had another plan. If he continued in his current direction, eventually he'd reach the road.

He slowed to a walk and moved in closer among the trees that lined the river. To limit the possibility of Bart following him, he moved from tree to tree, occasionally looking back. While Bart wasn't the brightest bulb in the socket, he had a hunter look about him that made Jackson extra cautious. Several times, he thought he heard footsteps. He'd turn, wait a minute, and watch. Nothing. Although his suspicions tried to persuade him otherwise, he continued toward the road. Taking a deep breath, he adjusted Cece's body. Instead of cradling her like he had been, he swung her up over his shoulder, squeezing her legs as he walked.

After some more pauses, adjustments, and assessments, he made it to the road. He laid her body on the ground and began searching through the foliage. Hastily, he brushed aside overgrown weeds to search the base of a tree. "Thank you," he said with a nod to the ground. He lifted a thick, dead branch. It was only three feet long but would do just fine. As he squatted by Cece, waiting, he began peeling off twigs until the branch was relatively smooth. He was ready for whatever came first: a car or Bart.

It seemed like hours that he waited until a car finally came rattling down the road. Waving his branch in the air, he frantically moved into the car's way. He pretended to pant as the driver rolled down his window and slowed to a stop. The vehicle was navy blue with a smashed left headlight—an easily identifiable feature. Jackson took a moment to reconsider his original plan and decided on a safer alternative.

"Hey there, fella, what can I do for ya?" the man asked with a smile. His teeth were yellowed and off-putting. Jackson moved quickly toward the window.

"It's my wife, Mister! She's terribly sick—been unconscious for two days straight! I ain't got no car to get her to the hospital!" He pressed his palm against his forehead and forced a couple tears.

"Well, don't you worry, Mister . . . "

"Leonard."

The man smiled. "Mr. Leonard, there's a nice, small town—Bomilton's the name—just back a short ways. As a matter a fact, I just came from there! Your wife can lay in the back, and I'll drive you! She'll be with a doctor in no time!"

Immediately, Jackson clarified his need: "No!" For an instant, he slipped back into the Italian accent he was trying to hide. Taking a breath, he continued in the local dialect. "That's mighty kind of you, but my wife's family lives in a small city in the direction you're headin'." He shook his head and looked down. "It's northwest of Ichacar. You familiar with the area?"

"Hmm . . ." The man shook his head. "I do know a couple towns out that way. As a matter of fact, I am heading to one right now. Perhaps I can drop you off there. You can make sure she's okay and call her family." The man paused. "You sure you wouldn't rather get her checked out in Bomilton and drive home after you know she is okay?"

Jackson went to lift Cece off the ground. "I know my wife, Mister. She'd want it this way."

The driver shook his head. "If you say so, Mr. Leonard. After all, you're the man behind this here operation! Now, let's get that wife of yours to a doctor."

Gently, Jackson laid Cece across the back seat. As he bent her knees to make room for himself, the driver corrected him.

"Oh no, you can sit up here, Mr. Leonard!"

He was taken aback. "That's quite all right, sir. If ya don't mind, I'd rather be with my wife."

"Come now, you can turn your head and watch her the whole time. Pardon me for the intrusion—I don't mean nothing personal—but it would make me more comfortable, seeing as how we just met and all."

By now, the whole event was taking too long for his liking. Bart could show up any moment. "Why didn't you just say so!" He hopped in the front seat. "Now, Mister, let's get out of here."

He watched as the driver clutched the steering wheel. The old man must have slammed on the gas because Jackson's head shot backward against the headrest. Buckling his seatbelt, he glanced back at Cece. Thankfully, she was still unconscious.

*** 

As the car drove off, Bart stuck his head out from behind a tree. "Now, that ain't right!" Frustrated by his failure to protect Cece, he turned and headed back to Bomilton. He figured he'd best be getting back to work. Besides, it was Monday now, and he had a client expecting his wood delivery today. If he didn't come through, it could hurt the long-term interest of his business. Word-of-mouth is a powerful thing in a small community; and as much as he wanted to protect Cece, his prior commitments prevented it. Besides, she'd be fine. He had a good feeling about this.

He stopped.

He didn't have a good feeling.

He couldn't stop thinking about their conversation last night. Did Mr. Connor really kidnap her? Something had to be done, but he didn't know what. He was hours from Bomilton with no cars in sight. Blood rushed to his face. Cece wouldn't be in the hands of a thug right now if he hadn't led Mr. Connor straight to her! How could he be so short-sighted? He refused to think the money had anything to do with it. He *couldn't* think that. It was a notion too repulsive to mind.

Realizing his jaw was clenched, he exhaled. Even if he wanted to do something, which he did, he couldn't. For the next umpteen hours, it was completely out of his control. All he could do was hope that she would be okay—that some Divine intervention would take place. He glanced back. The car was now a dot in the distance; in the heat of the moment, he'd forgotten to get the license plate number. Bart shook his head. If what she told him was true, the girl needed a miracle. A woman like that deserved a miracle.

## Chapter 25

### *Three to One*

As Tommy and Marley surveilled Jason, Tommy frowned. His wonderful, just slightly bad character was about to be compromised on a silly mission. If Marley complained about one more thing, he would snap. He tried desperately to distract himself from the annoying comments that flooded forth from his friend. Grabbing a chocolate bar from his back pocket, he opened the wrapper. His body had melted the treat, which now stuck to its foil covering. Finding he could not eat the treat as he would a regular candy bar, he began licking the wrapper.

He stood next to Marley on the sidewalk, a grayish-brown fence at their backs. To avoid suspicion, the two occasionally strolled down the street, looked in a shop window, went back to their post at the fence, looked over their shoulders to watch Jason, talked, leaned against the fence, and so forth.

They fumbled around all morning as they followed from a distance. They kept on the opposite sidewalk as he went to work and returned home. Although they were particularly proud of their creeping, it wasn't necessary. Their target appeared to be in a haze that kept him from noticing anything. Tommy was convinced that a tiger could have walked to the workstation, danced on its hind legs, sung a song, and Jason would not have noticed. Perhaps the tiger could have just eaten him and saved them the trouble of all this walking. He shook his head. Although he didn't wish any harm upon the man, Jason was unwittingly making him suffer. Marley had been driving him nuts. Up to this point, he was proud of his ability to tolerate the boss' antics, but his patience was wearing thin.

When Jason had returned home, they reclaimed their position across the street from his house.

Tommy sighed. "I'm pretty sure this is the most boring day of my life." As he spoke, an elderly woman inched her way across the sidewalk directly in front of the house. "Yep, no question," he confirmed.

"Would you quit your complaining?" Marley snapped. "Nobody likes surveillance, but you still gotta do it. All the experts do."

He got the feeling that only half of what Marley said was actually true. First of all, he was pretty sure that Marley *loved* surveillance. Even back in their heavier crime days, the boss seemed to take a perverse pride in the practice—perhaps because he thought that watching people made him an expert.

"If he's taking a break for lunch, why can't we?"

"You and your food." Marley rolled his eyes. "Say we do follow that stomach of yours and go eat. Then, that pathetic wretch comes home when we're gone, and everything's over because you're hungry. Do you want all this time we've spent to be for nothing? We'll wait."

He couldn't take it anymore. "I've had it up to here with you! First, you get mad at me for talking with food in my mouth. Then, my walk's too loud. Next, the way I lean against a fence looks suspicious. You get mad when I lick my chocolate off the wrapper. Now I can't eat lunch?" His voice rose.

"Pipe down!" Marley lifted his left arm and smacked him in the back of the head. "You'll compromise what we're trying to do here."

He let out a frustrated chuckle. "Yeah, my talking's really gonna cause a scene. Nobody cares that we're here! Do you see these people? You could count them on two"—he looked at the people and glanced at his hands—"four hands if you had them. Everyone is either at work or busy doing other stuff by now. So, don't try to tell me that anyone cares if I'm hungry!"

Marley blinked. "If you don't calm down, then I'll make you."

His tone was firm, but Tommy didn't care. Food was more important than being in the boss' good graces—at least for now. Besides, he was bigger than Marley and could win in a fist fight, especially with a meal at stake.

"How about this, Mar? What if Cece's watching us right now?" He gasped mockingly. "What if we're stalking Jason, and she's stalking us?"

Marley looked around. "You're right," he said kindly.

Tommy stopped, stunned. "I am?"

"Yeah, I've been a real jerk. Come here, Pal." The boss extended his arms as though offering a hug, but when Tommy came close enough, Marley thrust a knee into his delicate spot and sent him to the ground wheezing. "Now, back to business."

After a few minutes went by, something happened.

"There he is," Marley noted as Jason reemerged from the house with a woman.

Tommy rubbed his eyes. "It's Wendy!" he exclaimed. "She broke in while we was watching him at work, and he didn't notice anything suspicious?" He laughed. "What a doof!"

Marley rolled his eyes. "Someone else let her in, you moron!"

"You mean . . . "

"Some older folks live with him—probably his grandparents."

"Grandparents?" His face went numb. "But what they got to do with this?" He grabbed the boss' shirt and pulled his face within inches of his own. "If she hurts them, so help me!"

"Relax." Marley shoved his large hands away and straightened the t-shirt he had whined about wearing. He had made it clear that this attire was beneath him, but he would sacrifice for the integrity of the mission—or something like that. "They'll be fine. She's only there to seduce the guy anyway."

"Seduce?" His eyebrows furrowed. "You mean . . . ?"

"What? No!" The boss shivered. "I mean allure—deceive. Trick him into redirecting his affections for . . . you-know-who . . . onto Wendy. If the little traitor comes back, she'll be heartbroken just in time to die."

"Oh."

Tommy scratched his head and watched as Wendy hurried down the sidewalk and hopped in her car. He caught her eyes as she drove by; her quick wink sent a rush of blood to his cheeks. Looking over, he saw the boss blow a kiss at the car's bumper.

"Where's she off to, Boss?"

"I don't know," he declared. "The better question is: what's gonna happen when she gets back?"

The boss' grin was unsettling, his eyes wild as he stared at the man on the porch. Tommy's mind spun through horrific possibilities. Something bad was about to happen, and he had a front row ticket that he really didn't want.

# Chapter 26
## Seize the Moment

1:17 p.m.

After Wendy left Jason's house, she had searched out a local second-hand shop and purchased the cheapest dresser she could find. Thankfully, she had a story in mind that would make the piece of junk sound like a treasure—especially to weak-minded folks like Jason. As soon as she made her purchase, a willing gentleman loaded it into the trunk of her beige Honda Accord. Marley had given her the car last month, insisting that it was gold and radiant—like her. Gold. What a load of garbage. That thing was beige—the most boring color ever made. How he got the car, she didn't know, and frankly, she'd learned not to ask. It was a sweet gesture, and she was mature enough to recognize that without griping over the details.

She arrived back at her destination in no time. Removing her key from the ignition, she glanced at the house. Its white shudders and wrap-around porch were straight from a storybook. She sighed. Marley had promised that one day they'd live together in a house like that. He'd been saying it since the day he escaped from prison—the day he first laid eyes on her. Apparently, he had fallen in love at first sight. It took her a bit longer, but his persistence was irresistible. He made her feel like a rare gem, and she was delighted to be found by someone who cared. All the guys before him had just used her, and she was thrilled to finally be adored.

Reaching in her purse, she grabbed a tube of lip gloss and applied a thick, fresh coat. She rubbed her lips together and blew a kiss to herself in the rearview mirror. Marley loved her lips—said she was born to make men's hearts bleed. Today, however, the mission was different. She was going to save Jason from himself and break Cecelia's heart. From what Marley had told her, the woman was a downright awful person, and it was only fitting to take away everything, just like she had done to Marley.

Climbing from the car, she spotted Jason leaning against the white, wooden railing that lined the porch. He must have seen her, but he certainly didn't acknowledge it. Typical, self-indulged man. It would be easy to make him forget about someone else. The hard part was getting guys like this to get over *themselves*. Leaving the dresser behind, she proceeded to the porch and ascended the creaky steps.

"I'm back."

Jason jumped as though she'd startled him. Perhaps he hadn't noticed her arrival after all.

"That was fast," he replied. "Do you have the dresser?"

"It's in my trunk." Cautiously, she moved closer, like a hunter approaching a deer. "But first, I was hoping we could discuss the project in more detail." She tried to search his eyes, but he turned away.

She followed him to a corner of the porch. His muscles stretched out the back of his shirt. He was quite an attractive man. She could see why Cecelia had entangled him in her vicious web. There was a handsome ruggedness to him that made it all the easier to invest herself in the mission.

Noticing Jason was looking at her, she felt her cheeks flush. He had said something. What was it? She quickly refocused as he cleared his throat and extended an arm, offering her the first choice of seating.

Forcing a giggle, she scooted by. "That rocking chair is beautiful," she said with a smile, lowering herself onto the neighboring swing.

"Made it myself." He sat down and rubbed the chair's weathered arms.

"Impressive," she beamed. "Do you make a lot of your own furniture?"

"Yes. Now, tell me about this dresser of yours." Though his tone was friendly enough, she could tell he had no interest in getting to know her. She could fix that.

"You're all business, huh?" She chuckled. "Don't you ever just relax?"

He rubbed his hands against his face. "Listen. It's been a hard couple of days," he said, exasperation in his voice. "I'd appreciate it if we could just focus on the project. Sound good?"

Her eyes widened. "I'm sorry." She feigned innocence. "It's my fault, isn't it? I'm asking too much."

"No." He stood, leaving the chair rocking in its place. "It's not your fault. Really. I'd just prefer to stick to business."

"I just thought . . . " She paused. This guy was determined to keep her out. It was clear he was hurting, but for some reason, he wasn't angry enough to want revenge yet. The guys' note said Cecelia left him for another man. Most guys would be all over a new woman by now, seeking to throw the same daggers with which they'd been cut, but it seemed Jason was different. Any other day, she might have left and given him a few weeks to stew, but she didn't have much time before Marley wanted her back. She had to come up with a reason for him to let her in—a reason to trust her.

"I know work's important," she began. "After all, you gotta make money." Rising from her seat, she slowly approached the railing where he stood. "But I think that if your heart's happy, your work will be better."

"Is that a fact?" His eyes seemed to follow a squirrel as it scurried up a nearby oak tree.

She waited until his gaze finally landed on her. His stare was intense, his dark eyes beckoning. Something about the attention made her giddy. At last, an assignment she could get behind! Of all the guys Marley had her distract over the past few months, Jason was by far the most dreamy. "It is." She giggled. "There are scientific studies to prove it!"

He shook his head and looked away. Was that a smile she caught?

"So, what's been hard? Is it your fiancée?" The muscles around his shoulders tensed. "It is, isn't it?"

"Why would you ask that? Maybe I just had a bad weekend."

She shrugged. "Maybe, but I bet it's more than that. Matters of the heart tend to affect us most. You seem distracted, so I figured it might be about love. Am I right?"

*"Please, please! I love him! You've got to let me go!"* Wendy shivered as the memory of Cecelia's pleas shot through her mind. Where did that come from? Although Marley constantly reassured her that the woman was a traitor and murderer, the desperation in Cecelia's voice had made her very uncomfortable—so much so, that she'd left the room shortly thereafter. She shook her head and tried to focus on the present.

"I guess so," he responded sullenly. Finally, they were getting somewhere.

She had to keep digging so he could move past whatever was keeping him from hearing the truth. "I hope I'm not overstepping," she began. "But I heard some folks talking. They said your fiancée left you." She tried to squeeze out a tear, but nothing happened. "Is that true?"

He remained silent before answering. "News travels fast." He spun around and folded his arms. His legs crossed in like fashion, tanned skin peeking through the rips in his jeans. "I suppose. I mean, I didn't think so at first, but that was before the note."

"A note?" The plan was working. She watched as Jason went over to the steps and sat down. The silence was awkward, but she waited for him to continue on his own.

"I guess I'm not the one for her." He sighed. "And if that's true, it means she's not the one for me either." His eyebrows bent. "It's just . . . I really thought she was."

Wendy crept toward the steps, careful not to spook the man who was beginning to open up. Tucking her dress, she sat down beside him. She glanced at the intricately embroidered flowers across its hem. "I know how you feel," she started. "I didn't want to say it before, but that's why my fiancé left me. He met some woman, and apparently, they fell in love." She played with her fingers as they lay in her lap. "He didn't tell me until it was too late. He just . . . fell out of love. I didn't know that was possible."

Jason smirked. "You sound like me."

"But it *is*," she added. "It *is* possible. The best thing you can do—what worked for me—was accepting that it was over and moving on."

She waited through more silence. It was almost painful. She wasn't used to the process taking this long.

"She was the love of my life," he finally whispered, tilting his head toward the sky. He spoke as if to himself, or to someone seated in the clouds. "What should I do?"

There was pain in his voice that made her gut clench. This man's heart was broken—his pain almost tangible. Cecelia had really done a number on him. It wasn't fair.

"You move on," she answered. "It's the only way to feel better. You don't deserve what this woman has done to you, and if there's someone else, it means she's not coming back. You've got to let go of the idea of you and her. It's not what she wants, so it's never going to happen."

"The only other guy she dated was a jerk to her. She was miserable with him—she told me herself. No." He stood. "I can't move on until I know she's okay."

Wendy's palms started to sweat. The guys told her how manipulative Cecelia could be, but wow. It was evident that Jason knew nothing of her past. Perhaps she should tell him the truth about his precious bride. Then maybe . . . Before she could finish the thought, a better idea popped into her head. Her heart raced as she jumped to her feet. "Maybe it's not the same guy! It's probably someone else. Someone she thinks is better suited—"

"If he is better suited, then at least I'll know she's happy. But I have to know for sure."

"Of course, she's happy!" Wendy threw up her hands. "Nobody would leave a guy like you for someone less perfect."

"Thanks for the advice." Her compliment had obviously been lost on him. Although his words expressed appreciation, his tone said otherwise as he moved toward the door. "If you take your dresser to my shop on Elm Street, Derek will fix it for you. Just tell him Jason sent you, and he'll squeeze you in."

She was losing him. She had to think of something . . . fast. Her jaw hung open as he reached for the doorknob.

"I'm a private investigator!" she blurted out.

He stopped, his hand frozen in mid-air. Slowly, he looked back. "What?"

"That's what I do . . . back home . . . I'm an investigator. I didn't want to mention anything before . . . because I don't like giving people false hope . . . especially in a situation like this . . . but if it will help bring you closure, I'll investigate." Her armpits were sweating. The humidity certainly wasn't helping her remain cool in either sense of the word.

He rubbed the back of his neck as she continued: "Perhaps we can barter. You fix my dresser, and I'll find your girlfriend."

"You'd do that?" For the first time, hope shone in his eyes. "Doesn't seem like a fair trade. Shouldn't take long for repairs."

"And it shouldn't take long to investigate." Noticing a trace of skepticism on his face, she added, "But you have my word, I will find out who she's with."

Jason opened his mouth, then closed it. He waited, as if pondering whether or not his voice would work. "It's just that something doesn't seem right," he began. "She was happy the night of our rehearsal dinner—didn't act differently, wasn't pulling away, nothing. Then, all of a sudden, she leaves for another guy? The numbers don't add up."

"Fine." She wanted to roll her eyes but rolled them mentally instead. "I can look into the whole thing." Suddenly, she was aware of her intermingled fingers, twisting anxiously in front of her. Was she nervous? She didn't feel nervous, but then again, the butterflies had been a little distracting. She'd lied plenty of times. This should be no different.

She clasped her hands behind her and forced a steady breath. "Sometimes, we need to see things for ourselves," she continued. "Evidence can help bring closure." Plus, scrounging up some physical evidence of Cecelia's "choice" shouldn't be too hard, especially if she controlled the narrative as to what the evidence meant.

Jason nodded. "I need to hear it from her lips. If I can see that she's safe and happy, I'll eventually be able to move on." He shoved his hands in his pockets, drawing her attention to the muscly veins in his forearms. "I want to know the truth. Besides, it's the truth that sets us free."

She would have commented, but he kept talking.

"Now, where do we begin?"

"We? I was going to go—" She pointed toward her car, but Jason interrupted before she could verbalize her bogus plan.

"I'm coming with you." He rushed past her and started down the sidewalk.

"Wait!" She hurried after him, suddenly regretting her decision to wear heels. "We're going to the trouble of finding a woman who doesn't want to be found. Remember? Do you really want to be the one to find her? I realize how hard it would be to *see* your love with someone new. You don't want to do that to yourself. Trust me. I've worked plenty of cases, and client participation in the investigative part is always a bad idea."

He stopped abruptly, sending her jumping into the grass to avoid a collision. Composing herself, she gazed at his handsome face, his brows bent inward.

"I see your point," he started. "But abandoning Cece isn't an option. The thought of her with another guy is physically painful." It was true. Wendy could see it on his face. "But if she's safe, I can get over it. But if she's in danger, and something happens to her . . . " Pressing his lips together, he paused and closed his eyes. "Never mind. We're not going to let that happen."

There's that "we" again. "But—"

"Listen." He leaned forward. Somehow, his intense stare held a reassuring warmth. "If her ex is involved, she could be in trouble. I have to know. So please . . . take me with you."

Somehow, her simple plan turned into a task of immense pressure. How could she forge evidence with Jason on her heels—literally? A bead of sweat escaped down the side of her face. Perhaps something good could come of this after all. He was so determined to find Cecelia that he'd be spending every second with Wendy to do it. It was perfect. There was just one more thing . . .

"Okay, you can come, but keep in mind what I said before: some people don't want to be found. If that's the case with your girl, there's a chance we won't find her." She paused before quickly adding, "But I hope we do. I just want you to be prepared for any outcome." Her forehead was drenched. Of all the times to leave her purse in the car. No tissues. No relief. She felt like a hot mess. Hopefully, her smile was enough to reassure Jason of her sincerity.

He looked up at the sky. "God knows where she is, and if there's something good that can come from finding her, He'll lead the way."

There was something good for someone, but that someone wasn't him. This whole thing would be over in no time. She sighed. It seemed like this guy really was in love. A small part of her wished Cecelia had been honest with him. Jason didn't deserve the pain he'd feel when he found out their relationship was built on lies, but disappointment was a part of life.

She swept her tongue across her mouth. It was sticky and in desperate need of bubblegum. She looked toward her car. Ah, well . . . the show must go on.

## Chapter 27

# *Missing Mrs.*

2:15 p.m.

Cece's eyelids fluttered open. She looked at the gray ceiling and felt sick as her body jerked about. Throbbing pain shot through the back of her head. She winced. There were two distinct voices in the front seat, both of which sounded drenched with the same thick accent. Shifting her eyes to the side, she saw Jackson's profile as his mouth moved in conversation. Of course. Who else? She tried to think clearly, despite a pounding headache. The pain was so intense that it was hard to focus on anything else. All she wanted was release from her misery. First her heart and now her head? It didn't seem fair. Assuming Jackson was keeping a close watch on her, she closed her eyes. *Please, God, give me strength.* She paused and reconsidered her prayer. With restrained tears pressurized behind her eyes, she continued silently, *And thank You for keeping me alive.*

As she lay quietly, trying to determine whether the driver was friend or foe, the pain in her head brought back memories of the kidnapping. Although it was difficult to think, she forced herself to concentrate. The pieces seemed to be coming together . . .

*While walking home from the restaurant, she had passed a thin alley between two competing convenience stores. Abruptly, she was grabbed from behind, one hand over her mouth and the other across her waist, and dragged down the narrow passage.*

The mental image made her grimace.

*At first, she had thought it was a silly, pre-wedding prank. After about ten seconds, she knew otherwise. Frantically, she fought to get free, kicking and flailing her limbs in every direction. She thrust her high heel into the shin of her captor. He immediately released her, grabbing the leg as she ran screaming. That's when she saw a figure at the end of the alley. Although the person was not dressed in black like the rest, it was difficult to make out his or her distinct features. Thinking that whoever it was would save her, she began to slow and was jerked backward.*

Cece caressed her wrists as she remembered.

*Someone tied her hands while the other held her tight. She felt suffocated and repulsed as the larger being restricted her. Would they beat her? Rape her? Kill her for no reason at all? She realized that there was a very real reason someone could want her dead. Too bad they didn't understand that taking her from Jason was all they needed to do to impart the most painful punishment upon her smitten heart.*

As the horrific scene flashed through her brain, she watched from a distance as though living in a terrible nightmare. The gang proceeded to wrap a rolled bandana around her face and up into her mouth. The rest was still hard to remember. The image of a room kept appearing— that, and her body tied against a chair with her mouth wide open. Shaking her head, she winced.

By now, she figured that the driver must be clueless. Jackson probably fed him a line of some kind and was using a phony accent as cover—a move not uncommon from her former colleague. She could sit up, reveal the truth, and watch his look of disappointment; however, if the driver was truly innocent, she didn't want to risk his life to save her own.

Getting involved would be better than just lying there, so she sucked back her emotions and prepared for war. Slowly, she arose in the back seat.

"Hello," she screeched. The car swerved, sending everyone off balance.

"What . . . ?" The driver frowned as he looked back at her. "Well, I'll be! Your wife appears to be okay! I haven't seen many miracles in my time, but I reckon this is one of them! Her voice seems a little gone, but it ain't nothing serious."

Jackson found her eyes in the side mirror. "I can't believe it myself. Darling, you're all right! I couldn't be happier, my sweet wife!" He reached a hand toward her face, but she pulled away.

"Wife?" Although it still hurt to speak, at least she was able to produce some type of noise, however reptilian it may have sounded.

The driver's eyes widened. "Sounds like someone's in the doghouse!"

Jackson looked from her to the driver and back. The smirk on her face must have infuriated him, but she didn't care.

"Yeah, when's a guy ever out of the doghouse? Spent about half my life in that thing!" he said with a fake chuckle.

"Ain't that the truth, Brother!" the driver responded. "Why, the missus always seems to have me in there for something! Don't get me wrong, now; I love the woman, but boy, she sure does like to run things!"

Jackson kept glancing back at her. Noticing his persistence, she kept her eyes forward and hoped to give him nothing.

"Excuse me, sir," she crackled. "I understand what you're saying, but the man you see next to you is always in the doghouse because he *is* a dog." Her throat, head—everything above the neck—begged her to stop speaking, but her heart wouldn't have it.

The driver gave a big, hearty laugh as Jackson shook his head. "You see the way she treats me? And to think I was so worried about her." His voice quivered as he looked out the side window.

His performance must have convinced the driver because concern fell upon the elderly man's face as he stopped laughing. "Oh, now, look at your husband, ma'am. He was full of concern when he thought you was sick. Maybe he can get a pass or something."

"A pass?" If only he knew she was "sick" because of her supposed "husband" . . . maybe then he wouldn't be saying anything about passes.

"Thanks, Mister, but that's not necessary," Jackson replied. "I haven't been a great husband the past year and don't deserve a pass." He looked at her, and for a moment, she almost believed his sincerity.

There was silence until the driver pointed out a sign for Youngsburg City.

"Youngsburg?" she asked, her heart beating faster. "You mean, we're near Ichacar?"

"Yes, ma'am. Continue on this road a few more miles, and you'll be there."

"Can we go, please? I'll pay you!"

Jackson shot her a sharp glance through the side mirror.

She waved.

"Don't worry, honey!" he insisted. "As long as you're all right, we'd best be picking up some supplies in Youngsburg. We can get a ride to Ichacar later today, okay?"

She shook her head. "No, I need to go now!" She wanted to tell the driver her situation but feared what Jackson might do. "Happy wife, happy life, am I right?" She giggled, hoping the driver would agree.

He laughed. "I would drive you there, ma'am, but I got me some business to do here in Youngsburg. Tell you what: if you ain't found a ride to Ichacar by four this afternoon, you meet me at the car, and I'll take you there. My business should be over by then."

She sighed. It wasn't ideal, but if she had to wait, she could. At least they were going somewhere with a large population.

After a mile of driving in silence, the car pulled into Youngsburg City. The driver parked at a meter along the side of the road across from a strip of buildings. To the right of the vehicle sat a wooden bench freshly painted in a coat of kelly green.

"Now, remember, if you can't get a ride to Ichacar, be back by 4:00 p.m. We'll meet by this here bench—"

Before he finished, Cece slipped out of the left door and ran, leaving it wide open. She didn't have to look back to know that Jackson was following her. Her heart raced as she sprinted across the warm pavement, her bare feet slapping the ground. She swerved in and out of the oncoming people, hoping to lose the nightmare that followed. He might be cunning, but so was she. If he wanted her, he'd have to catch her, and she wasn't about to let that happen.

## Chapter 28

*Puzzles*

2:30 p.m.

Jason and Wendy spent the early afternoon hours walking from Bartinelli's to Cece's apartment. Wendy had originally objected to walking, but once she replaced shoes that she'd called "feet haters" with a pair of black Pumas, her opinion changed. She'd grabbed her purse, which she'd explained had essential tools for their investigation, and followed Jason to where the rehearsal dinner took place.

They walked back and forth for what felt like hours. They tried the shortest route, the back way, and even an unconventional path—in case Cece decided to make some extra stops on her way home that night.

"I still don't understand what constitutes a viable clue," Jason said as they headed back to Bartinelli's. "What am I looking for, specifically?" He glanced over at Wendy; her eyes were glazed as she stared forward.

"We can't identify specifics without knowing what happened," she finally replied. "The clues are supposed to tell us the story. We can't just make up a story and find clues to match. That'll lead us to the wrong conclusion." They continued a few more steps. "Please don't get mad at me for saying this." She stopped and grabbed his arm. "But there may be nothing to find."

His heart sank, but he wasn't sure why. He knew the chances were slim of discovering evidence that contradicted the note he'd received, so he shouldn't be disappointed. Still, he had hoped that *something* would turn up. Anything.

"It's possible you're in denial," she continued, a squishing sound following each chomp of her gum. "You're trying to find something to discredit what has already been proven true, and that's hard." A large, pink bubble popped over her lips, and she sucked it back in. "Plus, you're prejudiced."

"What? Why?"

"Oh, wait." Her eyes darted from side to side as if searching for the answer. "Not prejudiced. *Biased*. You're biased." A proud smile flashed across her face, but she turned as though trying to conceal it.

Jason followed her lead as she continued walking.

"You want a certain answer, and you're looking for something that points to that answer. But if your answer is wrong, you won't find that something because it doesn't exist."

A million thoughts flooded his mind. Was she right? Was he so desperate to prove Cece's continued love for him that he refused to accept the truth? Was he romantic and hopeful, or just plain pathetic? He didn't want to know the answer.

As they continued down Maple Lane, Bartinelli's came into view. Jason lowered his eyes to the sidewalk ahead of him. A series of small stones were scattered across the cement, probably from the rock beds that framed a brick mailbox nearby. He swung his right leg as he stepped forward, contacting a stone. He watched as it skipped across the street and landed in front of the alley beside Betty's Bakery. After walking a little farther, he froze.

Wendy continued another twenty feet before acknowledging he'd stopped. "What is it?" she called.

After checking for cars, Jason jogged across the street and peered down the alley. There was something on the ground about halfway down. "I think I found something!" He waited impatiently as Wendy sauntered over. "What's that?" He pointed toward the unknown object.

"Probably just garbage or something." She put her hand around his arm and pulled. "Come on now; we can't waste time."

Shaking free from her grasp, he jogged toward the object. "A bandana," he called, stooping to pick it up. The black fabric was rolled and knotted. "Looks like someone was wearing it!" Shaking off the dirt, he waved it at Wendy, who remained at the end of the alley. "Come see!"

"No, thanks!" she hollered back. "I'm good here. Hurry up!"

His eyes returned to the dusty ground. There were several sets of footprints—at least three that were clear. One looked like it belonged to a large man wearing sneakers. Another was probably some kind of dress shoe—he could tell by the lack of tread. The third . . . He froze. Such small, narrow feet. Those tiny feet were so precious, so familiar. His heart raced as he gently placed his foot beside one of the prints. "Cece?"

"Jason," Wendy called. "We have to keep searching. Plenty of people wear bandanas. It's nothing. Now, let's go find some real clues!"

Following the prints, he came to a halt where they disappeared and tire tracks began. Nobody drove in this alley, so why would a vehicle be back here? He glanced up and down the brick walls: no doors or windows. Heaviness entered his lungs as his fingers went cold.

Turning, he ran toward Wendy. "We've got to go."

"Where?"

Noticing her struggle to keep up, he slowed.

"I think Cece's in trouble—"

"For the last time," Wendy huffed. "You can't just make up evidence!"

He stopped abruptly and felt her collide with his back. It sent him off balance, but he lunged forward and caught himself before falling. Turning, he stared into her eyes. "I'm not. Not this time. Something happened, and I can prove it!"

She raised an eyebrow. "Oh?" Her voice cracked. Coughing, she cleared her throat. "Sorry. Almost choked on my gum," she explained, momentarily adverting her eyes. She returned her attention to him. "What happened?"

"I think she was forced to go somewhere . . . " He couldn't bring himself to say kidnapped. It was a lot to process. He couldn't think about it too hard, or emotion would consume him. He had to stay focused and find out what happened before it was too late—but that was Wendy's question, wasn't it?

"*Forced* to go?" She threw her arms out. "You got that from a bandana? This isn't the movies."

"I know, but you've gotta believe me—"

"Listen," she interjected. "I know you're hurting, but you need to recognize that you're in denial. She left you a note, right? What did it say?"

He chuckled and looked away.

"It said she left you for another guy. At least, that's how I interpreted it when you showed me just this afternoon." She chomped her gum harder as though it would emphasize her point. "Did the note change since then? Did the bandana somehow sprout lips and start spewing a story you want to believe?"

Something ignited inside him. Why should he accept the initial appearance of the situation when it contradicted what he knew to be true? He'd had enough of Wendy's negativity. He needed to get out of there.

"I understand what you're saying," he said through clenched teeth. "But an investigator is willing to examine *all* the evidence." Realizing his fists were also clenched, he fought to relax them and rubbed their sweat against his weathered jeans. "If you want to help, all I ask is that you go look at the footprints in the alley. Form an opinion for yourself."

Without awaiting a rebuttal, he peeled away.

"Where are you going?" she called after him.

He didn't respond. He needed to form a plan. Should he contact the police? He should. Definitely. But then what? He'd seen enough mystery movies to know that if Cece was taken two-and-a-half days ago, she could be long gone by now.

*Please, God.* He threw the gate open as he ran up the walkway toward his house, leaping over a squirrel that dashed across his path. *Keep her safe.*

***

The thick air rested upon Wendy's shoulders. Jason's discovery could've been bad news. Thankfully, the evidence was easy to wipe away. It was nothing a little shoe shuffling couldn't handle, and since he didn't get a picture of the prints, they were now gone for good. His determination, however, was not.

Scanning the area, she saw a bench across the street from Betty's Bakery. As she drew near, she noticed the rustic artistry and wondered if it was one of Jason's creations. There was no denying his talent. The rocking chair he had made was beautiful.

She could see herself owning a porch like his someday, relaxing on a sunny afternoon with the man she loved. Her dress flailed as she sat down.

As soon as she sat, she caught two figures in her peripheral vision heading toward her. She didn't need to turn her head to know exactly who they were. Any number of things gave them away—be it their extreme height difference, their constant jostling, or their all-around awkward movements, she'd know Marley and Tommy anywhere.

"Hey, babe," Marley slid beside her. "Ouch! What the?" He grabbed the bottom of his thigh.

"Something bite you?" She laughed. She was still unsure whether she should tell Marley about the footprints, and until she decided, she needed to act normal—put the whole thing out of her mind.

His snarl didn't hinder her amusement. "I think I got a splinter. Could this good-for-nothing town possibly get any worse?"

"I don't know." Smiling, she grabbed his brimmed hat and tapped his filthy loafers with the tip of her sneaker. "Looks like someone got bit by the country bug. Now, honey, are you feeling a little Ich-y?" She giggled as the two men stared at her. "Oh, come on. That was a good one! Ich-y, get it? Like 'itchy' and 'Ichacar'? You got bit by a bug that made you love this town?"

Marley rolled his eyes. "Good thing you're pretty, 'cause your sense of humor needs some work."

"I could say the same about that outfit, but I won't."

"Burn!" Tommy crossed in front of her and sat on the other side. "She got you good, Mar!"

She watched as Marley dug his fingers into the sides of his head. She could only imagine how exasperated he must have felt after a day with Tommy. He'd never been fond of the man but insisted on keeping him around. Although he refused to disclose the reason why, she figured he needed the muscle. Tommy was big, and Marley enjoyed using the physical strength behind a pliable mind.

"Wendy?"

It was Marley, snapping at her for some reason. He had been awfully moody since this whole thing with Cece started. It made her wonder if there wasn't something more to the story.

"Yes?"

"Are you almost finished? 'Cause that scene just now didn't look good."

She folded her arms. "You're spying on me?" She glanced over at Tommy, who quickly looked away, then back at Marley. "Look, I can understand you watching the guy's house, but following us . . . me? You said you trust me!"

"This isn't about you!" He shot to his feet. "When will you get that through your tiny, little head?" Spit landed on her face as he yelled.

"Then what's it about Marley?" She angrily wiped the spittle from her cheek. "What's it *really* about? Do you actually want justice, or is this just revenge for the way she framed you—a way to heal your bruised ego?" She paused. "Or is it something more?"

Marley opened his mouth, but nothing came out. His eyes searched her face. As she glared at him, Tommy's voice emerged from behind.

"Of course, it's revenge!" he answered cheerfully. "That ain't no secret. He's hated her since the moment she called the cops." He wiped his sweaty palms against his shirt and reached in his pocket. "Didn't help that he was sweet on her. Gum?"

She glanced back to see a mangled silver stick in his hand. "Already got some." Her hair flipped as she turned back to Marley. "Sweet on her?"

His fingers curled into fists. "I hated her. Everyone with a brain knew that! We just needed her to stick around for a few more jobs. That's it!"

"And that's why you want to keep punishing her, even after death? All for some vengeful love game? I thought Jackson said the deed was done."

"He said that, but after the way he disappeared earlier, I know she's still out there. If they'd drowned her like we planned—" He glared at Tommy. "—I would have found her body, pinned in the water beneath a boulder." He returned his attention to Wendy. "Do you think there was a body? No!" he fumed. "Now you're getting all righteous on me? That little worm is a murderer, remember? She deserves to die! That's how you stop murderers from killing again."

Tommy butted in. "But she didn't—"

"Zip it, Tommy!" Exhaling, he leaned toward her. The heat of his breath brushed against her mouth. "She's guilty, okay? We've got to stop her before she ruins more lives." He grabbed a strand of her hair and delicately placed it behind her ear. "Now, if you can't steal his heart, at least keep the bum occupied until we finish the job. Can you do that?"

She tried to pull away, but he grabbed her face. "I love *you*, Wendy, and that will never change."

Signaling to Tommy, Marley stepped away. Tommy squeezed her shoulder as he passed, his smile full of innocence and comfort.

"Now," Marley began. "If you insist on being left alone, we'll head back to our place—but if you realize you need help, or if something doesn't seem right," he smirked, "call me."

Evidently, her nod was enough to satisfy him. She was glad she hadn't told him about the footprints, but she wasn't sure if her decision was fueled by pride, anger, or regret. As she watched the two unlikely comrades walk away, a heaviness fell upon her. She was encompassed in a smog that nearly took her breath away. Exhaling, she struggled to suppress her thoughts. There was nothing wrong with Marley's intentions. If the law wouldn't protect the world from a murderer, someone else should, right? He was a vigilante, fighting injustice for the greater good. Never mind the fact that they stole for a living. They took only what they needed; it turned out they just happened to need a lot of stuff.

She closed her eyes and rested her head against the back of the bench. Marley's words played in her mind like a CD that held fifteen tracks of the same confusing song. She had known most of the words already, but these were new. Had she been singing along to a catchy tune without knowing what she was actually saying? She had thought the meaning was clear, but there seemed to be a few words still missing that could change the entire song.

## Chapter 29

### No Looking Back

June 22, 1990

Cece went airborne as the car sped over a small hill in the road. She was riding in the passenger seat of the gang's lifted station wagon. Marley had bragged about his role in the job for days—how he hot-wired the car and drove it away within minutes of his entry. Therefore, he considered the vehicle his, which is why he currently drove. Jackson interjected during Marley's storytelling with the fact that he was the one who distracted the owner with his good looks and charm. In either case, the whole gang traveled in the vehicle tonight, as per usual.

As they drove the maroon car—a color Marley enjoyed likening to "dried blood"—over a small, country road, Cece reviewed the plan in her head. She'd slip in through an obscure opening that led to the basement window, use a screwdriver to pry it open, and creep about the house to see if anyone was home. She frowned at the tool in her hand. What was wrong with her lately? Knots kept building in her stomach; it was almost like a ball of rubber bands that continued to grow with everything she did, a lingering discontent.

She forced a smile and looked over at Marley. "You really meant what you said, Mar?"

He glanced to the side. She was a beautiful young lady, although a bit rough around the edges. At least, that's what he'd told her. "You bet, sugar." He winked and kept driving.

It was almost a year now since Marley had proposed. She remembered the moment as though it'd just happened.

*Marley came home and tossed a tiny velvet box toward her spot on the couch. It landed in the bowl of popcorn she'd just made, scattering the buttery pieces across her lap. Furious, she chucked it back at his face.*

*"Whoa," he said. "Just look inside before you attack me." He tossed the box back, and this time, she caught it. When she opened it to see an engagement ring, she couldn't help but laugh. There was no way she was getting married. Not after what her parents had gone through. Before she could object, Marley's words stopped her. "Just think about it."*

*The weeks following, she thought hard. Why was he doing this? To keep her around, no doubt. She'd threatened to leave the gang before, mostly when they refused to see things her way. Perhaps now, Marley had found a solution to that. She couldn't decide if his attempted manipulation was insulting or impressive. She had been determined to reject the proposal until a particular thought changed her mind: as soon as the gang exhausted their usefulness, she could divorce Marley and get half of his stuff. Talk about a good heist! That outcome had her smiling for months. She didn't even care when Tommy informed her that Marley had pick-pocketed the ring from a guy on the street. Her future ex-husband was saving money, which ultimately meant more for her.*

*Thoughts of that masterful plan had fueled her for months, but as Marley kept postponing their trip to the courthouse, she'd become surprisingly needy. She somehow found herself wanting his claims of love to be true. How was that even possible? She hated love.*

*The past three months were confusing at best. The desire for love had crept up so gradually that by the time she realized how she felt, it was too late. After years of thinking otherwise, she had finally wanted someone to care. She wasn't even sure it had to be Marley—just someone. Something was missing from her life, and she couldn't quite put her finger on it.*

Cece turned her head to the right and gazed out the window, watching the tall, black trees forcefully pass by. Dark clouds covered the canopy of stars that shone behind them. She liked clouds. Not the light, happy clouds, but the angry ones, the bulky clouds that curled their fists and punched perky feelings in the face. Deep clouds that wore their bruises for all the world to see—they didn't hide their emotions; they embraced their pain and rained their frustrations upon those below. In a way, she admired their bluntness. That's the thing about nature. It isn't human and, thus, doesn't struggle with self-identity or projecting the right façade.

She stared at the clouds. There they were: tough and mean as ever, blocking the annoying twinkle beams behind. Although she could not see them, she knew they were there.

"I guess nobody will be making a wish tonight," she said sullenly, forcing a faint chuckle as she looked back at Jackson, who sat behind her. He met her eyes, then glanced outside.

"Why do you say that?" Tommy chimed in. He always seemed eager to talk when Marley wasn't involved in the discussion.

Looking at the sky, she replied softly, "No stars out."

"Aw, too bad for Ms. Anderson. She could use a wish tonight!" Marley drummed his steering wheel as he laughed.

"Who stinkin' cares if there are stars out or not?" Jackson huffed. "If people wanna wish, they'll do it anyway. Wishes are just superstitious hoopla that people do to indulge themselves in a momentary fairytale. Serious people do real stuff—like pray or something." He rolled his eyes and looked back out the window.

"Don't get heated with us!" Cece unbuckled her seatbelt and turned around. "You think you're the smartest person in the world, but everybody knows people who make wishes do it when the first star appears!"

"What's the deal with you and stars?" He shook his hands as if he were shaking her head. "They're just stars!"

"I hate stars! I'm saying I'm happy that—"

"What?" Jackson interrupted, laughing. "Are you kidding me, Kid? You love stars! That's all you ever talk about!"

"No," she corrected, infuriated by his accusations. "I sometimes talk about clouds covering the puny stars; but that's not all I talk about . . . and I'm not a kid!"

He shook his head. "You listen to me," he said, leaning forward. He brought his face within inches of hers as she glared back at him. "Whether it be about the stars being covered—dim, distant, whatever—you talk about them. What I don't get is why you don't come out with it and face who you are."

"I don't know what you're talking about," she declared. She tried to turn her head away, but he grabbed her cheek and kept her attention. "And who do you think that is?" Her voice was cold.

Still looking firmly in her eyes, he replied, "I think you're a girl who wants to make a wish. You want to have a hopeful quality about yourself but can't find a way to fit it into that hard exterior of yours." He threw her face away and leaned back. "You've got a façade, Kid. We all do—kind of like those clouds you like so much." Smirking, he looked over at Tommy and grabbed a cookie from his hand.

"Why would I put up a front? I don't have to impress anyone. This is who I am, so why don't you just drop it?" Cece whipped her head forward, determined to ignore additional comments.

Jackson laughed. "You don't need wishes, Kid. Wishes are futile. The stars can't hear you, and most certainly can't make your dreams come true. What you need is something real."

Her eyes shifted to the side mirror as he spoke. When he looked her way, she turned abruptly and pretended to assess her screwdriver. "Who cares about that stuff? Let's do this!" she declared, squeezing the handle.

"That's my girl!" cheered Marley.

After giving him a high-five, Cece turned and looked back out the window, waiting. *Something real.*

As they neared their destination, Marley steered the vehicle off the road and around the perimeter. The gang bounced about as the car rolled over the uneven, grassy terrain. After passing a few buildings, Marley shut off the headlights and slowed to a stop.

"There it is. That home there on the left," he said. The gang leaned toward the windows on that side of the car and looked out.

"You sure Ms. Anderson lives there?" Cece questioned.

"You bet she does. Just saw her unlock the front door and walk on in two days ago," he reassured her. "Now, she was supposed to be going out of town yesterday, so you, me, and Jackson can go in as planned. Tommy, you wait out here and start the car if anything goes wrong."

"A big home . . . two floors, three if you count the basement." Cece pointed out the obvious. "Does anyone live with her?"

Without hesitation, Marley answered, "At least a daughter—around seven maybe. Haven't seen anyone else."

"A daughter?" She realized by the look on his face that she must have sounded surprised or hesitant.

"You ready, Your Ladyship?" he questioned with an eyeroll.

She frowned and opened the car door. Guiding it gently to a close, she tucked her screwdriver—handle first—into the back pocket of her black jeans.

"Don't screw it up, Kid," Jackson whispered from the back seat. She scrunched her nose at him and proceeded cautiously toward the house.

After locating the basement window, it was a matter of seconds until she had opened it and slid into the home. She landed lightly on her narrow feet and crept across the floor in her thin, black slippers. Nobody in the basement. She navigated the winding staircase, cautiously placing her feet to avoid creaks, and emerged onto the main floor.

The house was well-lit, thanks to light that poured in from the street. It cast shadows of the window frames against what appeared to be a living room wall. In the hallway, in front of Cece, was a small, lit candle. It was an immediate red flag. Someone was home. She paused, shifting her eyes slowly around the space. Nothing.

As she explored the floor, carefully opening and closing doors in order to determine the number of people in the home, she entered the light of the family room. She swiftly glanced about, fully aware of time restraints and the expected rendezvous time at the front door. Four minutes and thirty-eight seconds remained.

Immediately realizing that nobody lay upon the sofa, she tip-toed toward the staircase, glancing at the wall art as she went. While her eyes wandered, they locked on an item that sat peacefully on the fireplace mantel. She stopped and stared at the piece. Suddenly, she began walking toward the mantel as though it compelled her to draw near. Reaching out her glove-covered hand, she delicately lifted a wooden cross. It was approximately four inches high, two inches wide, and was mounted on a stained wooden base. What was she doing? She had four minutes and ten seconds to check the upstairs. There was no time for this.

*No time for Me?*

Where did that thought come from? She shook her head and blinked. Hastily, she put the cross down and turned back toward the staircase. *Something real.* As the words came back to her, she stopped, frustrated by her inner struggle. She huffed and shifted her body back toward the fireplace and grabbed the cross. As she stuffed it in her back pocket, the base overflowing out the top, her eyes caught hold of a framed quotation over the mantel:

> *When I consider your heavens,*
> *the work of your fingers,*
> *the moon and the stars,*
> *which you have set in place,*
> *what is mankind that you are mindful of them,*
> *human beings that you care for them?*
> —Psalm 8:3-4

She felt a warmth in her stomach—a new clarity that hadn't quite been there before began to arise in her thinking and in her heart. These words spoke straight to her—words in a home of someone she'd never met were somehow meant for her to read. Was God speaking to her? She remembered her grandmother telling her about Him before she'd passed away, but that was a long time ago. Cece had been seven at the time, and her parents had refused to take her to church or answer any questions. For years since then, she'd been hiding . . . from the law, from love, from connection . . . perhaps even from God. But here, in the Anderson home, He had found her, anyway.

As she stood before the mantel in thought, there was tapping at the window. Startled, she snapped her head sideways to see Marley and Jackson looking in at her. They made hand gestures toward the door, indicating that she had better get moving. She frowned. She still had over three minutes left. Glancing back at the special quote, she sighed. Perhaps she should get moving. The guys wouldn't understand if she stopped now and explained what had happened.

Leaving the mantel, she glided up the stairs and surveyed the final rooms. There was a teenage boy in one, nobody in the master bedroom, and a young girl with a woman in the final room—it must have been Ms. Anderson. Cece crept toward the ladies as they slept. She was skilled at this by now and had no concern that they'd awaken.

The room was sky blue with a light pink border around the ceiling. The pink swirls were dotted with pastel yellow and purple flowers of all sizes illuminated in the window light. She approached the tiny bed. It looked like the mother had been holding her little girl on her lap while she read a bedtime story, and they fell asleep. The book still lay opened on the bed. Cece stared. She had heard that some mothers read to their daughters, but she'd never witnessed it. Shaking her head, she turned and went to meet her comrades.

"Three upstairs: one boy, a little girl, and Ms. Anderson," she reported after unlocking the front door.

"What took you so long?" Marley scolded.

"I'm only a minute or two late. What's the big deal?" she questioned, as loudly as she could without causing a scene.

"Cool it, you two," Jackson interjected. "Cece, get back in the car. Now, Mar, let's find the money and get out of here."

As she began to head back to the car, Marley grabbed her arm. "Not this time. You stay with us." She glared at him. "You heard me! Get moving!" Resentfully, she listened and continued to search the home.

The group spread out: Marley went upstairs; she headed downstairs; and Jackson remained on the ground floor. Before long, she reported to Jackson with no success. While he silently boasted about his findings, handing her a piece of the loot, she heard a scream from upstairs. The piercing noise was followed by a loud thud and crying. She looked frantically at Jackson as a door slammed shut.

"What? Who are you?" It was a young male's voice speaking above.

Another crash filled the house. She jumped. Looking up the staircase, she saw Marley storming down the steps, shaking his hand. "Let's get out of here," he ordered. Cece followed, confused about what had happened. "No, not you!" He held out his hand to stop her.

"She saw my face," he began. "You've gotta finish the job."

"Finish it?" she questioned.

"Yeah, you're the worm." He quickly caught his mistake. "I mean girl! You're a girl! You're lighter on your feet. Plus, you won't get in trouble if Ms. Anderson comes to. Nobody will believe you were capable of any of this. Say you were sleepwalking." He turned away from her and began to leave.

"Sleepwalking? What if that doesn't work?" She hated the whole idea. After all, she thought Marley, of all people, would be looking out for her. "Jackson already found some money; let's just go!"

"If it doesn't work," he continued, "then kill her. Kill them all."

She looked at him, and for the first time, all she could see was darkness looking back.

"We need the money. Do it."

Cece froze and glanced at Jackson. He was mad. "Hey, no way, man!" he fumed, moving toward her fiancé. "We've got rules, and it's your own fault for getting yourself into this mess!"

"Fine. No killing," Marley mumbled. "But if you don't get out of here and tell Tommy to bring the car around now, the neighbors will come over, and then we'll all be in trouble."

Jackson looked back and forth between her and Marley. "No killing," he declared, and took off toward the backyard.

As Marley began to follow, she stopped him. "But what if something happens to me? I thought you wanted me around?"

"I do, babe." He put a hand on her shoulder. "After all this is done, we're gonna get married just like I said we would. That way, you can stick with the gang forever, and we never have to part." With a crooked smile, he stared into her eyes. "Now, if they don't cooperate, kill them. It's the only way."

"For what? You to escape?" Her voice grew louder. "If you care about me, why is it always about you and keeping you safe?"

His eyes widened as he stood silently, but it lasted only a moment. Rolling his shoulders back, he glared down at her. "What's all this emotional nonsense? Just get up there and do what you have to do!" he demanded.

"You know what? I'm not marrying you. I'll never marry you. All you care about is yourself! There's a little girl up there." It was all she could do to keep from screaming.

"Then it should be easy."

That was it. Swinging her arm back, she struck him in the stomach. He groaned and hunched over. Using her screwdriver, she struck the back of his head, knocking him unconscious, then placed the money from Jackson in his back pocket.

Hastily, she ran upstairs and opened the door to check on Ms. Anderson and her daughter. "Hello?" She grabbed the woman's head and tapped her cheeks softly. After receiving no response, she ran to the bathroom, filled her hands with water, and carried the water to where the woman lay. Gently, she sprinkled the victim's face until she awoke, coughing. Cece then moved toward the unconscious little girl, checked her pulse, and carried her toward her mother.

"Who are you people? What are you doing with my daughter?" Ms. Anderson questioned as she began to cry. Her voice shook with each word.

"Don't worry," Cece explained, "I'm here to help you." She dropped the woman's daughter in her arms. "She'll be okay," she said. "Might have a headache, but you'll both be fine."

"What? I don't understand. Who was that man?"

Cece glanced out the window: no cars and no witnesses.

"He's a thief . . . and, potentially, a murderer." She looked over at Ms. Anderson, whose tears poured down as she rocked the little girl. "Shh," she tried to console her. "You're okay now. I've got to go!"

"Wait!" the woman called. "Where are you going? Please stay with me!" she pleaded, reaching toward Cece's arm.

"Don't worry; I'll call the police on my way out. They'll be here in no time." As she jogged to the doorway of the bedroom, she turned one last time. "I saw this on your mantel downstairs." Reaching out her hand, she revealed the cross.

"Keep it," the woman sobbed. "It's the least we can do for your help."

Cece smiled. Leaving the room, she noticed the teenage boy down the hallway. He was rolling on the ground, groaning as he held his nose. A small stream of blood dripped from his hand to the floor, creating a puddle on the wooden boards. Although she wanted to help him, there wasn't time. Marley could wake up any minute, and she had to get out of there. After using Ms. Anderson's phone to call the police, she ran over her ex's limp body and returned to the car.

"Where's Mar?" asked Tommy.

"He's not gonna be joining us for a while," she replied.

Jackson raised an eyebrow. "Us?"

"Yeah . . . He won't want to see me, anyway." She watched through the back window as they drove out of town. Red and blue police lights flashed in front of the house, where she had been just moments ago. Slowly, she turned forward in her seat, holding the wooden cross in her hand. Stroking its smooth surface, she pictured the motionless, little girl, the bloody face of the groaning teenage boy, and Ms. Anderson. Her face bore such agony and fear; she recognized them well, for the most part. The fear was familiar, but the agony was different; it held something foreign and strange. It almost seemed like Ms. Anderson really cared about her children. Perhaps she even . . .

"You okay, Kid?" Jackson reached his hand back and laid it on her knee.

"Yeah." She sighed. "At least, I will be."

# Chapter 30
## Escape Me

March 14, 1994
Monday, 2:46 p.m.

The flesh on her feet pressed firmly against the pavement as Cece ran. Distracted by her will to survive, she barely noticed the stones and dirt that clung to them. As she turned sharply into Kingston Alley, the tip of her large, right toe stuck against the concrete, sending her flailing forward. The ground flashed before her eyes. Adjusting quickly, she stretched her arms forward and transformed the fall into a somersault. As she rose, an aching throb plagued her toe. She tried to run, but the injury wouldn't allow it. She looked down in disappointment and proceeded to run using the heel of her right foot.

Like a broken wind-up doll, she continued making her way through the alleys of Youngsburg, occasionally glancing back to ensure she'd lost her captor. Thus far, there had been no signs of Jackson, but she wasn't convinced. He was as good at remaining undetected as she was. In fact, she wouldn't be surprised to find that he'd somehow gotten in front of her. Being mindful of the possibility, she peered carefully around corners before choosing her direction of escape. She intended to find a way to Ichacar that involved her safety and Jackson's arrest.

Still running, she frowned. This was a game to him. She knew it. He couldn't care less if she lived or died as long as she was alive long enough to acknowledge his victory. He was always competitive, a legend in his own mind. Although his associates knew he was good, no one except Tommy would verbally acknowledge his greatness. He was a slick, arrogant shadow, and it pleased her to rebel against him.

As she emerged from another alleyway, she noticed the faded white sign with black print that read, "Main Street." There must be shops around here somewhere. Shops meant heavy foot traffic, and where there were people, she could disappear. In the time it'd take to flip a coin, she decided to take a sharp right toward what she hoped would be the hub of Youngsburg. The plan was to find a store with a phone. Along the way, she would secure an alternative means of transportation back to Ichacar. No matter the cost, she was determined to make it home today. Whatever money she owed, she would certainly repay upon arriving home, assuming someone would take her word for it.

***

Nanna Moore sighed as she nestled back into her wooden chair at The Cozy Café. Although using public restrooms was not ideal, she made an exception for emergencies. All that tea she'd consumed with Veronica had certainly led to an emergency. She looked at the empty tabletop. Nothing except a steaming cup of tea and its porcelain saucer remained. Perhaps she should have said no to another refill, but the hibiscus flavor transported her to a spring garden. With each sip, she imagined freshly watered leaves, young flowers in bloom, and vibrant colors bursting into the world. Nanna chuckled. She and Veronica had discussed this topic countless times. Veronica still insisted that lemon tea tasted more like the essence of spring. Lemon tea. So silly!

Nanna delicately reached for the handle and wrapped her opposite hand around the teacup. Its warmth radiated through her, warming her chilled limbs. Although most folks were out and about in t-shirts, what many considered a warm day was not warm to Nanna. Drawing the cup to her lips, she took another sip and returned it to the saucer. She reached for the ends of her crocheted shawl and pulled it tighter around her shoulders, watching as folks passed by. She loved this table. By now, it was *her* table. Being that the café was directly in the middle of town, two tiny tables on either side of the door classified as outdoor seating. Every time she frequented the establishment, one of those tables—if available—was hers. Mondays at 12:30, however, she and Veronica had a standing reservation.

By now, her friend had come, sipped tea, shared stories through tears of laughter, and left, leaving Nanna alone with her thoughts. She looked at her watch: 2:49 p.m. Veronica sure was a talker. My, how time flew when they got together! Glancing toward the middle-aged couple seated at the table across from her, she caught Joey's eye. His smile made her heart happy. He was such a nice, handsome boy—tall, slender, with deep brown skin. Several evenings a week, Nanna would sit on the café deck and people-watch while he closed. Many nights, they found themselves talking and laughing about the future. Somehow, Joey managed to tickle her funny bone in ways she didn't think possible. The way he told such animated stories, she couldn't help but chuckle. Today, of course, he was pleasant as always. She should probably go so he could seat someone else at her table. She certainly didn't want to hinder his tips.

As she positioned her hands firmly on the handles of her chair to stand, something peculiar caught her eye. Across the street was a tiny woman, couldn't weigh more than one hundred pounds. Nanna released the handles and leaned forward in her chair.

The woman must be in a hurry. She wore a lovely violet dress that looked a bit tattered at the bottom. Nanna shook her head. She certainly could've finished the hem better than that! This woman ought to find a different seamstress, immediately.

# Chapter 31
## *Hibiscus and Overreacting*

2:51 p.m.

To Cece's initial satisfaction, she found stores and a decent number of people. She steadily slowed to a brisk walk and attempted to move with the flow of foot traffic. Glancing back occasionally, she was focused on finding a store and calling Jason before Jackson could interfere. She preferred not to see her old colleague again but knew the chances of that were slim. He was bound to show up somewhere, and this time, she'd be ready.

Looking up, she read white letters that were printed clearly above a black, wooden door, "Bobs and Barbers." It was probably a hair salon. A quick peek in the window proved her guess correct. Three white mannequin heads with various-colored wigs sat eerily on display. She assumed they were intended to entice customers, but their unsettling appearance seemed like it would have the opposite effect.

Cautiously, she extended her raw hand and pulled on the door handle. Locked. It was Monday. She forgot that not all stores were open on Mondays: a fact that she knew all too well. As she turned to continue on her mission, she froze. A closed store could be just what she needed . . . No. That wasn't who she was anymore. Closed meant closed. She squeezed her eyes shut. There's no time for this! Without an additional thought, she turned about the sidewalk, passing three people in the process. She returned to the door with a bobby pin that she'd obtained from an unknowing donor. In a matter of seconds, the door was open, and she entered. After concealing her entry, she continued toward the front desk.

A phone. Focusing on the target, Cece moved swiftly toward the telephone that sat on a long desk at the side of the store. Her heel was becoming more tender with every step, but they were steps that must be taken. Putting her memories on hold, she grabbed the receiver with one hand and dialed with the other.

*** 

Catching herself drifting in thought, Nanna returned her attention to the present. What was the woman doing at Bob's shop? She paused. Yes, it was Monday, which meant the shop wouldn't open until tomorrow morning. She considered yelling across the street to inform the woman, but no sooner did she cup her hands to her lips than did the tiny stranger walk right inside the door.

The breath left her lungs. Shock rendered her body motionless. She thought for a moment. Perhaps Bob was doing the woman a favor. It was possible, right? Before she could answer herself, a dark-haired man entered the shop, too. He didn't look friendly at all. Although the small woman wasn't up for any fashion awards, at least she didn't appear troublesome. Perhaps that's why he was at Bob's shop—to soften his sharp edges. The sun reflected off his hair, highlighting an exorbitant amount of grease—or hair product—either way, it was excessive.

As she grasped the handles of her chair again to stand, she took a deep breath and released her clutch. She was overreacting. It wasn't her place to interfere, although it would have been helpful if Bob had informed her of his plans to break schedule.

# Chapter 32

## The Things You Know

2:55 p.m.

The phone rang five times.

"Hello?" a raspy voice answered.

"Hello, may I please speak to Jason?" Cece whispered, still struggling to produce noise from her vocal cords.

"Huh? I can't hear you. You'll have to speak up."

Again, she reached down in her gut to pull out enough sound for what could be her final request. "Jason! I need Jason!"

"Who is this?"

"It's me, Mr. White. It's Cece!"

"Of course, you are," a deep voice echoed from the doorway.

She turned sharply as the phone dropped from her hand. It hung, swaying back and forth as the black, coiled cord bounced up and down. Jackson. She reached her hands back to touch the counter behind her and inched her way to the other side.

Jackson smirked. "It looks like you didn't miss me as much as I thought," he said playfully, clearly amused with himself.

"You're in the wrong part of town, Pierson." She looked around the store to determine a means of escape. "What do you want, anyway?"

With each step, the dark figure in front of her grew more horrifying. His eyes were narrow and tired, his face stained with dirt. The one thing that remained untouched was his slick, black hair—that and the overgrown ego that she detested more than the man himself.

"What do I want? Ha, at least you've still got your sense of humor." His shoes squeaked as he sauntered toward the counter.

She didn't respond.

"You're serious?" He mockingly pointed his finger at her. He must have realized she *was* serious because he straightened and withdrew his former playfulness. "You left. Ditched us and didn't leave a number."

She remained silent as she continued to move down the back of the counter.

"There's also the little matter of you betraying us, calling the cops, and leaving your lover for dead." His agitation was growing; she could see it in his countenance.

Clenching her fists, she couldn't restrain herself. "He wasn't going to die. But that's your thing, isn't it? Lying! You manipulate people into doing what you want—it's what you're paid to do!"

Jackson shook his head and smiled. She was angry at herself for playing his game.

"Yeah, it is. Practice makes perfect, Kid. That's why I'm the best!"

She rolled her eyes.

"I must say, you still got your touch." Pausing his walk, he waited. His eyes followed her until she finally stopped by the cash register. "We thought you went and got honest. Found good. Whatever it was you left for."

"I *am* honest."

"Ha." He chuckled. "If you were honest, you'd own what you did. Take pride, like me." The man blew on his knuckles and rubbed them against his jacket.

"I'm not like you, Jackson," she declared, her throat begging for mercy.

"I see. Then you aren't hiding from the law. You came clean, confessed, did your time. What else should I expect from a righteous person like you? No wonder you don't know why I'm here."

She glanced down. Was he right? She wasn't the same person—at least, she didn't think she was. She hadn't thought it necessary to turn herself in. God had forgiven her, so why bother the police?

She remembered her conversation with Jason on this very subject. It was five months after they met; she didn't understand the connection she felt to him, but in some way, she knew he could be trusted—and not like the illusion of trust she experienced in the past. That had been a trust that required you to watch your back and keep one hand free. Her trust of Jason was something different entirely.

*He sank his forehead into his rugged palms and sighed; he said nothing.*

*"I need you to respond," she sobbed.*

*"I don't know what you want from me, Cece. What am I supposed to say to that?"*

*She wiped her sleeve across the fountain of tears on her cheek. Slowly, she inhaled and exhaled, trying to relax herself. "Say you forgive me."*

*With a look of sorrow, Jason turned toward her. He reached out his hand and placed it on hers. "It's not about that," he said tenderly.*

*She felt a glimpse of hope.*

"I forgave you before you told me. I've said it before, and I'll say it again. There's nothing you could tell me about yourself that would ever change my feelings for you. My love for you doesn't have qualifications." He continued softly as he moved closer to her, "You live your life as best you can and adore God, and I adore you." He turned his face from hers and stopped.

Unsure if it was an acceptable time to ask, she decided that she must clarify what he had said. "I don't understand what the issue is."

He stared at the wall. "I know you're apologetic for your actions." Silence lasted for a frozen moment. Finally, he continued, "Is there a part of you that thinks you should come clean?"

She shook her head. "I still don't understand what you want me to do."

Locking eyes with hers, he reached out and touched her hand. "I won't force you to do anything. I support you one hundred percent. I'm simply saying that you ought to consider going to the police—you know, take responsibility. It might help bring relief to the people who were victimized."q Shocked and hurt by what he said, she rose from the couch on which they were sitting.

"I knew it," she declared. "You're exactly like them!"

"Cece," he interjected, his voice mellow and low. "It would tear me in pieces to see you punished for anything. I would rather see myself locked away for life than see you in pain."

"You don't mean that."

"Yes, I do."


"That's why you'll come with me," Jackson finished as Cece returned to the present. He was now much closer to where she stood, obviously taking advantage of her momentary inattention.

"In your dreams!" She squeaked as she shoved the register over the counter and hobbled toward the door. As she pushed it open, she felt a pair of arms wrap around her stomach and pull her back inside. She flailed as Jackson dragged her from the windows. There was no way this was happening. Kicking violently, she fought for freedom until the room went black.

# Chapter 33

## *Only Hope*

3:00 p.m.

Ed looked at his watch as Jason jogged toward the house: 3:05 p.m. It had been ten minutes since he received the phone call, and he wasn't sure whether or not to bother his nephew with the details. Besides, what if it was nothing? He didn't want to raise his concerns, or hopes, for no reason. Unfortunately, he had made the impulsive mistake of telling May and was convinced that although he explicitly instructed her not to, she would divulge everything.

While his wife's eyes were on the street, Ed watched her. He hoped to catch her attention and transmit the look; she would know what the look meant. She must have been oblivious to him because she did not look over once. Finally, when Jason made it to the porch, she jumped to greet him.

"Hey, there! How was your walk, or . . . run? Best enjoy the indoors on a damp day like this. Goodness me, I'm about soaked!" She fluttered her hand in front of her face like a fan. "Why'd you go running in jeans?"

"I was handling business, Auntie May." Jason's face was straight and firm.

Ed knew that now was not at all a good time, but his wife tended to impose her will on others. If she wanted to talk, there would be a conversation whether someone liked it or not. Although this time, while she was still talking, her target veered right and hurried upstairs.

***

When Jason got to his room, he slammed the door. He stormed toward his desk and flipped it over, sending its contents crashing to the floor. "Why?" he roared at the ceiling. Grabbing his Bible from the nightstand, he threw it across the room. It crashed against the wall, its pages falling open as it landed. "How could You let this happen?"

He jerked his head from side to side, searching for something to rip. Spotting the disheveled maps on the floor, he reached down and started tearing them in pieces.

"She's not there! She's not here! God knows where she is, but He won't tell me! What if something happened to her?" He glared up through bent brows. "How *dare* You!" He pointed at the blank ceiling. "How could You sit back and let whatever happened happen? You were supposed to be watching over her! She gave her life to You, and You failed to intervene when she needed You!" Picking up a pencil, he broke it in his hand. "I *trusted* You!" Moving forward, he punched his fist through the drywall. The pain in his hand was nothing compared to the rage within him. He wanted to scream.

A sudden tap at the door sent his head bolting toward the sound.

"Jason? Are you okay?" The knob started to turn, but the door was locked. "Can I get you anything, honey?" It was Auntie May.

Taking a deep breath, he clenched his teeth and waited. He didn't want to lash out, but he knew that's what would happen if he opened his mouth.

"I'm right downstairs if you need me." The gentle voice stopped. He waited a minute to be sure she had gone.

Turning, he spotted the wooden cross he had brought back from Cece's apartment. Lurching toward it, he grabbed it, ready to throw it out the window.

*Will you throw Me away?* The faint voice stopped him in his tracks. Looking down, he frowned at the cross in his hands.

"You threw her away first!" He dropped the cross and collapsed as it hit the ground. "Why?" He pounded his fist against the hardwood like a judge calling for order in the court. All he wanted was justice, but it was clear that wouldn't happen. "You watched as she went back to a life she hated, or even worse—what if she was kidnapped! She must have been scared, and You didn't give her courage! She needed You, but You didn't come through!" The words were not enough to convey his feelings, and with a loud groan, he bowed his head against the floor and wept.

His chest ached. His stomach turned. He had never felt so abandoned and alone. Until now, he had always known God was on his side. He hadn't feared or doubted in the face of adversity because God was his strength. Even amid trouble, he knew that God would take care of him—like when his dad left. Although he didn't understand it, he knew it wasn't God's fault. In fact, God was the best Father he could have. This time, however, things were different. He knew Cece put her faith and trust in God. She believed He would be with her always, so where was He now?

"How can You be all good, and then sit back and watch these things happen? Don't you care at all?" He held his chest as he rolled over, hoping the pressure would keep his heart from tearing. "I need to find her! I need to know she's okay!"

*I have never left you, and I never will. I am with you. Though you push Me away, I will keep loving you. You can't outrun My love, and she's not beyond My reach.*

Laying with his back on the floor, Jason felt tears rush down his temples. They were relentless, as though he had no choice but to let the rush continue.

*Forgive.* The Voice went on. *Forgive as I have forgiven you.*

Reaching for the cross that lay beside him, he held it before his blurry eyes. He didn't know who God wanted him to forgive, but the thought was difficult to process. He just wanted to see his betrothed again—to hold her in his arms one more time and to know she was safe. He wanted to do *something,* but there didn't seem to be anything he could do.

Closing his eyes, he hugged the cross to his chest. "I should have been there, God. You entrusted her to me, and I failed." He sniffled as tears continued pouring down his face. "I can't do this alone. I need You. You're my only hope."

# Chapter 34
## *An Alternative Arrangement*

3:15 p.m.

"Mar! Mar!" Tommy extended an elbow, careful not to injure his sleeping associate. He didn't care much for grumpy, tired Marley; and furious, tired Marley was even worse.

The boss moaned as he attempted to roll over.

"Wake up!" Growing increasingly frustrated at the lack of response, he reached across the couch and pinched Marley's nose.

Coughing, the boss awoke. "What's the matter with you?" he roared, throwing Tommy's hand to the side.

"Jackson's on the phone!" He waved the white receiver in Marley's face.

The boss rubbed his eyes and leaned forward. "What did he say?"

"He said, 'Tommy? Good. I got news . . .' then I hurried over to wake you."

He watched as Marley's face grew red. "Find out what he wants," the boss said through clenched teeth.

"Right." He put the phone back to his ear. "Jackson? Boss wants to know what's up. You confirmed what we thought, right? She is dead." He nodded at the boss, who just rolled his eyes.

"I got her." Jackson's voice was calm, as he expected it would be. What a rock. "I'm just not sure what to do next."

"*You* don't know what to do?" The words flew from his mouth like cold canned spinach. It was an unfortunate reflex. Cautiously, he shifted his eyes to Marley. The boss had flames shooting from his head. Before he could object, Marley grabbed the phone, but said nothing.

Tommy wished he could warn Jackson that the listener had changed, but it was too late. The mumbling sound coming from the phone told him his friend was still speaking, but he couldn't make out what was said.

Marley sneered. "Having second thoughts, are we?" He stood, taking the cordless phone with him. "Is that right? Of course, it didn't come out the way you intended. I see." His crazed expression made Tommy's skin crawl. "Well, then, meet us back at the river, three-hundred klicks north of where we parked the other night."

"A klick? It's the length of one stride . . ." He paused; obviously, Jackson was correcting him. "Whatever. Just meet us at the road then. I want to see her before we climb that awful terrain anyway. We're leaving from our place now. At least an hour, maybe faster since I'm driving." He glared at Tommy.

Marley was silent for a moment, obviously listening to something else. "I don't care. Just get there." He hung up and threw the phone at Tommy.

He tried to duck, but the device hit him in the arm. "Ouch." He grabbed the offending spot. "What's the matter, Boss?"

"She's not dead," Marley snarled, reaching for his jacket.

Thinking quickly, he responded, "That just means you get to do the deed yourself, like you wanted, right?" Tommy tried not to smile, resisting his present self-admiration. He was clever, too, whether Marley would acknowledge it or not. Sure, he'd screwed up some missions in the past, but he was getting better with time.

Marley's grin was all the thanks he needed, which was good, because he knew full well that he'd receive no thanks otherwise.

"Grab your things and let's go."

As the boss retrieved his fancy shoes, Tommy threw an array of snacks in a plastic bag. He met Marley at the door, followed him to their ride, and climbed inside.

The boss tapped his fingers against the steering wheel and looked over confidently. "Time to rendezvous with that rotten worm."

Tommy bit his lips as he reached for a bag of chips. The bag shook like a mouse stuck in a hungry cat's litterbox. "Whatcha planning to do?"

"You'll see. Shut up and keep watch." Pressing the two starter wires together, he smiled as the engine rumbled. "Gotta love that new car sound, you know it?"

Tommy felt the boss' eyes looking through his skull.

"Well?" he insisted.

"I thought you didn't want me to say nothing."

Marley rolled his eyes. "Forget it."

"It ain't new, anyways. It's an old station wagon that you hot-wired from a junkyard this morning."

"It's new to us!" the boss huffed. "And it has to be inconspicuous, so people don't . . . never mind. At least it still works. Just watch the road."

Tommy looked forward. He wanted to say something else, but Marley's incoherent mumbling typically meant he was mad. Still, he couldn't help it. "Shouldn't we take the van?"

He watched as Marley's hands clenched the wheel and began twisting slowly, as though winding a rope or wringing a bothersome neck. Tommy leaned away and braced himself.

"I ditched it." It wasn't the outburst he'd expected. Relieved, he exchanged glances with the boss. "With all this rigmarole, somebody might have seen us."

He nodded as he stared at the road in front of them. What did Jackson mean when he said he didn't know what to do? Was he having second thoughts about Marley's plan?

He glanced at Marley, then back at the road. It wouldn't be the first time that Jackson did things his own way. He had always managed to make it look like he'd followed the boss' plan—"to keep the peace," Jackson had said. Tommy stuffed a handful of chips in his mouth. He didn't see how it was possible for Jackson to pull something like that now. If he were being honest, Tommy didn't understand the gang's harsh actions toward Cece. 'Course they were mad, but she was family. Families get mad at each other all the time. As far as he was concerned, that's part of what made them family in the first place.

Sighing, he rested his head against the padded seat cushion. His pulse throbbed. Things were bad, and they were about to get a whole lot worse. At least it would all be over soon. He just wished it would end before Marley asked him to do anything else; but at this point, that seemed unlikely.

## Chapter 35

## *Harm's Way*

3:30 p.m.

Jason's eyes shot open. He looked at the wall clock: 3:30 p.m. Somehow, he had fallen asleep after calling the police. Chief Wilson promised to check out the alley when he got a chance and offered to issue a missing persons report to the surrounding communities. Although he hadn't sounded convinced of foul play, he mentioned that if Cece saw the report, she could contact their office to confirm her safety—which he would then tell Jason. It was a good first step, but Jason needed more.

Although he wasn't sure what really happened two-and-a-half days ago, he was determined to make sure that Cece was safe . . . but what if she was? What if she *did* choose to leave after all? The thought was still raw and painful, like an open wound. The truth would be medicine poured upon his heart, and though it might sting at first, healing would follow. *God, guide me.* He looked up. *You know where she is and how she feels. If there's something I can do, please show me.* Pausing, he sighed. *And give me strength to face the outcome.*

Sitting up, he rolled his shoulders back and stretched his arms. Cracks cascaded from his shoulders down his spine. He scanned the disheveled room. Broken pencils, torn papers, flipped furniture—almost nothing was in its rightful place. Looking over, he saw his Bible, sprawled open upon the floor. He rose and retrieved the book, gently lifting it in his hands. It was open to the book of Romans. As he glanced down, a verse jumped off the page. It was Romans 5:8.

*"But God demonstrates his own love for us in this:*
*While we were still sinners, Christ died for us."*

Closing the book, he walked over to the window and gazed outside. The thick, white canopy that hung over Ichacar was beginning to dissipate. Looking closely, he could see a pinkish-orange hue brushed lightly across the sky. He noticed the clouds, the bushes, the leaves being tossed about by a seemingly strong wind. Although he tried desperately to focus on the present, he couldn't suppress memories of the woman he loved. The harder he tried, the harder his heart fought back.

Cece constantly took notice of the sky—dark, light, orange, gold, red—whatever the color, she marveled. He remembered her likening it to a large canvas on which God paints masterpieces for the world to see. Every day, she seemed blessed by the new exhibit.

*"Jason, look! Quick!"*

*"What is it?"* he questioned, *fully aware that his attention should be on driving.*

*"Look at the sky over there."*

*He twisted his neck.*

*"On the right. Do you see it?"*

*"Yeah, it's nice,"* he replied, *returning his eyes to the road ahead.*

CAITLIN M. SMITH   211

*"I love when the clouds are thick and shimmery like buttered mashed potatoes. You can't quite see the sun because it's tucked behind one of them."*

*"You don't like the sun? Perhaps you should become nocturnal,"* he suggested with a wink.

*She slapped his arm playfully. "No, you know what I mean. You can see the sun's rays shining down from behind that cloud. They look like beams of light from Heaven." She smiled and laid her head against the headrest, all the while looking out with wonder.*

*"Very poetic—perhaps you should write."*

*She shook her head. "I don't know. I'm not very good at that."*

*"Everyone has to start somewhere, right?" He reached over and took her hand. They sat quietly for the remainder of the drive; nothing needed to be said.*

As Jason reminisced, he couldn't help but wish she was there to see this particular painting. She would love it. He imagined what they would be doing if she were there. They'd probably be seated on the front lawn—she in his lap, resting firmly against him. She was so easy to hold. On this evening, he would pull her hair back and kiss her forehead. She would comment on the beauty of God's artwork and probably fall asleep in Jason's arms. After a few moments of resting peacefully together, he would gently scoop her up and carry her inside before heading home.

Turning from the window, he brushed a tear from his cheek, put the Bible on his bed, and went downstairs.

\*\*\*

May White immersed herself in knitting while she anxiously awaited Jason's descent. Her hands worked furiously, looping and pulling yarn with two thin rods. Her mature fingers remained firm in their task, as trained soldiers, despite their owner's present disposition. As she looked from her scarf to the clock back to her scarf, and then over at Ed, she struggled with what to tell Jason. Should she tell him about the phone call? Ed seemed to think it would make matters worse, but she disagreed. What if the person on the phone *was* Cecelia? She shook her head. It couldn't be. Stuff like that only happens in the movies. Cecelia couldn't be in trouble. It was just . . . just . . . absurd.

Thirty painful minutes later, Jason came downstairs. He smiled dimly at her and proceeded to the kitchen. She dropped her project and followed closely behind. Prepared to make her presence seem like a coincidence, she went straight for the crockpot lid, eyeing Jason as he opened the pantry.

"Looking for somethin' in particular?" she asked, setting down the lid and grabbing three potatoes.

He shook his head. "Just a snack to hold me over. I'm going out for a while."

Should she worry Jason with her suspicions if she wasn't one hundred percent certain? "Okay, then. You'll want to be home by 7:00 p.m." Her hands moved quickly as she peeled the rough vegetables. "I'm making my famous beef and potatoes!" She watched as he closed the pantry and picked up an apple from the counter.

"I'm not sure I will be."

Her heart began to race. "Why not? Where are you going?" Clearing her throat, she took a deep breath. "I mean, is everything okay, honey?"

Although he didn't respond, his face said it all. Of course, it wasn't okay. He was clearly upset. She shouldn't tell him about the call. It would only add confusion to his current situation. Grimacing, she turned away and reached for a masher.

"Not yet," he answered. There was a short moment of silence before he continued. "Are you feeling all right, Auntie May?"

"Me? Why would you ask a silly thing like that?" She was now demolishing the potatoes that were no match for her anxious arm. As she kept her eyes averted, a warm hand appeared upon her shoulder.

"What is it?"

Throwing her instruments down, she motioned toward the kitchen table. Jason followed her, and they sat down.

"Honey, there's something you should know," she whispered, looking back toward the living room. Her nephew leaned in. "Now, don't get your hopes up, because I'm really not sure if it's anything."

"What?"

Summoning her courage, she sighed. "Your uncle got a call today from a lady—sounded like she was in some kind of trouble."

"What? Who was it?" he demanded.

"Well, Ed said it was real hard to make out what she was saying—something about her voice."

His eyes widened. "What'd she say?"

She raised her head slowly and looked at him. "She claimed to be Cece, and . . . " She paused. "Ed said there was a loud noise and what sounded like a man in the background."

Jason stood. "When did this happen? Did she say anything else? Where is she?"

"Please keep your voice down! We weren't sure whether or not to tell you because if we were mistaken, we didn't want you to get worked up. It could be nothing."

"I don't think you're mistaken. Something's not right." Pushing his chair aside, he rushed from the room.

***

As he went upstairs to retrieve the maps, he prayed that one of them was still intact. Numerous thoughts flooded his mind and prevented him from focusing on a single one. True, he didn't quite know *where* to go, just that he *had* to. Within seconds, he was out the front door with nothing but his wallet, sections of torn paper, and a raging heart.

"Mind if I come along?" Wendy's voice called from across the street as she approached his car.

He shifted his eyes to see the smile on her face.

"Really? You still want to help?" he asked. As the words came out, he realized that he'd need someone to help piece the maps back together while he drove.

She shrugged. "I visited the alley. While the footprints could mean anything, I suppose we can give your theory a closer look. Why not?" Her quick steps brought her to the side of his car in no time. "Where are you off to, anyway?"

"To find my bride," he said, unlocking the doors.

"If you say so." Opening the passenger door, she stopped. "I'm sorry about what I said about your hunch. You don't give up easily, and I like that. Every lead is worth investigating—I, of all people, should know that."

Jason smiled; however, the momentary relief that a sleuth would accompany him was swiftly followed by overwhelming sadness. The love of his life was in trouble, and he didn't have the slightest idea of where to go. At least he was letting someone help. Derek would consider that significant progress, but Jason wasn't sure this counted. It was easy to let someone help if it meant finding Cece. Her well-being was all that mattered.

Realizing he hadn't responded, he looked at Wendy. "Could be dangerous. Can you navigate?"

She hesitated.

"Is something wrong?"

"No," she said through an awkward smile. "It's just that I'm not so good at directions, but I'll give it a fair shake."

"Then, hop in." Without another thought, he threw the map scraps in her lap and started the car. Feeling the engine rumble, he fixed his eyes intently on the street before him and began to drive.

"You know," Wendy said, drawing his attention, "I don't think I've ever seen someone who believed in another person the way you believe in your fiancée. What if she isn't who you think she is?"

He would be lying to say he hadn't toiled over that very question, but the truth remained the same. He loved Cece, and nothing would change that.

"It might not be easy," he began, "but what she does doesn't change the fact that I care about her." He thought for a moment as he slowed to a stop sign. "You said before that I was in denial; and maybe I was at first, but now I have hope." His heel ticked up and down as he waited for an ice cream truck to cross. "Denial refuses to see the truth, but hope sees what is true and chooses to believe that heartache isn't the end. It doesn't close the book before the story's over. When it comes to Cece, I just want to know that she has a happily-ever-after."

As soon as the truck passed, he stomped on the gas, and the car went racing forward. He didn't know where he was heading nor what he would find when he got there. His mixture of emotions confused him. All this time, he had been wanting Cece's departure to be an accident and to know she still loved him. Now, the matter of her affections didn't seem as important. He needed her to be out of harm's way, and he would have given anything to know that was true.

# Chapter 36
## For You, Of Course

3:32 p.m.

Jackson surveyed the shop one last time. He had managed to put everything back in its place, including the cash register that he intelligibly pieced back together. He was nearly certain the device wouldn't work, but at least it wouldn't arouse suspicion from people passing by. Nobody would notice anything amiss until the shop opened tomorrow and some unfortunate employee found the dysfunctional register. By then, he would be long gone; and given the fact that he'd wiped away Cece's fingerprints, so would any chance of cops uncovering what happened here.

His eyes followed the ceiling line, confirming once again that there were no security cameras. The checkered wallpaper looked like a 1960s kitchen threw up on the walls; the dizzying effect of its black-and-white pattern made him question his initial determination. Now, he was sure of two things: there were no cameras, and he would rather grow a knee-length beard before coming to a barbershop like this.

He looked down at Cece's body. She was wrapped tightly in a compilation of black capes that had been draped over the chairs of several cutting stations. The capes, plus a heavy supply of duct tape, were all he needed to make her unconscious body look like a new carpet ready for delivery. Of course, he left a few small holes at her head so she could breathe. While he wasn't sure of his endgame, it was important to leave his options open.

Hoisting her over his shoulder, he carried the makeshift package outside and plopped it in the trunk of a black Mercedes. He grinned. It looked nothing like a person—evidence of his mastery over all things inconspicuous.

Slamming the lid, Jackson circled around to the driver's door and scanned the streets. No one was giving him unnatural looks—no one except an old lady, whose glasses told him she couldn't see that far, and a beautiful redhead across the street. Flirtatious gestures from a random woman was hardly suspicious. It'd become a natural part of his life for years. On any other day, her juicy, red lips and gorgeous smile would warrant a date, but there was no time for that now. Returning her attentions with a nod, he slid in the car.

***

Tapping her heel against the floor, Nanna had waited—partly, to confirm her suspicions about Bob extending hair favors, but also to see the greasy man's new look. The minutes dragged on until finally, the greasy man had emerged carrying a large, black tube. Retrieving a pair of thick-rimmed glasses from her purse, she'd thrusted them on her face and squinted. The man's hair was exactly the same, and there was still no sign of the blonde woman. That was enough.

"Joey! Joey, hurry!" she called. Pedestrians' eyes shifted toward the deck as their owners continued on their way.

After a few moments, Joey appeared at Nanna's side. "What seems to be the trouble?"

"Look!" She pointed across the street. "Outside Bob's shop. That man just put a tube in his trunk!"

"He probably got a haircut, Nanna. Don't worry."

"The shop's closed. It's Monday." Fear gripped her heart. She firmly reached up and grabbed his shirt to pull his face toward her own. "Something isn't right. The woman's still inside!"

He freed himself from her grip and stood upright. "What woman?" Sighing, he continued, "Fine, I'll check it out."

Lacking the sense of urgency she desired, he turned to cross the street.

No sooner did Joey turn than the greasy man's car pulled away. As the waiter casually made his was across the street, Nanna climbed to her feet and tried desperately to discern the license plate number. By the time she'd jotted something down on her handkerchief, Joey had returned.

He offered her what appeared to be a sympathetic smile. "The door was open, but there's no woman. I'll call Bob to come lock up. In the meantime, can I interest you in another cup of tea?"

"There was a woman, and I've got the greasy fellow's plate number," she insisted, waving her handkerchief in the air. "We must call the police before they get away!"

"But, Nanna—"

"Listen." She clenched the handkerchief and looked him in the eyes. "Something's wrong," she declared, pointing down the street. "And that man is getting away. Please, Joey. Call the police. We need to do something!"

Whether he believed her or not, Nanna didn't know, but Joey finally called the police and let her explain what had happened. She even gave them what details she could remember about the car, including the direction it was heading and her best guess regarding the license plate number.

When she hung up, her heart felt like it was trapped within a cage in her chest. She tried to calm herself with deep breaths. In and out. In and out. She didn't know what the man and woman were up to, but she knew something wasn't right. Hopefully, the police would heed her warning and send someone immediately, but there was nothing else she could do to convince them. It was in God's hands now.

## Chapter 37
## One Hour

3:40 p.m.

Pulling free from the city, Jackson smirked with satisfaction as he gradually increased speed. With a sense of relief, he exhaled and spun the wheel left. One hour. Everything should be over in one hour: the chase, people questioning his skills, Marley's constant obsession. He exhaled. Sometimes, the self-proclaimed boss infuriated him. Not even sometimes—all the time. Marley was becoming more and more of a liability. His behavior was unpredictable, which made it harder to counteract when necessary.

"I guess it's you and me, Kid," he stated, turning his head sideways to address the lady in his trunk. "You chose this," he continued aloud, although she was probably still unconscious. "Tell me, does it taste good? I've got half a mind to drop your scrawny body on your heartthrob's doorstep." He snickered. "He couldn't handle it. You think he's perfect. Ha! You're in for disappointment, Princess, but that's life. Get used to it."

## Chapter 38

# Melt Me Down

3:50 p.m.

Gazing out the passenger window of Jason's car, Wendy sighed. A twisting agony tangled her tongue, rendering her with nothing to do but breathe. She shifted her eyes toward the man driving. His muddy brown eyes were fixed on the road. That stare sitting above such sharp cheek bones showed a determination that was almost unsettling. He cared so much, and what for? A liar? Cece didn't deserve a man like this, and Jason shouldn't feel compelled to travel the world looking for someone who—if Marley got his way—would never be found.

Reaching in her purse, she pulled out a new stick of bubblegum and popped it in her mouth. Her teeth went to work like a boxer hitting a punching bag. She crushed the wrapper with her fingers, opened it back up, and crushed it again. Looking back at Jason, she caught his eyes as he glanced over.

"Is something wrong?"

She shoved the wrapper in her purse and laughed. "Of course not. Why do you ask?"

"For a second, it looked like you weren't sure you wanted to go through with it."

Her heart stopped. "Go through with what?"

"Chewing that piece of gum." He said with a chuckle, though the noise lacked the sound of happiness. "Looked like you wanted to fold it back up in that wrapper."

"But once you chew it, you can't put it back." She chomped harder. "Its consistency is different; plus, the shape is all wrong." Fiddling with her purse strap, she continued. "It's too late to put it back now. I'd have to spit it out, but then it's no good to anyone. I want to salvage what good can come from it. Otherwise, it's just a waste."

"And you don't waste gum," Jason added.

"Right."

An awkward silence hovered over them.

"How much longer 'til we reach your office?" Jason didn't take his eyes off the road.

Wendy reclined against the headrest as she gazed out her window. "Not long." For the past ten minutes, she'd struggled to think of her next move. There was no office. Where could she take him that would *seem* like her office? The gang's place was certainly not an option. Marley would kill her.

She squeezed her eyes shut as a flash of darkness shot across her memory. Muffled screams, kicking, hoisting, an expression of horror she'd never forget . . . Doors slamming and the wink of gratitude. With a gasp, her eyes shot open, and she pressed her quivering fingers into the aching temples of her head. Cece deserved it. She was a traitorous murderer, who had backstabbed the gang. She needed to learn her lesson.

But Jason? She looked at her blind companion. He seemed like a nice guy. He didn't deserve Cece's lies. Someone needed to tell him the truth, even if Marley would disagree. She took a deep breath.

"Are you going to make it?" Jason questioned with a hint of sarcasm. "You seem more distressed than me, and believe me, this isn't my ideal Monday."

Her body tensed as she sat upright, barely using the padding on the back of her seat. "Look," she began. "I don't know how to tell you this, so I'm just going to say it: your fiancée is a liar."

Jason looked at her. Sorrow filled his eyes. "I guess if she chose to leave me, that might be true." Silence filled the air. His chest moved out and in as he breathed. "But I would never want her to be unhappy just to fulfill a promise. Even if I wanted to hate her, I can't. My heart is drawn to her, and if she did leave, I just want to know she's okay. I want her to know that I love her. If she needed to leave me to be happy, it'll break my heart; but it will heal. I just want her to be happy and safe. I guess that's what happens when you fall in love with who a person is. If she chose to leave, it doesn't mean that she's a different person; it means that she believed leaving was the right thing to do, and I could never blame her for that. I could never take away the woman that she's become by blaming her or accusing her or telling her she did something wrong by trying to do what she thought was right. I mean, second to Jesus, she's my hero. If you only knew what she's been through and what she's overcome, you'd love her, too." He smiled. "I've been waiting my whole life to find a woman like Cecelia Burbin, and far be it for me to let my pride lose her. No. I'll fight my pride and keep my good opinion of her. Nothing's going to take that away from me."

Wendy pursed her lips. She almost wished she didn't need to share the secret that would surely crush him. "Breaking an engagement? That's not what I mean. I know you think she's perfect—and trust me, we all want our significant others to be flawless—but Cece is dangerous.

She killed a mother and two children during a robbery!" She gently placed her left hand on his thigh. "I'm so sorry, Jason, but you deserved to know. This woman isn't who you think she is. You deserve better."

She watched as his expression remained constant. He was calm—too calm.

"Did you hear me?" she persisted. "She killed people, as in *murder*. You can't trust someone like that."

She waited for what felt like an eternity. "Ms. Anderson?" he finally asked, removing her hand from his leg.

Her jaw fell open. "I . . . I don't know," she stuttered. "He never said the name, only that it happened."

"He? Who's he?"

"He's . . . um . . . well, uh . . . "

"Marley?"

She wanted to speak, but there were no words. Did Jason know? Had he known all along? Adjusting the skirt of her dress, she crossed her legs and squeezed them together. Hopefully, this would silence her twitching knees. "How did you know?"

"Cece told me about Marley, and she also told me about Ms. Anderson." He exhaled, and after checking his sidemirror, he continued. "Ms. Anderson was a single mother with two kids: a son and a daughter. Marley asked her to kill them one night during a botched break-in, but she refused. Instead, she knocked him out, called the police, and left the gang forever." He glanced over, then back at the road. "I don't know what Marley claimed, but Cece has never taken a life." A gentle smile graced his stubbly face. "A few hearts, maybe, but no lives."

Good thing Jason was handsome because his intelligence was certainly lacking. For some reason, he still refused to see the truth.

"That's not how it happened. Marley told me—"

"Wait. You spoke to Marley? Were you part of his trial?"

Blood rushed to her cheeks. How could she make such a careless error? Thankfully, Jason's excuse was perfect. "I'm not permitted to discuss it," she began, playing into his assumption. "But that's not important. The point is he told me all about her."

"And do you trust him?" Jason's jaw flinched. He was clearly aggravated, though she appreciated his attempt to harness his emotions.

Her words from earlier smacked the back of her brain. *She killed people—as in murder. You can't trust someone like that.* She froze. It was too much. First, she found out that Marley once had a relationship with Cece—a fact which he neglected to mention. Now, the story he told her about why Cece deserved to die might not even be true? What else? Did he even love her at all?

"How can you trust Cece?" she countered. "Maybe she's the one who lied."

"Maybe," he said, "but she didn't have to tell me anything. She *chose* to share the truth about her past. She insisted that I know everything about her before deciding to love her."

"And you still fell in love?"

He smirked. Perhaps his frustration was subsiding. "I had already fallen. Nothing about her past could have changed that."

Wendy threw her head against the seat and let it roll left. "Have you ever wanted something so badly that you'd do anything to get it?"

"I think I've got an idea what that's like."

Turning, she tried to relax as she stared in the side mirror. "So do I." Tears welled up in her eyes. She couldn't do this anymore. "I'm so sorry, Jason." Though she could feel his eyes on the back of her head, she kept her face averted. "I didn't know." Her words shook. "I thought she deserved it, but he lied to me . . ." When the first tear fell, it released a stream that poured down her cheeks.

"Sorry for what?"

The sincerity of his voice twisted the wrench that already stabbed her foolish heart.

"I'm not an investigator, but I do know what happened to Cece. If we hurry, there might still be time to save her."

"Save her?" his voice rose. "From whom?"

"From Marley," she sobbed. "We can't let him find her before we do."

"Marley? You mean he's behind all of this?" His voice was tense, his forearms flexing as he tightened his grip on the wheel. "And what do you mean 'find her'? Where is she?"

Wendy had been too distressed to realize that they had stopped along the side of the road. Jason's full attention was on her, but she wouldn't return the favor. No matter how upset she got, no one needed to see her mascara-drenched raccoon eyes.

"The gang had her at first, but then she supposedly got away. They're all looking for her, but if we hurry, maybe we can find her before it's too late."

"Too late? What's that supposed to mean?"

"It means we can't waste time sitting here talking." Slowing her sobs, she swallowed hard. "Last I heard, they hadn't found her body yet, which means she might still be alive. But if she is, and they find her first . . . nevermind. Let's just get to her before they do. It's the only way to keep her safe."

In seconds, they were back on the road, driving ninety miles an hour in a fifty-five zone. She told Jason where his fiancée was last seen and informed him that Bomilton and Youngsburg were the towns closest to where Cece was left at the river, assuming she had made it to a town and wasn't stuck in the woods somewhere. Marley, however, had insisted that she'd be heading back to Ichacar. Without debate, they decided to head through Youngsburg and across the river to Bomilton.

Pressing her head against the window, she released a quivering breath. Her heart was in conflict with itself, and no matter which side won, there would still be a loss.

# Chapter 39
## *Belief or Disbelief*

4:10 p.m.

"Say something."

Jason barely heard Wendy's plea. Somewhere during her explanation of what had happened to Cecelia, he had zoned out. A bead of sweat ran down his face. He had never felt this sensation before. It was a gut-wrenching sense of loss that smashed through him like a wrecking ball. He ached for the woman he loved. How he wished he could have taken the beatings for her, carried her pain, and stood in her place. He would have done it all—given his life, even—to keep her safe.

His heart wasn't broken; it was shattered—obliterated—and that was for the pain he knew his fiancée must have endured. He couldn't even think about the possibility that she was dead. He wouldn't allow his mind to go there. Cece trusted God, and although Jason wasn't able to protect her from what had happened, God could heal her body, restore her heart, and bring her through.

"There is no situation from which God can't bring about something good."

"Huh?"

"I will trust Him," he declared, as though reminding himself. His breath was heavy, the words falling from his lips like lead. "I trust

Him. He's protecting her. I trust Him. It's going to be okay." Feeling a quiver in his last words, Jason swallowed hard. He would not let his emotions get the best of him. He needed to think clearly and keep his heart open to hear from God. He needed direction. He couldn't do this alone.

"This is Youngsburg," Wendy whispered. Her words solemn. "Do you still want to start our search here?" She paused.

Looking over, he saw her eyes surveying the buildings. Her cheeks were stained red from tears, though she had managed to collect herself significantly in the past five minutes. She glanced at him with puffy, brown eyes. "You know her best. If she came to the city, would she be at the police station?"

Jason shook his head. "I think if she were here, we would have passed her on the road. She probably would have gone to the police and gotten a ride back to Ichacar. We took the main road to get here, and I didn't see any police cars. I highly doubt they would've driven the long way." Slowing to a stop, he tapped the steering wheel as the traffic light stayed red. "Let's keep going."

The logic made sense. It was unlikely that Cece was here; and even if she was, the police could take her back to Ichacar, and Auntie May would care for her until he returned home. Plus, Wendy explained that the criminals who took Cece wouldn't risk bringing her to a big city during daylight. The risk of being seen was too great. If they found her first, they'd want to take her to a secluded location.

"Then it's on to the river?"

Sensing an unease in her voice, he noticed Wendy's knee bouncing in his peripheral vision. "What's wrong?"

"Nothing. It's just that . . . " She twisted her fingers together. "You remember the spot I showed you, right?" Reaching in the back seat, she withdrew a large map that she'd pieced together with the help of clear tape.

"Yeah. Park on the east side of Patterson's Bridge and travel north on foot. She could be anywhere, but they left her on that—" He got choked up again. Exhaling, he continued, "They left her on that side of the river."

"I'm sorry I couldn't be more specific. I didn't go with them." Her knee continued to bounce. "I know Marley said she deserved it, but I couldn't bring myself to watch."

The instant the light turned green, Jason slammed on the gas.

"I just . . . I can't . . . " Glancing over, he saw Wendy's fingers twisting anxiously in her lap. "Stop the car," she whispered.

Before he could process her request, she threw her jittery hands on the dash.

"Stop!" she yelled.

Slamming on the brakes, car tires screeched behind them. A series of honks followed. "What? Do you see her?"

"No," she declared, pushing her door open. "I can't go with you. If the guys find out I helped you, they'll never forgive me." She climbed from the car and ducked her head down. "I've heard you reap what you sow, and I don't want to reap vengeance from Marley the way your girlfriend did."

Jason shook his head. "Maybe you'll reap mercy, as you chose to show mercy by coming forward."

"Maybe." She hesitated. "Now, go."

As the door slammed, Jason stepped back on the gas. He had one goal: find Cece and bring her home. He glanced at the speedometer in his shaking car: 101 miles per hour.

*\*\*\**

Wendy watched as Jason pulled away and the traffic jam behind him straightened out. Turning, she hurried to the nearest payphone and dialed the operator.

"Operator. How may I direct your call?"

"I need the police. It's an emergency."

# Chapter 40

## A Decision

June 22, 1990

"So that's it, huh?" Tommy questioned as he paced about the room. The gang had moved into an old apartment building a couple years back. Although the white walls were now brushed with a stale, yellow tint, it was enough to keep the group warm until they saved enough money to move into a better hideout. Marley had been promising future luxury for years; they'd have an indoor Jacuzzi, a pool table, separate bedrooms, and a huge television set. Just a few more gigs, and they'd have enough money. It was always a few more.

Cece hadn't stopped moving since the gang returned from Ms. Anderson's place. Quickly, she grabbed, rolled, and stuffed her clothing into a ragged suitcase. This was it. She had to act now while the bravery was still there.

"So, you're ignoring me now?" Tommy's irritation was evident, although Cece wasn't concerned. She had bigger things to worry about than the angry teddy bear who questioned her. He stopped pacing and stepped forward, grabbing her shoulders and bringing an abrupt halt to her progress. "You talk to me!" he shouted.

"Don't bother," Jackson stated as he leaned against the side wall of the room. "A girl who leaves her people in the dust and backs out on the only ones who ever cared about her isn't worth it."

Cece rolled her eyes and pulled away as Tommy released her. "Thank you," she said sharply. "You know that's not how it is, Jackson." She continued packing her belongings. "I made my decision, and now, there's no backing out."

"What do you mean?" Tommy asked.

"We left him behind. Anybody in his position would be angry; and Marley's already angry all the time anyway, so you figure it out."

"But I thought you two was getting married." He sounded genuinely concerned. "He's gonna be heartbroken."

"I'm pretty sure he'll survive." Apparently, she let out more attitude than she had intended. Rushing toward the kitchen to pack some food, she kept her eyes forward, hoping the others would drop it and focus on something else.

"You think?" It was Jackson. Of course, he wouldn't let it go. That'd be too convenient. She paused and gave him a look. Squinting her eyes, she peered deep into his.

"Yes, I do."

"Huh, couldn't have saved that for the altar, could you?" He chuckled. "You aren't as tough as I thought you were."

At that, she grabbed the last soda and threw it in her bag. "That's it!" She stormed toward Jackson, who remained still, leaning against his wall. "You want the truth? The police back at Ms. Anderson's? She didn't call them—I did. And you know why? Because Marley's a jerk!" Her blood boiled as heat rose to her face. "I don't care what anyone says! Killing's wrong. You know it. I know it. Tommy knows it. Marley couldn't care less!" She was yelling now, which must have irritated Jackson. He straightened and gestured for her to lower her voice, but she didn't. As he moved toward her, she walked backward and continued her confession.

"Not only did he not care, but he wanted *me* to do it. *Me*! Why me? I don't know, but I bet you do!"

"Calm down," he replied. "Just what are you implying?"

"Marley doesn't want me around," she declared. "I was just his insurance policy in case anything went south on a job! I'm the expendable one—isn't that right?" She threw her arms forward and pushed him away. "Not anymore!"

Tears welled up in her eyes. Although she hadn't believed in love, part of her at least wanted Marley to like her. As angry as she was at how he behaved at Ms. Anderson's, it still hurt to learn that she meant nothing to him. She was his tool—his foolish, disposable tool. Perhaps she'd been fooled by her own wishful thinking, but not anymore.

She stared at Jackson. "Try to deny it if you want, but you know the truth!"

Zipping her bag, she hurried to the front door; but as she was about to open it, Jackson's voice emerged from behind. "One more question, Cecelia." His tone sent chills down her arms. She stopped and turned to face her questioner. "What was Marley doing when you called the police and left Ms. Anderson's? He probably insisted on coming with you, no?"

Her stomach was filled with knots. There was something wild in Jackson's eyes—something that made her bones shiver, though she tried to appear unshaken.

"He was down," she declared with a deep breath. "He asked me to kill her, and I refused. He didn't listen, so I showed him I was serious."

Jackson slowly inched closer.

"Stop right there! So help me!" She grabbed the door handle, preparing to run out.

He paused. "Let me get this straight," he began calmly. "Marley asked you to kill someone, insisted that it be you instead of him; you wanted none of it; you smacked him, called the police, and ran out of the house?"

She nodded. "It is what it is. I didn't want anyone to get hurt—you know that. Please, Jackson, you of all people should understand. You *know* Marley wanted to cross the line! You heard what he said!" Fear gripped her heart as she waited for him to respond. She just hoped that he would let her leave. She could try running now, but he'd catch her if he wanted to. She must make him understand.

"You set him up."

"He deserved it! He needed it. He was going to hurt someone!" A tear escaped down her cheek.

Stepping forcefully toward her, Jackson leaned in. She braced herself as he spoke.

"You listen to me, Girl. I ought to make you pay for using us against Mar the way you did. Is he confused sometimes? Sure, but the decision you made to leave him behind wasn't yours to make." He stood upright. "You want the truth? Marley was probably arrested, and if so, we'll read about it in the papers tomorrow. Will he get out? Someday. Will he break out? Maybe. But in both of those scenarios, he ends up out of prison." He leaned toward her again, so close that she could smell his breath. She would have turned her head, but she didn't want to appear intimidated. "And he'll come looking for you; you can bet on it. By leaving us now, you're not doing yourself any favors. Yeah, you did wrong, but maybe—just maybe—if you stay, Tommy and I will let you earn back our good graces. We might even help you when Marley comes back. But if you leave, you won't have just one enemy; you'll have three."

Cece felt her jaw shaking. She clenched her teeth, refusing to let them chatter. Talk of Marley's return didn't scare her. With Ms. Anderson and her children's testimonies, she imagined he'd be in jail for quite a while. Tommy wasn't a threat either; he was a big softy. If he did come after her, she was convinced she could talk him out of anything. But Jackson—he made her nervous. When he was pleased with her, she could trust him to protect her at almost any cost. On the other hand, he was a perpetual nightmare when angry. He didn't snap right away; it was just the constant worry of when and where you would turn and find him right behind you.

She shook her head and wiped the rebellious tear from her cheek. It angered her that the tear didn't obey her strict, internal order not to cry.

"I have to go, Jackson. I can't live this way anymore. I just can't." With that, she opened the door and hurried up the hall, down a flight of stairs, and out the building into the unknown.

***

"Wow," Tommy began. "You just let her walk out like that?"

"Girl's still got a heart like a bull," Jackson replied. Both men were silent as they collapsed on the couch. "Something definitely got to her."

As the two sat quietly in the apartment, they couldn't help but wonder what would become of Marley. He'd most likely be convicted, but of what? Would he ever return? More importantly, would he rat them out to the police? Jackson looked over his shoulder at a window that opened toward the street. The little brat had gone too far, and soon enough, she would pay. There was no way Marley would forget what she did. It was one thing to cross a sane man, but betraying a power-driven maniac? That was just stupid.

"What happens now?" Tommy scratched his head and reached for a bag of chips. "You really gonna side with the boss man? I know what she did ain't cool, but you wouldn't have killed the old lady neither."

"I guess we'll see." He cracked his neck and kept his gaze toward the window. "She'll learn her lesson, one way or another."

"Welp, we both know you're the best teacher."

Jackson's eyes shot sideways at his wise friend. Rising, he went to the window and looked down. There she was, standing at a bus stop, oblivious to the weight of her actions. He watched as the bus pulled up and she stepped inside, probably thinking she'd already won. Boy, was she wrong; but the more confident she felt, the more delightful his victory would be. Within seconds, the bus pulled away, carrying the traitor inside. He watched as it disappeared into the distance.

"Until we meet again, Miss Burbin," he said with a grin. "And we *will* meet again."

# Chapter 41
## *Recognition*

March 14, 1994
Monday, 4:25 p.m.

A sudden jolt brought Cece back to consciousness, sending her body bouncing up and down. She tried to move her arms, but they were restricted by what felt like a duffle bag. Her legs were pressed together, making it difficult to kick free.

"Help!" she squeaked, but there was no way anyone would hear her. Judging by the jostling, she was obviously in a vehicle. She rolled her eyes. It was Jackson's vehicle.

Without hesitation, she kicked her legs, lifting her knees as high as the container allowed and thrusting her heels downward. As she fought to break free, distressing images flooded her mind. She saw herself tied to a chair. A blindfold covered her eyes as a man laughed in her face. His breath was a burning pile of garbage, stinging her nose with each word he spoke.

*The man eerily brushed her face with the back of his index finger. "Smooth—you've been taking care. I wonder why that is." His voice was deep and hollow, clearly an attempted disguise.*

*"I thought you said she was getting hitched," another masked voice chimed in.*

*There was tension between the two men—she could feel it. If they didn't get along, perhaps she could use that to her advantage. As she contemplated a clever response, she was struck on the face. A muffled shriek escaped her lips as her head flew sideways. There was a gag in her mouth, and it tasted awful.*

*"I can give you money," she mumbled, struggling to maintain her composure. "Is that what you want? Lots of money . . . if you just let me go! Please!" She couldn't think. She could barely breathe. Her chest convulsed as she wheezed.*

*"I don't believe you," the first man sneered.*

*As he uttered the words, someone struck her face. She let her head fall to the side as the bitterness of blood filled her mouth. Sensing the man nearby, she jerked her body, trying desperately to move the chair away from the creature who tormented her.*

*"How does it feel?" he taunted.*

*As she continued to struggle, he grabbed her face and held it between his hands.*

*"No!" she tried to scream.*

*His breath violated her face as he leaned in. "It's no use. Nobody can hear you!" he growled. "You're mine."*

*He struck her again, this time hitting her right forearm. Pain shot through her bones.*

*"Stop it!" As she fought to break the restraints, she felt a body against the back of her chair.*

*"That's enough." It was a new voice.*

*A loud thud made her jump. It sounded like something hit the floor.*

*"Thank you," she said, hoping one of the thugs had a change of heart.*

*"It wasn't for you," the voice replied. "You two can have your lovers' quarrel on your own time, not mine."*

*Heat rushed to her face. "I don't even know him!" She paused. "Is that what this is about? Please, you have the wrong woman. Take me home to my husband!"*

*"What's that now?" the voice questioned.*

*"Take me to my husband!"*

*"I know what you said; I'm just surprised that a saint like you would lie. You gotta face the hard facts—you don't have a man anymore. The only man you have right now is me, and I'm not feeling very appreciated. Perhaps you should convince me to keep you around."*

*Cece frowned. "I don't understand. Who are you? What do you want?"*

*"I guess you'll have to figure that one out on your own, Miss Smith." The bone-chilling edge of a needle crept its way up her leg. "Clench your teeth, Kid. This won't hurt a bit."*

*Kid.* Cece bounced to the present as she hit the trunk wall.

"Sorry, Short Stuff," Jackson's creepy voice called. "Don't hurt yourself back there. I'd like to keep you fresh for our company!"

*Kid?* She couldn't believe she was so blind. Even with the voice changer, she should have known it was Jackson. Shifting her eyes down, she tried to assess her body for scars, but she was wrapped too tight. Wishing she could remember more, she closed her eyes and tried to think. Nothing. Something happened beyond the needle—something that had abolished her vocal cords. Why else would her voice be crushed into unrecognizable fragments?

Frustrated at her lingering memory loss, she raised her head and dropped it back against the floor. Pain shot through her skull and down her spine. She kept forgetting about that tender spot that hadn't fully healed. Growing increasingly angry with herself, she laid her head sideways and fought the pain. As much as she tried to deny it, she knew if somebody deserved what was happening, it was she. Were each deception a brick in life, she would own enough to build a mansion. Ignorance would be her maid and disappointment, her butler. Why did she think a lying life would treat her well?

*Jesus*—were it not for Him, she would still be living a wretched illusion.

As she lay motionless on her side, a single tear broke free. That tear led to an outpouring of humility that traveled across her nose toward the trunk floor. According to her mom, crying was a loss. Each tear was a reason why she wasn't strong enough to make it in the world.

*"Wipe your tears and keep playing," the stern voice said. Sobbing, young Cece wiped a runny nose across her arm and placed quivering hands back on the piano keys.*

*"Arrogance is unacceptable. You think you can perform better than Sally Loubull without practice?" Storming away from the expensive instrument, Mama mumbled, "Fancy me being stuck with such a worthless human for a child."*

*"I can't play with my left hand," Cece called out. "I didn't learn it in lessons yet."*

*She watched as Mama whirled back around and glared at her. "Learn it yourself! Sally Loubull is playing at level six in the concert, and you, little girl, are nowhere close! You play this and don't embarrass me." Turning to resume her exit, she continued, "Thursday is the concert; you learn it by then. You earn your way in this world, Cecelia. People who don't perform aren't needed or wanted by anybody. You'll do well to know such things."*

Earning a place in the world—it took her years to recognize the flaw of that mindset. Each day of her life, she had tried to win the approval of people with no idea she was already adored. Jesus took her way of thinking and completely transformed it to a point at which she could finally live with the comfort of knowing her value. It all came back to the night she prayed with Jason.

*"God forgives you, Cece,"* he declared, *tenderly placing his hand on her shoulder.*

*"I said a prayer. I didn't do anything, and you tell me He forgives me? I don't get it." She did believe and meant each word of her request for Jesus to live in her heart. Forgiveness, however, had to be more complicated.*

*Jason looked at her with warmth in his eyes. "God doesn't require us to earn His mercy. He gives it as a gift. You don't earn it; you receive it—you choose to accept it."*

*"You can say that, but you don't know what I've done. Maybe God forgives others, but why would He pardon me?"*

*He remained silent for a moment before speaking: "When you make something outstanding, you like showing people, right? Artwork is hung on the fridge, in a living room, and all over the walls. Did you ever make something you were proud of?"*

*She thought for a second and then nodded.*

*"God created you. When you recognized yourself as being His, it made Him smile. You didn't know who you were before, but you know now. From this day forward, you're in His family. I imagine if God had a fridge in Heaven, your picture would be all over it!"*

*Trying to hide her pleasure, she continued to argue. "But I haven't done anything worth recognizing."*

"God doesn't measure our accomplishments by what the world thinks. Have you ever read the Psalms?"

She shook her head.

Reaching for a piece of paper, Jason patted her knee and wrote something down. "Read this before you sleep tonight."

Receiving the paper, she tried to make sense of it.

"First, this is the name of the book in your Bible. Second, you find the number indicating a chapter in the book. Do you mind?" He motioned toward her bedroom, and she nodded. Quickly, he rose and retrieved the worn Bible from her nightstand. Showing her each step of the way, he opened the Bible and navigated to the part he asked her to read.

As Jason stood to depart for the evening, she arose and gave him a hug. His warm embrace was comforting—unlike anything she had experienced before. There was something different about Jason Porter, something mysterious and wonderful.

"Remember," he began as he opened the door, "He will be with you through everything and won't leave your side."

After he left that night, Cece returned to her Bible that was still open to the part he had asked her to read: Psalm 103:11-12. Relieved, she pulled the leather book close to herself and carefully studied the words. Although reading was still somewhat difficult, she was now able to sound out almost any word.

> For as high as the heavens are above the earth,
> so great is his love for those who fear him;
> as far as the east is from the west,
> so far has he removed our transgressions from us.

"I call you a sight for sore eyes," a muffled voice seeped into the trunk where Cece lay. Little did she realize the car had been stopped, and she had no idea for how long. She listened closely. *Tommy.* Why was he meeting them? She had to break free if she had any chance of defending herself. Whispering a prayer to God, she bent her knees one last time and kicked as hard as she could. The bag ripped as her legs broke loose. Moving quickly, she inched her way out of the bottom of the bag and adjusted her dress. Hopefully, she hadn't made enough noise to attract attention from the men outside.

Attempting to stay calm, she searched the enclosed space for a sharp object. To her delight, she caught sight of a set of jumper cables in the bottom left corner. Wasting little time, she peeled away options before finally arriving at a plan. Somebody would be disappointed today; she just hoped that somebody wasn't her.

## Chapter 42
# Back to Where it Began

4:33 p.m.

Tommy's fingers tapped incessantly against his thighs. He glanced at the clock as Marley drove; one minute had passed since he last checked. He sighed. Time had never moved more slowly. Well, except that one time when Jackson bet him he couldn't drink a jumbo slushy and get through a full-length movie without peeing. Tommy knew he could do it! But even if he couldn't, who cared? It's not like they paid to get in. The only cost to them was the slushy—an expense certainly worth having. By the time the movie was over, he nearly broke Jackson's face as he leapt from his seat and raced to the men's room. He snickered. Good times.

"Something funny?" Marley scowled, shifting his eyes toward the passenger seat.

He smiled. "'Member that time Jackson got a bloody nose at the theater?" Thinking back on the situation, he couldn't contain himself. "The look on your face was priceless! You got so mad . . . thought we was on a job without you!"

"Shut up!"

Tommy flinched, nearly hitting his head on the car ceiling. Marley's sour mood was normal, especially lately with all this Cece stuff.

"Goodness, Mar, I'm only kidding," he offered.

"I don't care." The boss' teeth were clenched as he glared at the car in front of them. He was like a cheetah stalking its prey.

Tommy shivered. "What are you—"

"Will you please!" Marley's face was growing red. "I don't *care* what you think or what you say . . . As a matter of fact, want to know what I care about this very minute?"

Spit flew from Marley's mouth, and although he knew it was a trap, Tommy couldn't resist asking. "What?"

"I wanna know why in the world I got stuck with an idiot like you! And what's Jackson's problem? Fool better have a good excuse for second-guessing me . . . or else!"

"Or else what, Boss?" he asked, trying to ignore the "idiot" part. Despite countless lessons from Jackson, it was still hard to ignore Marley's vicious zings. *"Don't worry, man,"* his friend would say. *"You're smart; old Mar's just hard at showing his appreciation."*

Tommy would look back at his comrade. *"If that's true, he's got lots of work to do. He ain't so good at talking."* Honestly, if he had to decide, he'd say Marley would rather not have him around. But Jackson said otherwise, and he was always right.

"Or else he'll get what's coming," Marley answered. Pursing his lips, he threw a fist into the stereo.

Tommy froze, watching as Marley withdrew his bloody hand and slowly returned his hand to the steering wheel. Trying desperately not to laugh at his agitated companion's pain, he thought he'd help by graciously continuing their conversation.

"Oh, man . . . sounds scary."

Glaring at him, Marley reached his good hand under the front of his seat.

"I bet Jackson has a really good reason for whatever he's doing," Tommy continued. "You know what?" He glanced at the clock once more. "I bet he'll have everything straightened out before we get there."

Marley returned to his upright position and tossed a shiny device in Tommy's lap.

"What's this?" he asked.

"My utility knife," the boss retorted. "Sharpened it just last week. Wanted it fresh for her."

"Her? I thought we were talking about Jackson."

"You . . . " Marley huffed. "I can use it more than once! We'll see how useful Jackson decides to be. He's really messed up this time!" He paused. "Wait a minute. What do you mean he'll have everything straightened out? What aren't you telling me?"

"I . . . umm . . . I mean . . . "

"Just say it!"

Sighing, he turned his face away. "Maybe he's already punished Cece." He hated even thinking such things; but she had betrayed the family, so it was only right that there be consequences.

Marley reached over and yanked his knife away. "Well, for both of your sakes, you better hope he hasn't done anything foolish. If she isn't there when we arrive at the river, it better be because she's dead—and I want to see the body!" He paused. The sides of his mouth rose in a creepy smile that gave Tommy chills. "But we'll have more fun if she's still alive."

Tommy forced a chuckle, then faced forward. He understood why Marley claimed to hate her, but was she really so bad? She and Mar used to get along just fine when they were engaged. At least, until Cece started acting all funny. Sure, she had always been a little strange, but then again, so were they. There toward the end, however, she started getting all awkward and weird, talking about ideas and things that made no sense.

Marley exhaled. "What am I saying? Of course, he'll have the girl." Before Tommy could speak, he continued, "Jackson's got a huge ego. He's a cocky crook, and cocky people don't like to be proven wrong. It's actually good she's not dead yet. Now, I'll get to do it myself and watch her pathetic face beg for mercy as I rip her heart out."

A combination of shock, confusion, and horror flooded over Tommy. His eyes were locked wide open as though he had spotted a mouse running across his bedroom floor. He didn't dare look over, disgusted by his perverse leader's gruesome dream.

Feeling a shift in momentum, he cocked his head to see the speedometer: forty-five, fifty, fifty-five, sixty, sixty-five . . . The red needle pointed farther and farther right. Marley's fists were white as he squeezed the wheel, his right knuckles still spattered with blood from the stereo incident. The man leaned forward with a crazy grin.

Tommy frowned.

The grin became a snicker; the snicker became a laugh; and soon enough, the boss was laughing uncontrollably as the needle continued to turn.

"What are you laughing at, Mar?" he asked casually. He forced himself to chuckle. What he really wanted was to tuck and roll out of the vehicle, but he knew that could be fatal in his current physical condition.

The boss gasped. "Oh, man. The sweet taste of victory!" He beamed. "Did you see her the other night? She was terrified! I've never seen her so scared."

Tommy remembered. He had heard the screams. "Yeah, she was pretty upset," he added with a sigh.

"And the way she panicked when I pelted her that first time!" Marley roared. "She's still the worthless, little worm she always was. I should have told her it was me. I can just see the look on her pathetic face now!"

It was a hard night to forget.

*Tommy and Jackson had gone to grab a quick snack down the hall and had left the room for only three minutes, tops. Cece's bone-shattering cry made him nauseous. They ran back to the room as soon as they heard. After what had happened earlier, they should have never left the boss alone with her.*

*"Marley!" Jackson roared. He reached for the doorknob. It was locked. Swiftly slipping his hand in his pocket, he pulled out a pin and unlocked the door.*

*Raging forward, he thrust the heel of his shoe into Marley's right shin. The boss yelped and hunched forward. In a swift follow-up, Jackson thrusted his fist in an uppercut to Marley's stomach.*

*"Thank you!" Cece's eyes were still covered, but her mouth restraint had been removed. Marley seemed to take perverse pleasure in hearing people beg.*

*"It wasn't for you," Jackson replied. "You two can have your lovers' quarrel on your own time, not mine."*

*After they said some more things to which Tommy paid no mind, Cece started screaming. They were ear-piercing, gut-wrenching screams.*

*Tommy grimaced as he covered his ears. "Do something," he insisted, agitated at the ringing in his eardrums.*

*He watched as Jackson looked around, but the mouth restraint was nowhere to be found. Acting quickly, Jackson moved toward him. "Sit."*

*He sat.*

*"Give me your shoe. Hurry!"*

*Shaken by the intensity of the moment and by the terrifying screams of their prisoner, he struggled to get one of his shoes off but finally managed. Jackson took it and threw it backwards. Aggressively, he reached down and pulled Tommy's white sock off and tied it around Cece's mouth. Thankfully, she was small, and Tommy wore high socks.*

"Ha!" Marley gave a final roar as he slammed the brakes and spun the car off the road. At last, they stopped, although parked perpendicular to the road.

Tommy opened his eyes. There was a black car sitting twenty feet away, and a man was getting out. It was Jackson. Unbuckling his seatbelt, he opened the door and stumbled out of the car. He looked around to see if Cece was somewhere near Jackson's new ride. Nothing. Of course not. Jackson wouldn't have her out here in the open. Encouraged by the sight of his friend, he jogged forward, although his breath could hardly keep up with him.

"It's you!" he called.

"You bet it's me." Jackson smirked. "Quick, we gotta talk before Marley gets here."

"What do you mean? He's right over there . . . "

"Yeah, I know," he said quickly. "Now, listen, I got her in the trunk, but she's still alive."

Tommy felt instant relief and concern all at once. "Alive?"

"For now, but here's what we're gonna do . . . "

# Chapter 43
## *The Unspoken*

October 26, 1991

Cece lay atop the orange autumn leaves, her arms sprawled out as she gazed toward the fresh, blue sky. She felt the long grass beneath her hands and delighted in the dew drops that covered it. What a gorgeous morning. Fiery leaves mimicked the sunset, flaunting their colors on windblown trees. When a leaf would fall, she'd watch it dance freely through the sky before finding its home on the ground. In change, there was beauty—a beauty that emerged from countless hours of rain and shine. A beauty that resulted from growth, maturity, and a life well-lived.

As she breathed in the smell of grass and pine, she closed her eyes. Life was finally good. She had a cozy job with Mrs. Jones' quilting business, and she was getting pretty good at it, too. She now had free reign on most of her designs, which meant creating blankets from the images in her mind. Whatever she could imagine, she could make, as long as they had the right fabric.

Mrs. Jones paid her well. It was enough to make rent plus utilities at her apartment in downtown Ichacar. She had food, shelter, and Jason. Smiling, she exhaled. She had never expected to meet a man like him. In fact, she was convinced they didn't exist. She'd always felt like an afterthought in the lives of others, until he came along. He was so . . . different—like a breath of fresh air.

"Hey there, lovely lady! Mind if I join you?" It was him. Opening her eyes, she grinned and patted the ground next to her.

"I saved you a spot," she said.

As he went to lower himself, his foot slipped, sending him flying to the ground. "I just couldn't wait to join you." He laughed, looking at the new grass stain on his pants. "That's one for the record books!"

She smiled. "You have many talents, and I guess falling is one of them!"

Rolling over, he tickled her stomach. She laughed and jerked her knees, trying not-so-hard to break free. "Truce! Truce!" she cried, resting her head against his chest.

"The times I've spent with you are some of the best memories of my life," he said, gently squeezing her arm and pulling her close.

"I know," she said. "I mean, me, too . . . my time with you. It's been great." Grimacing, she could feel herself blush.

"I knew what you meant."

He had a way of making her feel better about her imperfections. It was as though he appreciated her for who she was, not who she could or should be.

"I love you, Cecelia Burbin."

Her heart stopped. She could feel dizziness setting in as she sat up, her hips sinking into the soft ground. She should say something, anything, but she had no words.

"Is something wrong?" He sat up beside her.

"You love me? What do you mean, you *love* me?" she snapped, struggling to navigate the sudden turmoil that struck.

"I . . ."

She stood. "What do you want from me, anyway? Just tell me." She began pacing, stomping on the crisp leaves and watching them crumble. "I refuse to play this stupid love game!" Standing, he moved toward her and reached out a hand, but she pushed it away. "That's what this is to you, right? A game? You just want to use me like everyone else! Well, I've had enough," she yelled as she ran toward the parking lot to retrieve her bike.

"Wait!" Jason called, but she kept running. "That's not what I meant! Please, hear me out!"

Stopping abruptly, she turned, arms crossed. "Why should I? So you can convince me to do whatever you want? So you can tell me how to remain in your good graces? I don't need love, and I don't need you."

"Cecelia . . . "

She looked up and caught his eyes. They were glossy, but she didn't know why. Gently, he extended a hand, probably expecting hers in return, but she didn't oblige. She just stood and stared, reluctantly awaiting his explanation.

"I don't love you because of what you can do for me," he began. "I don't expect anything in return, and I wouldn't want you to try to 'earn' my love. I care about you because of the woman you are: your faith, your heart . . . you. I've gotten to know you—there's something about you, and it's not what you can do for me; it's something God has placed inside of you. I'm falling in love with you, Cecelia Burbin, and love isn't about earning affection or striving to be good enough. It's about selflessly caring for another person. I want to do what I can to make you happy, not the other way around." Slowly, he stepped forward and touched her shoulder. "You don't have to say anything.

My love doesn't come with a list of expectations," he continued. "Except for that smile."

She smirked, slightly frustrated he broke through her anger. Could what he was saying be true? Is that what love was supposed to be? She liked Jason, a lot, but she had never thought about using the L-word. She hadn't tried to figure out her feelings. She just felt—and enjoyed— the experience of feeling. Somehow, it was comforting to not attach a word to it. Whatever their relationship was, it was great, but labeling it meant facing the reality of how relationships typically end up: dead.

"I don't know how to be in love," she whispered. "I'm not even sure I understand what love is." She was getting choked up. Swallowing hard, she turned away, only to find Jason emerge by her side.

"That's okay," he said cheerfully. "I'll show you."

Grabbing her hand, he led her to a picnic table and hoisted her up. As she sat, he untied her shoe and took it off.

"Love is taking my shoe?" she questioned sarcastically.

"No . . ."

"It's giving my shoe back?"

"No." He smiled. "Love is seeing that you don't have a shoe and offering mine in its place."

Removing his sneaker, he put it on her foot and tied it. She wiggled her toes, amused by the oversized piece of footwear she was given. "What else?" She beamed.

"Let's see." He looked around, then ran toward her bike and hid it behind a tree.

"Hey! My bike!" She laughed. "Is love buying me a new one with fancy bells and whistles?"

"No, although I could do that if you'd like," he replied with a wink. "Love is seeing you don't have a bike and offering you mine to ride home."

"But what about you?"

"I'll walk." He extended a hand. Reaching for it, she jumped off the table. "Love is caring about someone else and putting their needs above your own. Not because they require it. It's a gift you give. And when two people love each other . . . " He wrapped his arms around her waist. "You both give, and you both receive. It's continuous, like a waterfall that never stops flowing."

Moving closer, she hugged him, squeezing his back in her hands. "I want that. I want that with you. I just hope that God will teach me how."

"He will." Jason pulled back and looked into her eyes. "He's already started."

# Chapter 44
## For They Shall See God

March 14, 1994
Monday, 4:45 p.m.

Cece laid quietly, jumper cables in hand, awaiting the moment when the trunk would open. The wait wasn't long. As the first beam of light shot horizontally across the floor, she kicked the roof up and thrust the sharp jumper teeth onto Jackson's fingers: right hand red, left hand black.

"Ouch!" he hollered as she rolled out of the trunk and stood. Before she could make a run for it, Tommy grabbed her arm and sat her down on the car's bumper.

"You trying to get us killed?" he asked with a look of worry.

She glared at Jackson and clenched her teeth. "What do you want from me?"

"What an interesting question."

A chill shot down her spine. She knew that voice—that awful voice. She turned her head to see another figure from her past approaching.

"Marley."

"Present! Although, I must say . . . I'm somewhat surprised you are." He glared at Jackson. "I see you're right! The current certainly moved her body downstream. So far down, in fact, that somehow, she found land!" Pausing, he took a deep breath and continued. "You know," he said as he circled around in front of her, "I'm kind of glad you're still here. After all that fun we had the other night, I was thinking you may want to go a few more rounds in the ring."

He came toward her. Jerking forward, she spit in his eye. Tommy laughed as Marley wiped the glob from his face.

"You think that's *funny?*" he barked, instantly returning his attention to where she sat. "Spit, huh?" He smirked. "I can work with that."

She watched as he signaled to Tommy. In seconds, she was swept up from the bumper and carried through the untrimmed grass. She kicked and squirmed as Tommy struggled to keep her arms contained.

"Yo, Jackson, come grab her feet!" he called toward his friend, who was trailing behind.

Jackson's concern for the road had not gone unnoticed. She had seen him glance back more than once.

"Forget that. You grab her feet," he retorted.

"Why should I get kicked? I'm the one doing all the work here!"

"Who said she's going to kick you?"

A few more back-and-forth exchanges, and Jackson was firmly holding her hands while Tommy carried her feet. She felt like a flimsy hammock in a thunderstorm. Marley led the way, strolling along with his typical arrogance.

After a short time had passed, the rushing water grew louder. Was this the end? After everything God had brought her through, could these really be her final moments? *Please, God.* She looked up. *I don't know how, but I know You can rescue me. You're the best Father I've ever known, and You can make a way.*

"Put her down over there," Marley directed, pointing toward a large boulder.

The others followed instructions. As Tommy released her legs, the sole of her right foot collided with what felt like a needle but was likely a sharp rock. She squealed, then clasped her lips together. She hated to give her captors the satisfaction of hurting her.

"So, Jackson," Tommy started, seemingly oblivious to her pain. "I'd really like to do the plan right about now. Is it time yet?"

Cece frowned as he shook his head.

"Not quite."

Marley pulled a knife from his pocket and approached her. He was five feet away when she heard an unexpected noise.

"Stop!"

It was a warm voice—firm but kind, intense yet endearing. It was handsome, and she would recognize it anywhere.

"Don't move," the voice continued as Jason emerged from the grassy distance.

"How did *you* get here?" Jackson questioned sharply. He looked at Marley with daggers in his eyes, but their leader just smiled.

"Oh, but I'm so happy you could join us, Jacob!" Marley declared with a fake tip of an invisible hat.

"Jason!" Cece beamed, ignoring the sharp pricks to her throat. "You're here! How did you find me?" She couldn't help but smile.

"I'll always find you. Are you okay?"

As he stepped closer, Marley raised an arm. "Not so fast." He inserted himself between them.

"Move," Jason demanded.

"You see, I would," he started, "but I'm actually here to warn you. You see, she's no good to you."

He squinted. "That's not true."

"Oh, but it is. Your fiancée over there . . ." Marley leaned to the side just enough that she and Jason locked eyes. "She's as good as dead, and now, so are you." Grabbing Jason's arm, he threw him against a tree. "She and I were an item once, and my, oh my, the awful, disgraceful things she did." He sneered. "She stole an old lady's cane on a bet! Yep, I bet her she couldn't do it without being seen, but guess what? She did! An innocent, old woman minding her own business and eating lunch, then poof!"

Cece watched as the shadow from her past unveiled more of her secrets. Although she and Jason had discussed her past, he never asked for details. She could only imagine what he must think.

"That's enough, Mar," Jackson insisted, but it did nothing.

"And this one time—I'll never forget—she pretended to date a guy so she could get him out of the house while we robbed him blind! Ha! Guy never saw it coming."

"I remember that!" Tommy exclaimed as though her deceit was a good thing.

Cece felt the fight leave her body; she deflated as shame engulfed her heart. He was right. After everything she had done, she didn't deserve a man like Jason. She deserved to die. If the penalty for sin was death, she should've died a hundred times. She looked toward the sky. Thankfully, God hadn't given her what she deserved. He gave her grace and forgiveness. It was a gift—not because she earned it, but because of His love for her. He took her past wrongs away—"as

CAITLIN M. SMITH   261
far as the east is from the west"—and she wasn't going to let anyone come dragging them back.

"That's not who I am," she declared, a fire burning in her heart. "I made mistakes, but that's the past. I have a new future to share with the man I love." Smiling, she met her fiancé's eyes.

"That's enough!" Marley drew his knife and pressed it against her man's cheek.

Jason shoved his hands against the villain and pushed him backward. "Don't," he warned.

Signaling to Jackson, Marley and he raced forward and pinned him back against a tree, Marley's left arm shoved up against his throat.

"Don't hurt him!" Cece croaked, watching the knife graze his skin.

"She's just using you," Marley raged. "Once she'd gotten what she wanted, she'd be gone. Her death will be my favor to the world. People like her don't change; they expire."

Jason jerked his arms, but Jackson held fast. Slowly, Marley sliced his face with the knife, letting blood drip down his cheek.

"Mar!" Jackson shouted. "That's enough! You said you wanted her; now let's take her and go!"

"Shut your trap!" He grinned. "Besides, it'll be more fun this way!"

A soft melody of sirens began playing in the distance.

"Marley . . . " Jackson glanced over his shoulder toward the direction of the noise.

"Any last words?" the crazed boss asked.

Watching the knife pointed at her beloved's neck, something arose within Cece. She thrust her heel into Tommy's knee and drove her head into his chin. Breaking free from his hold, she ran toward Marley.

As he turned, she clasped her fists together and knocked him under the chin. He collapsed, the knife dropping to the ground beside him.

She glared at Jackson, his dark eyes staring straight back. Amidst his anger, she saw sadness. It was the first time she'd seen this emotion from him, and she was sure he didn't intend to show it. Before she said or did anything, Jason threw him to the side and ran toward her.

The sirens were growing louder. She watched as Jackson waved at Tommy.

"Let's go!"

"But what about the plan?" he answered.

Jackson pointed at the ground. "No need. He's down. Now, let's get out of here!"

"Wait!" Marley gasped. "We're not done! Get them!" He pointed toward her, but nobody moved. "You worthless fools! Do something!"

Ignoring the directive, Jackson turned back and jumped behind his struggling boss. He wrapped an arm around his throat and squeezed.

"Tommy! Help!" the man wheezed.

Heavy car doors slammed in the distance.

"Uh, Jackson?" Tommy's voice shook.

"One . . . more . . . second." He kept squeezing.

Cece watched as Marley flailed his arms, his face turning red, then purple as he finally passed out.

"Is he dead?" Tommy asked.

"No." Using his shirt, Jackson placed the knife handle back in Marley's hand. "He'll come to again. Now, let's move!" The two took off jogging.

"Wait!" Cece called, keeping her eyes on Jason.

No response. They were gone.

"Are you okay?" She pressed her hand against his cheek, trying to stop the bleeding.

Footsteps and voices came closer. "We've got movement down here," one declared.

Jason gazed at her with a soft smile.

Tears began pouring down her cheeks. "I think the cops are here. They'll take care of you."

He kept his eyes on her as beads of sweat ran down his forehead.

"Freeze!" a deep voice boomed.

She froze.

"Put your hands up!"

She raised one hand; the other remained on Jason's cheek.

"Back away from the man."

"I got it," Jason whispered, replacing her hand with his own.

Slowly, she stepped backward.

Three additional officers emerged on the scene. One went toward her and began asking her questions, while two others helped Marley. The officer with the deep voice, who appeared to be the leader, approached her future groom.

\*\*\*

"Don't move, sir," the large man told him. "Do you need an ambulance? Where were you between 2:50 and 3:30 p.m. this afternoon?"

Jason frowned at the officer. "Three-thirty? Why?" He fought to conceal the pain of his wound, though it seemed to be growing worse.

"Sir, an eyewitness reported a break-in. Said a woman fitting that lady's"—the officer pointed at Cece—"description broke into a barber shop this afternoon."

Jason looked at her. He saw concern in her eyes and somehow knew it was true.

"Sir?" the officer insisted.

"It was me," he answered, pressing harder against his face. His left hand dripped with blood.

"What was you?"

"It was me," he reiterated. "I forced her to break in for me. She had nothing to do with it. She's innocent."

The officer looked him over. "What about that man on the ground? What happened to him?"

Jason looked at the unconscious criminal, then over at his bride, and back at the officer. "That man attacked me." He grunted, then paused. "Found out about the thing."

"The thing?" The officer raised an eyebrow.

"You know . . . " The ground spun as he struggled to finish his thought. " . . . the store thing."

Looking at the ground, all he felt was anger and nausea. After what these people did to his beloved, they should be locked away for years. How dare they . . . As he continued to think, a memory interrupted him. It was the conversation he had with God the other day. *Forgive as I have forgiven you.* He didn't want to forgive. He wanted to kill these men for what they did to Cece and for how worthless they made her feel.

As time stood still, he stared at the collapsed criminal. He saw the face of Jesus appear where Marley's face once was. *While we were still sinners, Christ died for us.* The words were clear, as though someone were speaking directly to him. Carefully, he exhaled. He himself was among the undeserving to whom forgiveness was given. Somehow, he would do it. He would forgive. It was the only way to move forward in the true freedom God had for him and his bride-to-be, and they would never look back.

***

The sound of helicopters caught Cece's attention as she gazed at her beloved. She didn't know exactly what he and the officer were saying, but she herself had exercised the right to remain silent. She should have taught him that.

"Excuse me, Miss." One of the officers who had been interviewing her returned from speaking with Jason's officer. "We've arranged for the three of you to receive medical attention." He appeared to be staring at her bruised arms. "Two choppers from the nearest hospitals are on their way to transport the two most urgent cases. The third individual will ride with us, but we won't know who that is until the EMTs get here. After medical examination, we'll get your official statement."

"I don't need life-flighted," she insisted, but the decision was not up for negotiation. The EMTs would decide. As the helicopters drew near, she requested to speak with Jason. Keeping her at a safe distance, the senior officer consented and remained by her fiancé's side.

She reached her hand forward, and he took it in his. Tears poured down her dirt-stained cheeks as she leaned in. "I love you, Jason Porter."

The police officer frowned, though she doubted he could hear her over the frantic helicopter blades.

Jason looked at her. "Your eyes are so beautiful, like shining stars in a hazy sky. I love you, too, and nothing will ever change that."

She sobbed. He made her feel like the most special woman in the world, yet so humble and blessed all at once.

He softly released her hand and touched her cheek. "You're so special; and when I get out of prison, we'll get married and spend our lives together. I'll love you more and more each day and be the happiest man in the world."

Her heart froze when she heard the words, "out of prison." What did he mean? He must have sensed her confusion as she glanced at the officer beside them because he offered a comforting smile.

"I told the officer everything, about how I forced you to break into the shop for me."

"You what?" she exclaimed. "Why would you . . . "

"Trust me," he insisted. "No matter what I did earlier today . . . " He looked at the officer and back at her. "Remember, it's because I love you. I love you, Cecelia Karen Burbin." Gently squeezing her hand, he slipped a piece of paper into it. She cupped the treasure so nobody would notice.

She watched as the EMTs rushed both her nemesis and groom to temporary safety. An officer offered to carry her to the police car, but she politely declined. After painstakingly limping on her heel through grass and dirt, she finally made it to the vehicle and climbed inside. With everything that had happened, she'd forgotten about her wounded foot, but now, the pain was back. Nevertheless, she had wanted to ride with Jason. Actually, she wanted to do everything with Jason. After the past few days, she never wanted to be apart.

Her eyes followed the helicopters as they soared through the sky and out of sight. As she rode toward the station, she carefully prayed about what to say. She wanted to be honest and wise, traits that she knew God would help her learn and traits her groom already possessed. As she sat on the black leather seat of the police car, she opened a slip of paper that Jason had slipped to her just moments before they rushed him away. Slowly, she read:

*For I am convinced that neither death nor life,*
*neither angels nor demons,*
*neither the present nor the future,*
*nor any powers, neither height nor depth,*
*nor anything else in all creation,*
*will be able to separate us from the love of God*
*that is in Christ Jesus our Lord.*

Romans 8:38-39

# Chapter 45
## *When*

10:43 p.m.

Pain oozed through Cece's body as she walked down the sterile hallway. Her crutches clicked between each step of her good foot; her right foot dangled behind her, still recovering from the newly applied stitches. Though her feet were safely nestled in the fuzzy, yellow slippers Auntie May had brought, their comfort didn't erase her physical pain.

Thankfully, the medical tests were now over. The way the doctors had run every test known to man made her feel like a newly discovered specimen in a science lab. Auntie May reassured her that they were only doing their job and that the assessments were necessary before she visited Jason. The final list of injuries included a few minor cuts, the stitch-worthy puncture in her foot, a severe case of laryngitis—which was finally clearing up—and an anterograde concussion, which they explained could account for her memory loss as well as her blackout in the pottery store. The best thing about the list was that it meant she was still alive, and Cece knew Who to thank.

After a few more clicks, the officer—whose name was Paul—looked at her. "This is it." He nodded at the man standing guard by the door. The man stepped aside as she entered, Paul close behind.

As she stood gazing at the patient who had saved her life, her eyes filled with tears. A scar started at his left cheek bone and ran three inches down his face. Auntie May said he had gotten thirty stitches in surgery. The area was shaved smooth of the stubble that normally graced his handsome face. Lowering her eyes, she watched his chest rise and fall as he breathed. It was *because* of him that she was still breathing. God had rescued her, and He had used the bravest person she knew. Jason was a good man, and he deserved to be safe.

Scanning the room, her eyes landed on Derek. He was sitting on the far side with his elbows resting on dirt-stained jeans. His torso was leaning forward with his head bowed against folded hands. Auntie May said he had come as soon as he could, and Cece was thankful he was here for Jason while she couldn't be.

After a moment, he looked up at her. "He's gonna be okay." She could hear the compassion in his voice. Standing, he came closer and offered a sideways hug.

She returned his assurance with a nod as tears escaped down the sides of her face. "Thank you." Her words were soft and delicate. "Can you please give us a minute?"

As Derek excused himself, explaining that he'd been meaning to check out the vending machine, Cece moved toward Jason.

She had contemplated what to say since the moment she'd read his note. Back at the river, she would have run away with him and spent their lives together. Now that her head was clear and she had time to think about it, she realized how selfish that would be.

Even if the police found Tommy and Jackson, who had disappeared into the woods, there could still be someone out there who wanted to do her harm. She had stolen from a lot of people over the years, and any one of them could come looking for vengeance. Although God had forgiven her, she knew that not all people were that forgiving. She couldn't put Jason in that kind of danger—not if she truly loved him. If she loved him with the selfless love that he demonstrated to her, she would sacrifice her own desires to keep him safe.

The tears flowed harder as she gazed at the man she loved. She longed to be nestled in his embrace as they lay on the park grass, staring up at the starry sky.

Taking hold of his hand, she gave it a gentle squeeze. "I love you, Jason Porter," she whispered, unconcerned with what the police officer might think.

She had told Paul everything about the past three days, including the truth of what happened at the barber shop. He knew now that Jason was her fiancé and had provided a false confession to protect her. Although Paul wasn't thrilled about the deception, he said they would need Jason to recant his confession. Once that was done, he would be free from any charges.

As she went to pull away, she felt tension in her arm.

"Cecelia?" Jason held on to her hand, keeping her near. "Aren't you a sight for . . . eyes?"

She smiled, unwilling to waste time wiping fluids from her teary face. "For eyes?"

"I'd say 'a sight for sore eyes,' but the truth is, you're a beautiful sight for any eyes."

Delight warmed her cheeks as she laughed. "Don't look at me," she sniffled. "I'm a mess!"

Jason smiled, but only half his mouth moved.

"Is it numb?"

"I sure hope so." He winked. "Half a smile isn't enough to express the joy in my heart."

She frowned, "Joy? Now?"

He held her hand tighter, keeping his gaze fixed on her. "I didn't know what had happened. For a moment, I didn't know if I'd get to hold this hand again." His eyes twinkled in the light of the hospital lamp. "Now that I am, I want to hold it forever."

*Forever.* If she was going to tell him, now was the time. Her face scrunched as the tears grew thicker. Her beloved's facial expression was hidden behind the watery wall.

"I can't go through with this, Jason . . . with us."

For a moment, her sobs were the only sound in the room.

"What about what you said at the river?" His voice was calm. "About sharing our future?"

"I know I said that." She gasped. "But it wouldn't be fair to you." Her chest heaved as she fought to control her breath. After wiping her face against the sleeve of her hospital gown, she exhaled. "As long as I'm in your life, you could be in danger, and I love you too much to put you through that."

Paul approached her and waved a tissue in her face. When she accepted it, he returned to his place by the door. She blew her nose. "I can't even begin to describe how I felt when Marley held that blade to your face. You could have been killed, and all because of me. I won't be selfish this time. If I want to protect you, I need to let you go. It's the only way."

Though her voice was still froggy, it was certainly audible, and Jason had heard everything. He rolled his head back and looked up at the ceiling.

"Say something," she insisted.

Locking his eyes with hers, he reached a hand toward her face. She leaned in as he rested his calloused palm against her cheek. "Thank you," he whispered.

Her stomach fell. She couldn't believe this was actually the end. The wrench in her heart was too much. She had to get out of here before she completely fell apart, though it might be too late for that.

"Thank you for loving me that much, my beloved Cecelia." His thumb caressed her wet face. "Let me ask you something: Do you want to marry me?"

Pursing her lips together, she nodded. "But I don't want to put you in harm's way."

"You know, when I was looking for a wedding gift for my bride— that's you." He winked. "I looked up the meaning behind your beautiful name. Do you know what it is?"

Averting her eyes, she nodded. "It's nothing beautiful, though. It means 'blind.'" Laughing awkwardly, her gaze found his. "I can't say I haven't felt that way at times."

Jason's smile radiated compassion. "I think we all have." Removing his hand from her cheek, he took hers once again. Comfort filled her heart as their fingers intertwined. "But your middle name—Karen— means 'pure.' Multiple times in the Bible, God gave His followers a second name to represent their new identity and calling in Him. You once were blind, but now you see. Now you have a pure heart as a daughter of God. Is it a little dangerous being with a woman like you? Of course. You're strong, smart, talented, and brave. I'm in danger every day of falling deeper and deeper in love with you. But when it comes to danger from your past, that's not a factor in my desire to spend my life with you. The Cecelia I know doesn't have a dangerous past—only a bright, promising future—a future that I pray I get to share . . . if you'll have me."

Smiling, she let her crutches fall as she threw her arms around him. With her lips beside his ear, she whispered, "Do you mean it?"

"Absolutely."

She smiled so hard that her face could barely contain it. "I'm so happy to hear you say that."

His strong arms embraced her, covering her with warmth and love. "If God is for us, who can be against us?" he began. "With Him, there's nothing we can't overcome. Nothing can separate us from His love, and nothing ever will."

Their chests moved in unison as they breathed, wrapped in the deepest hug Cece had ever felt.

"Cecelia Karen Burbin," Jason whispered, his mouth still by her ear. "Will you marry me?"

Relaxing her grip, she pulled back just enough to gaze lovingly in his eyes. "Just say when!"

"When."

# *Epilogue*

June 25, 1994

Cecelia's eyes shifted to the clock: 8:29 p.m. It was almost time. She exhaled slowly as Auntie May placed the final touch behind her ear.

"There. All done."

She rose from her place at their makeshift salon, which consisted of a chair and the kitchen table. Thankfully, Auntie May had brought a pillow to place on the wooden seat, making the experience a little more luxurious and a lot more comfortable.

Looking in the mirror, she smiled. "It's perfect." She lifted her hand to feel the soft, yellow petals of the daisy in her hair. Tears filled her eyes as she turned back to Auntie May.

"Oh, no! Don't you start crying. You'll get me started, and I already did my makeup!" May's hands shot to her face and waved frantically.

Laughing, Cece went back to the chair and sat. "Okay," she said, collecting herself. "I'm ready."

She watched as Auntie May lifted a makeup bag from the table. "You still just want lip gloss and mascara?" Grabbing a powder brush, Auntie May swirled it in the air. "You sure you don't want any blush on those beautiful cheeks?"

"No, thank you." She smiled. "I imagine I'll be blushing enough without it."

Auntie May laughed and tucked it away. Pulling out the mascara, she bent toward her. "Let me see those eyes."

Cece shifted her gaze to the side as Auntie May applied the black polish to her lashes, following it with a single coat of gloss to her lips. "Well, melt me down and call me a puddle! You're breathtaking."

"Oh, stop it. You're going to make me blush!" Cece felt her cheeks as she hurried into the bedroom. She was thankful Miss Horner let her stay a few months longer. After everything that happened with the police and Marley, she was relieved to have her lease extended long enough to plan a new wedding.

Looking to where her dress hung in the closet, her heart raced. After three more months of waiting, the day had finally come. Initially, it seemed like it never would.

Officials were happy to have Marley back in custody. After several testimonies regarding his additional crimes, Marley was sentenced to life in a maximum-security prison. They hadn't even needed Wendy's testimony. According to Jason, the mysterious woman had helped him find Cece, but they were never able to track Wendy down to testify in court. Cece had been a little disappointed. She'd wanted to thank the woman for doing the right thing. Sure, she made some mistakes, but so had Cece, and she was ready to extend the same grace God had given her.

Although Jackson and Tommy were still out there, she wasn't concerned. Sketches of their likeness had been faxed to every county in the state, and with heat like that, they were probably long gone.

During her trial, the judge had been both merciful and understanding. She had been sentenced to fifty hours of community service at a foodbank in Youngsburg. Jason drove her every evening after work, Monday through Friday, and they served together. She cherished the time with him, laughing at his jokes as they washed dishes together in the large tub sink. He'd dab bubbles on her nose, and she'd pretend to scowl, though she secretly enjoyed every moment. Jason was not obligated to serve, he chose it, and the joy he brought to the experience made the work seem fun. Of course, that's always how she felt with Jason.

Shaking her head, she smiled. God had brought her through so much. He had given her a freedom unlike anything she'd ever felt, and it wasn't just the result of physical safety, though that was important. It was because now, the guilt was gone. God had brought light into her dark places; and as she surrendered the rooms of her heart to Him, He transformed them. One of those rooms contained her former crimes. Perhaps that's why Jason wanted her to confess before—he knew it would open a door that might otherwise have stayed closed.

It hadn't been easy, confessing. She remembered her arms shaking as she walked into the judge's office that day.

*Although she couldn't afford a lawyer, Mr. and Mrs. Jones had hired one on her behalf, insisting that she be represented by Ichacar's finest. While her knowledge of the law was quite good, she appreciated the credibility he would add to her case.*

*What troubled her most about confessing was not the act of admitting what she had done. God had already forgiven her. The hard part was realizing that soon, everyone would know about her past. They would probably judge her, but she couldn't blame them. For years, she had judged herself. How could she expect them to forgive so soon?*

*Pursing her lips, she refocused. Though her head insisted that people would reject her even more, her heart knew none of that really mattered. What mattered was her relationship with God. He would love her forever, no matter what, and if He wanted her to come clean, that's what she would do.*

*Standing in the judge's office, she realized he had asked her something. What was it? Her throat was dry, her lips stuck together. Instead of responding, she stared at him.*

*"Cece." It was her lawyer. "The judge wants to know what he can do for you."*

*Squeezing her fists, she fought to make the shaking stop. "Yes." Her voice quivered. "Your Honor, I'm here to confess."*

*He looked confused. Her trial for breaking into Bobs and Barbers had come and gone, and Marley's trial was still three weeks away. She had not yet been asked to explain the details of her association with Marley, though she was sure it would come up. She wanted to tell the judge herself— because she chose to, not because a court demanded it.*

*"Go on."*

*Again, she froze. Her lawyer had informed her of the penalties for her former crimes and insisted she wait before voluntarily incriminating herself. As she stood, her mind fought desperately to keep her secret.* If you tell him, everything you love will be taken from you. *She shook her head.* "Not everything."

*"What's that, darling?"*

*She refocused on the judge. "Your Honor, I used to work with Marley Rossi's gang." Taking a deep breath, she assessed his expression. "I'm guilty of larceny and countless burglaries. I know I can't change what I've done— though I sincerely wish I could—but I'm here to make it right."*

The judge seemed calm. Clearing his throat, he asked, "And did you yourself assist in, conspire to commit, or commit kidnappings, assault, or murder?"

"No, Your Honor. I left the gang when I realized Mr. Rossi's intentions to harm people. I should have left much sooner. It took some time before I recognized God's tug on my heart."

The judge rubbed his chin.

"It's not who I am anymore. I've been out of that life for years now, and I'm never going back. Now, I want to make things right with the people I wronged. I don't know how, exactly." She stopped and glanced at her lawyer, who gave her an uncertain nod. "But I'm here now, ready to accept the consequences for my actions."

Leaning back in his chair, the judge brought his fingertips together. "Marley Rossi, you say?"

"Yes, Your Honor."

"And you intend to testify at the trial?"

She nodded. "I will."

He sat up and rested his forearms against the desk. "I'll tell you what. The State will go lightly on you in exchange for your honest testimony in Mr. Rossi's trial. We'd like to keep him behind bars this time, and we could use your help."

Warmth washed over her as she stared at the judge. She couldn't believe it. Glancing at her lawyer, she saw that he, too, was staring.

Looking back, she blinked. "Really? That's all? But isn't there something else I can do? Surely, there's something."

He smiled. "Your testimony will be enough. Besides, it took me a while to listen to the Big Guy myself. We all need a fresh start, a little mercy, and a lot of grace."

Cece dabbed away a tear as she remembered. At this rate, there was no way her mascara would last. The judge had been so merciful, and she knew Who to thank for that. Ever since she accepted Jesus as her Savior, He'd been working in her heart and molding her into something new. Something beautiful. Something He'd created her to be. The freedom from her past was one more step in this grand adventure. It wouldn't always be easy—the experience last year was evidence of that—but God would be with her, offering hope and strength to face the day.

"Would you like some help, honey?" Auntie May stood by the opened door.

Cece looked back at her dress. The glass beads sparkled as they cascaded down the satin fabric, creating the appearance of windswept flowers. Reaching for the hanger, she lifted it and nodded.

"You're gonna be the most beautiful bride!"

Beaming, she caught Auntie May's eyes.

"I'm so blessed to have a daughter like you."

As May helped her into the dress, Cece fell back into her thoughts. She had told the Whites months ago that Mama wouldn't want to come to the wedding. After the new date was set, Auntie May lovingly insisted once again that she send an invitation. This time, Cece agreed. After everything for which God had forgiven her, she was finally ready to forgive. She sent the card but heard nothing back. As a matter of fact, she wasn't sure if the address was correct. For all she knew, her parents may have moved from her childhood home a long time ago. In either case, she felt peace. She had new parents now, and that was okay. Perhaps her birth parents were still out there; but she had decided to entrust them to God, hoping that someday, He might draw them to Himself in the same way He had drawn her.

She slipped on her shoes and turned. "How do I look? Fancy?" she smirked, raising an eyebrow.

"You look perfect, honey. Oh, I almost forgot!"

She watched as Auntie May hurried out. She heard the rustling of a paper bag and what sounded like plastic coming from the kitchen. In moments, May emerged carrying a bouquet of sunflowers intermixed with white roses.

Gasping, she extended her hands to receive the stunning gift. "You shouldn't have." Her eyes searched the flowers and greenery, marveling at their beauty, until she noticed a white quilted bow that held the bunch together.

"Oh, I know you didn't want 'nothing fancy, but Mrs. Jones insisted, and that woman just can't be stopped." Auntie May came over and stood beside her as they turned to face a mirror. "Beautiful. Honey, you make everything you touch look beautiful."

Within minutes, they were out the door, down the steps, and in Miss Horner's car. Although the park was within walking distance, Miss Horner had insisted on driving them. She emphasized it as the least she could do, and Cece was blessed by the gesture. Besides, this meant Jason wouldn't see her as she approached, allowing for a big reveal.

After all that had happened, she and Jason decided that a new venue was in order. When he mentioned the park where they first met, she instantly agreed. They would hold the ceremony under a starry night sky. It was a dream come true—a dream that she didn't even know she had.

She closed her eyes as they rounded the street corner. She knew that the park was now close enough to see. The anticipation was almost too much.

"We're here!"

It was Miss Horner's voice. With eyes still closed, she slipped off her shoes and, fumbling for the door handle, pulled the door open. She heard the flapping of flat shoes on pavement, followed by May's call.

"I'm comin' around! Just a minute!"

A soft hand took hold of hers and guided her from the vehicle. They moved forward, one slow step at a time—her bouquet in one hand, and Auntie May's arm in the other. A cool breeze tickled her chin as it swept a dangling curl from her forehead.

"Ed!" It was Auntie May again. "Ed! Tell Jason to turn away. He shouldn't see the bride until the music starts."

They continued to walk until finally, the gentle tug stopped. They must be at the aisle now. Cece pictured the three rows of white wooden chairs Jason had made, carefully placed on either side of the grassy walkway she was about to traverse. Inhaling, she let the familiar smell of pine engulf her as she lifted her closed eyes to the heavens.

"All right, honey. Open."

Obeying, she gasped. The sky was decorated with hundreds—thousands—of extravagant stars stitched perfectly across its deep blue fabric. She hoped for a clear night, and it couldn't get much clearer than this.

A pinching sensation stung her cheeks. Had she been smiling that hard? Despite the facial fatigue, she never wanted to stop. The joy she felt was beyond what her words could explain, and she would soak in every minute.

As the violinist began to play, she lowered her eyes and fixed them on the man at the end of the aisle. *Jason*. She loved that name. *That man*. His toothy grin must have matched hers, though his strong cheekbones added sparks to his smile that made her insides flip. Before she knew it, she was standing across from him, gazing into his warm eyes. Reaching up, she wiped a tear from his cheek as the music continued to play.

"Don't be so sad," she whispered, still grinning. "Is it because you aren't wearing shoes?"

Taking her free hand, he pulled her closer.

The pastor must have said the right things, but she didn't notice. Her attention was fixed on the man before her and the unexpected blessing he had been. At a time when she was new in her faith, still resisting love, God brought someone into her life who modeled what love really meant: It was selflessly caring for someone else, expecting nothing in return. When you loved like that and found someone who loved you that way in return, something special happened. She remembered being amazed that Jason could love selflessly—amazed, that is, until she understood Who his God was. He had once told her that it was God Who first demonstrated selfless love by sending His Son to die in our place, so we could have a relationship with Him. While we were sinners, though we didn't *deserve* it, God reached out to us. His love was unconditional; and when we have a relationship with Him, He gives us the ability to love others in that same way.

"It's time to put on the shoes," the pastor declared.

Her heart leapt. Although the ceremony was almost over, she suspected this would be her favorite part. She watched as Jason turned to receive a sneaker from Derek, who had been holding it safely in the front row. Seated next to him was Bart. Leaning forward, Bart handed her the second shoe. Together, the two formed a new pair—in Jason's size. As she reached out to offer her bouquet in exchange, Bart extended a comforting smile. She was glad he had agreed to come. After she had told her story to the police, they brought him in for questioning. She was relieved to learn that he wasn't involved in the original plot, and even more thankful that he had refused to turn her over to "Mr. Connor." Bart had clearly been misled by Jackson, though he confessed to initially not wanting to know the truth. Since then, he'd had a change of heart, and she, now more than ever, understood what that meant.

Facing Jason, she giggled as he knelt and reached for her right ankle.

Looking up at her, he began. "Cecelia Karen Burbin, I will always love you, and I will never stop putting your needs above my own. No matter the terrain, we will walk it together—the three of us. You, me, and Jesus."

She beamed as he slipped on the shoe and stood. Lifting his right foot, he wiggled his toes in the air. She laughed, touched by both the silliness and thoughtfulness of the gesture, but she didn't mind squatting in the grass.

"Jason, I didn't know what love was until I met you. It was hard for me to understand how God, let alone another person, could love me." She paused and shifted her eyes to the sky, then back at the man before her. "But I understand now, and I can't wait to spend every day of my life walking beside you." It took a little maneuvering, but she finally got the sneaker on his foot. The second she stood, he pulled her into himself. Leaning against him, she rested in his arms.

"All righty, you love birds. I now pronounce you husband and wife. You may kiss the bride."

She felt Jason's finger graze the bottom of her chin, lifting her gaze toward his. Looking up, she melted into the steamy pools of his deep brown eyes. The world around her became a haze as his lips drew near. His left hand gently pressed against her lower back, sending goosebumps down her arms as his lips met hers. They were soft and warm—firm, yet tender. Closing her eyes, she sank into the moment, cherishing the feelings that swirled within her heart. Tingles danced down her jaw as he slowly pulled away. The look in his eyes told her that this was forever. It reassured her that no matter what they'd face, he wouldn't let go. This was the start of a new beginning—a new life. The past was gone, and a bright future lay ahead. With God by their side, there was nothing they couldn't overcome, and they would overcome . . . together.

# Acknowledgments

First and foremost, I thank God. I remember sitting down with my laptop over ten years ago, a blank document open, and words flowed onto the page. God sparked the birth of this story, and when I stopped writing partway through, He breathed new life into it and helped shape it into what it is today. I am so thankful for His words, guidance, and inspiration. It is because of Him that this was possible, and I'm grateful for His loving presence every day.

I also want to thank you. I appreciate you so much and am honored that you chose to read Cece and Jason's story. I want you to know how much God loves you. You are valued and treasured by Him. He created you uniquely . . . wonderfully. You are one of a kind, and no matter how lost you feel, you're not too far gone for God. He loves you and is waiting for you to choose Him. He will free you from guilt and shame. He will forgive your past and give you a fresh start. There's no ocean, river, mountain, or valley great enough to separate you from Him. He will meet you right where you are. You aren't too lost to be found. His Son, Jesus, made a way.

To the incredible team at Ambassador International: Thank you for believing in this story and for investing time in a debut author. Your support means so much. To my editor, Katie Cruice Smith, who helped smooth the rough edges: your feedback and suggestions made a HUGE difference, and I'm so thankful for your contribution. God has blessed you with a cool gift, and I hope it continues to blossom as you use it to glorify Him.

Last, but certainly not least, thank you to the family and friends who cheered for me through this process. I appreciate your love and kindness. Thank you to my parents, who have watered the seeds God has placed in me over the years. To my husband, John: I am so grateful for you. Thank you for encouraging me to finish writing this story and for believing in my books. You love with such a selfless love, and I am blessed to be your wife. I would also like to thank the godly men and women who have spoken life over me. Keep shining, and keep your eyes on Jesus.

For more information about

## Caitlin M. Smith
and
*Love's Lost Star*
please visit:

*www.caitlinmsmith.com*

Ambassador International's mission is to magnify the Lord Jesus Christ and promote His Gospel through the written word.

We believe through the publication of Christian literature, Jesus Christ and His Word will be exalted, believers will be strengthened in their walk with Him, and the lost will be directed to Jesus Christ as the only way of salvation.

For more information about
AMBASSADOR INTERNATIONAL
please visit:

*www.ambassador-international.com*

*If you enjoyed this book, please consider leaving us a review on Amazon, Goodreads, or our website.*

When a prominent city official dies in a car wreck, Scott and Angela find themselves tangled in intrigue and deception. Together they search for the truth and discover that not all is what it seems.

Charlotte Hallaway needs to come to terms with her father's death. He had been her only family, and she wasn't handling her grief well. It was just supposed to be a few weeks of peace and quiet to process it all, but then she saw them—a drug deal and a murder within seconds of each other. And they saw her. Now running for her life, Charlotte boards a bus to escape her pursuers and wakes up the next morning in the woods without a memory of how she got there or of who she is.

After two and a half years of deep depression, anger at God, and guilt over the death of her husband and twin girls, all bestselling romance writer Jessica Lynn Morgan wants is to buy a house, get back to writing, and live out her life alone in peace, but once she moves in, the threat against her life becomes real. Clearly, someone or something wants her out. Now. Will her stubbornness cost Jessica her life?

Made in the USA
Columbia, SC
14 August 2022

65319595R00159